Benjamin Franklin

and

The Quaker Murders

Benjamin Franklin

and

The Quaker Murders

by

John Harmon McElroy

www.penmorepress.com

BENJAMIN FRANKLIN & THE QUAKER MURDERS
by John Harmon McElroy
Copyright © 2017 John Harmon McElroy

ISBN-13: 978-1-946409-10-2 (Paperback)
ISBN :-978-1-946409-11-9 (e-book)

BISAC Subject Headings:
FIC022000   **FICTION** / Mystery & Detective / General
FIC022060   **FICTION** / Mystery & Detective / Historical
FIC022090   **FICTION** / Mystery & Detective / Private
Investigator

Editing by Lauren McElroy
Cover Illustration by Christine Horner

Address all correspondence to:

Penmore Press LLC
920 N Javelina Pl
Tucson AZ 85748

To
Lauren McElroy
superb editor, empathetic critic
& loving daughter
whose devotion to this book
made its completion possible

Acknowledgements

I owe a debt of thanks to the late Samuel Grabb, MD, and to my granddaughter Onyria Gilmor Tschudy, ND, LDM, CPM, for checking the narrative for medical accuracy. Sara Button, another granddaughter, proofread the manuscript. My son, John Herrera McElroy, knowing of my interest in Franklin, encouraged it by buying me, long ago, one of the best of the Franklin biographies. My daughters Helen Britten and Lisa Button were also particularly encouraging and supportive, and Lisa and her husband Kevin provided needed computer support; my debt to my other daughter is acknowledged in the book's dedication to her. The counsel of my dear wife was, as always, unfailingly good; to say thanks for sixty years of love is hardly sufficient, Ony. To my sister-in-law Irene McElroy who read the completed manuscript (I'm sorry Bill, whose admiration for Franklin was as great as mine, isn't alive to see the final product) and to "Dub" Button (Kevin's father) whose help was very great indeed, your interest has meant a great deal. To my cousins back home in Pennsylvania, Gerre Slaugenhaupt and Joey Ann Mostow, I appreciate your saying you looked forward to reading the rest of the book after reading the first chapter. And of course to everyone at Penmore Press, especially Michael James who has taken me on as one of his authors, thank you.

JHM

Tucson, Ariz.

Prologue

This narrative features Benjamin Franklin (1706-1790) in the role of a detective. The story is set in Philadelphia, two years after the conclusion of the American Revolution, when Philadelphia was the largest English-speaking city in the world after London.

It should not surprise anyone that Franklin could have undertaken such a role since he was successful in so many undertakings. Master printer. Self-taught writer. Newspaper publisher. Creator of the best-selling annual *Poor Richard's Almanac*. Commander of a Pennsylvania militia company. Longtime secretary to the Pennsylvania colonial assembly. Founder of many civic organizations in Philadelphia and fundraiser for them. Inventor of the idea of matching funds, daylight savings time, the lending library, bifocal reading glasses, a medical catheter, the lightning rod, an efficient heating stove, etc. Author of the first systematic study of the Gulf Stream, based on observations he made on his eight crossings of the Atlantic. Writer of Pennsylvania's first state constitution. Internationally famous diplomat. A founder of the American republic. World-class research scientist whose discoveries in electricity led Scotland's oldest university to bestow on him an honorary doctor's degree in 1759, after which he was known as Dr. Franklin.

Having played so many roles, why not that of a detective? After all, a detective's observations and inquiries are not unlike the procedures a scientist uses in investigating the mysteries of nature.

JHM

Prelude

The three boys were playing Patriots and Redcoats on the waste-ground behind the stoneyard on Dock Street in Philadelphia that September day. Every blow they struck with one of their wooden swords—lopping off a scarlet-leaved limb of a sumac or laying low some tall weed—was accompanied by a yell of triumph. Scores of Redcoats were being slain, left and right, as they noisily hewed their way through the overgrown empty lot.

All of a sudden, David, the ten-year-old leader of the trio, stopped dead in his tracks and inquiringly stated, "Smell that?"

The other two Patriots also suspended their slaying of Redcoats.

"Smells like a dead horse," eight-year-old Rufus declared.

"It's from over there," Abraham said, pointing his sword toward an old, abandoned privy on the edge of the waste-ground.

"Let's go see," David commanded.

The boys moved off toward the necessary, and the nearer they got to it, the stronger the sour stench became.

When they reached the weathered wooden booth, they saw its splintered door and seat lying in front of it, along with several old crocks without handles, a tattered wicker jug, and a broken wheelbarrow, all of which had apparently been torn from and thrown out of the necessary. David stepped into the doorless privy, where the stink was strongest, looked down into its dried-out pit, and instantly backed out. Abraham replaced him and retreated just as abruptly after seeing the elongated canvas bundle in the necessary's cavity.

Rufus wanted a look, too, but his brother David grabbed his arm to prevent it.

"Come on!" he ordered. "We got to tell Mr. Maul!" And the three boys hightailed off in a bunch like three startled deer. By the time Rufus and Abraham reached the peaceful home of the Quaker stonecutter Jacob Maul, David was already banging on the door with his fist.

Chapter 1

It all started for Captain James Jamison after Sunday supper eight days later.

The family was seated around the Jamison dining room table conversing, when a barely audible knock was heard at the back door. Livy, who had cleared the table before sitting down with the others, sprang to her feet with her usual alacrity and asked her elderly mistress whether she should go see who was at the door.

"Please, Olivia dear," replied Grandmère in an English still colored by the intonations of her native French, "do see who it is. I can't imagine who is calling at such a late hour on a Sunday at the back door instead of the front."

Livy soon returned to report the presence of "a man in shabby dress" who refused to tell her his business except to say he needed to speak with Captain James Jamison.

James rose at once from his seat and, taking from Livy's shapely hand the candle she had used in answering the door, went to see what the caller wanted. As he passed his brother-in-law, Lawrence, he heard him say to Jane, James's twin sister, in a bantering tone, "The beggars have tracked your dear brother to his lair to better extract alms from him. A kind man and his money are soon parted."

Standing outside the back door, James found a man holding his hat in his hands, his thin, grey locks ruffled by the wind. He was, as Livy had said, poorly dressed and yet had an air of respectability as if he might have known better days before his descent into society's lower orders.

"How may I be of service to you, my good man?" James asked.

"If ye be Captain James Jamison, sor, I'm obliged t'yer honor fur speakin' wit' me," the man replied. "My name is Tom Wilson. I have a message t'give ye."

"I am the one you seek."

Wilson paused as if to gather his thoughts before saying, "If ye'd be so kind, Captain, as t'come away wit' me to a place nigh here, there's a gentleman wants t'speak wit' ye. He sent me t'fetch ye."

This turn in the conversation was not particularly to James's liking. The streets around the home he shared with Grandmère and Livy, which his deceased grandfather had built in the western outskirts of the city shortly before the war, were still unpaved, and most of the lots facing them had yet to be built on. No whale oil lamps like those which illuminated the city's innermost streets existed here; and on cloudy, moonless nights like the present one this part of town was as black as the inside of a cow. Jamison had no desire to leave his warm house at the invitation of a stranger to meet another stranger, even though the first unknown described the second one as "a gentleman."

"Who is this person who wishes to speak with me, yet does not come himself to state his business?"

"That I couldna say, an' it please yer honor. He nar give me his name. He only give me yourn an' pointed out yer house, an' where I was t' bring ye."

The man paused once more before adding, "The gentleman said I was t' have a ha' shilling hard money if I fetched ye, an' I'd be much obliged t' get it, yer honor."

From his appearance, James could well believe the man needed the money; and it was more out of a sense of Christian charity toward such a humble petitioner, and the initial impression of honesty Wilson had made on him than for any other reason, that he told the man to wait while he got his coat and hat.

When Lawrence heard what the caller at the back door wanted, he asked whether James would like him to go along on this errand, but was assured that would not be necessary since the man seemed quite harmless.

"Besides," James said, "I intend to take Grandfather's heavy stick from the hall cane stand, in case of any trouble."

As he leaned over to give Grandmère the kiss he always gave her when leaving the house, Jane exclaimed, "Do be careful, Jamie!" To which he replied, "Jane, you know I am always careful. Did I not return all in one piece from the war? Though my left hand was a bit the worse for wear! I'll be back in a wink, don't you worry."

After getting his hat, officer's greatcoat, a lantern, and his grandfather's oak cudgel, James joined his guide. Wilson conducted him but a short distance, to the backyard of a recently vacated house in the next street over, which was enclosed by a high board fence. There, seated on a chopping block, James saw a stocky, respectably dressed man smoking a clay pipe, his figure lighted by the partly shuttered lantern next to him on the block.

Without acknowledging James's presence in any way, or even glancing in his direction, the man handed his messenger the coin he had ready, and Wilson departed after bowing and touching his forelock to each of his benefactors in turn.

With his grateful hireling gone, James's summoner stood up, withdrew from an inner pocket of his coat a letter sealed in red wax and presented it to James, saying, "Please read this, Captain Jamison." Having delivered the missive, the man opened the partly closed shutter of his lantern and held it aloft to give sufficient light by which to read.

James appeared as puzzled as he felt, and the man said, "At your service, sir," and elevated his light a bit more, whereupon James broke the letter's seal and saw a brief message, without date, which read:

> My Dear Capt. Jamison,
>
> If you are disposed to oblige me, and are not otherwise engaged, I would like to consult with you later tonight at Franklin Court on a matter of some interest to me. Whether you come or not, I trust the grandson of my old confrere Samuel Jamison, whom I always found worthy of my trust, will not mention to anyone, not even your dear Grandmother, or your Sister, or anyone in your confidence, the request I am hereby making of you. My servant Mr. Mahoney will inform you of how I would have you enter Franklin Court to avoid being noticed, and the hour at which I can receive you. Please return this note to Mr. Mahoney after reading it.

The missive was signed, with a flourish, "Your obedient servant, B. Franklin."

As instructed, James returned to its deliverer this invitation from the greatest man in America after General Washington, a man he and Jane had been taught by their grandfather when they were children to revere; and Mr. Mahoney, after setting his lantern down and opening one of its panes to gain access to the candle within, twisted the invitation into a spill and burned it to an ash.

There was never any question of James's response to the request from Franklin. The illustrious man had been a friend of his deceased grandfather Samuel Jamison from their early manhood when they were both ambitious mechanics starting out in life and active in the Junto, the mutual improvement club the young Franklin had organized among aspiring leather-apron workers like themselves.

James therefore told Dr. Franklin's manservant to inform his master that he would be pleased to attend him, and received from Mr. Mahoney instructions on how he was to gain admittance to Franklin Court and the hour at which he was to come. With this exchange, James's interview with the taciturn servant of Dr. Franklin came to an end, and he returned home, having been gone but a short while.

Lawrence, Jane, Grandmère, and Livy were eager to have the story of James's mysterious summoner. But, mindful of Dr. Franklin's admonition not to reveal his request, and indeed honor-bound not to reveal it, James was equally eager not to tell them the truth of the matter. The problem was how to satisfy their insistent curiosity, which had to be assuaged in some way.

It occurred to him that Lawrence's quip regarding beggars coming to the house to extract alms from him might be useful, and he said the man at the back door had taken him to see a gentleman who wanted to build an institute for the education of paupers out near Harris's Ferry, on the banks of the Susquehanna, where land was cheaper than it was in Philadelphia, an institute that would qualify them in useful employments for the benefit of themselves and society. James said he had refused the gentleman's solicitation, despite the worthiness of his project, because he could not provide the name of a single person known to James who had endorsed the plan or given it support.

A discussion then ensued as to why the gentleman had not come to the house in his own person at a decent hour on a weekday, instead of sending a messenger. James said he could not account for the man's behavior beyond the motives he had already described.

Grandmère wanted to know if the man was a foreigner, for, she said, she had heard there were many recently landed foreigners in Philadelphia these days proposing schemes of improvement. Lawrence agreed with her that he had noticed more foreign reformers in the city since America's recent overthrow of royal government, which apparently had given Europeans the notion that Americans were open to any proposal for the perfection of the human race. Recalling Mr. Wilson's accent and diction, James said the gentleman's speech suggested he might have been from Ireland.

This led to a spirited discussion of utopian ideas, and the remainder of the evening was passed in conversing on such general topics, until Jane pronounced it time she and Lawrence returned home to their little Samuel and James.

Soon after their departure, James informed Grandmère he had to go into town to tend to some business, and because he was not sure of the hour of his return she should not wait up for him. Grandmère, as always, received this announcement without inquiring into the nature of his errand, and only advised him to dress warmly for it was a frosty night, being well aware of his aversion to cold. James said he intended to wear his officer's greatcoat.

After hearing Livy and Grandmère retire, James came down from his room as quietly as he could so as not to disturb them and left to keep his appointment with Dr. Franklin.

Because of the lateness of the hour, on his walk into town he saw only three other pedestrians and the vehicle of a nightman making his rounds to empty privies. As he turned the corner into Market Street, gusts of wind sent a broad sheet of yellow leaves—the result of early, heavy frosts—tumbling by starts and stops across the brick pavement in front of him, bringing to mind engravings in the history of Russia he was reading of the swift Mongolian cavalry called the Golden Horde that had overcome everything in its path.

Arriving before the ponderous carriage gates to Franklin Court, James did as Mr. Mahoney had instructed him to do and gave them a single rap of his stick as he passed by. He then proceeded to the corner of Third and Market, where he stopped, turned around, and went back the way he had just come until he was once more in front of the gates. Having thus seen in both directions that the street was empty, James rapped twice on the gates and was instantly admitted through the small door in one of them by Mr. Mahoney, who had been waiting for these signals.

Stepping through the postern, he found himself in the vaulted brick tunnel large enough to admit carriages that pierced the continuous row of houses and shops facing Market Street. The massive gates and masonry of the tunnel muffled the sound of the wind in the street. Mr. Mahoney wordlessly led him through this enclosed, hushed space, the lanterns they carried projecting dancing shadows on the tunnel's curved ceiling.

As James and Mr. Mahoney emerged from the tunnel's stillness, their lanterns began to flicker wildly as the wind entered the vents at their tops and buffeted the candles inside. As they proceeded along the bricked carriageway by this fitful light, the branches of the trees planted alongside thrashed noisily above their heads in the wind, sending falls of yellow leaves into the lantern light.

Upon reaching the broad turnaround in front of Dr. Franklin's story-and-a-half carriage house and stables, Mr. Mahoney unlatched a gate which led to a graveled walk around a small oblong of grass bordered by a low hedge of privet. Looming over this token lawn was the dark mass of Dr. Franklin's three-story mansion-house.

Once inside the mansion-house with the door shut behind them, the sounds of the boisterous night were entirely silenced. A solitary candle burned in a silver candlestick on an elegant little table opposite the dimly lit, square, rather small entrance hall, from which a plain staircase steeply ascended.

"This way, sir," James's usher said, gesturing toward a double door to his left, and showing Dr. Franklin's guest through it and into a large dining room with heavy, damasked drapes of a rich blue color drawn across its tall windows. Against all four walls of this spacious room, wherever the absence of doors, windows, and fireplace permitted, were stacked barrels, wooden boxes, and trunks of various sizes, shapes and finishes, along with several wicker hampers and burlap-covered bundles. An unusual uniformity of pleasant warmth and the smell of camphor permeated the room's atmosphere.

Setting his lantern on the hearth, Mr. Mahoney went back out into the foyer and returned with the candle from there. With this, he lit three of the candles on one of the candelabra on the dining room's gleaming table and asked James to please wait here, if he would be so kind. Then he retrieved his lantern from the hearth and, taking it and James's lantern by their top rings in one hand, and the foyer candle in his other, retired from the dining room, leaving James to pass the time as best he might.

The first thing he did—something he was prone to do—was to count the number of chairs around the dining room table, which were sixteen on the sides and two at each end. Then he inspected and counted the bundles, hampers, trunks, wooden boxes and barrels piled along the walls, which numbered sixty-three, each of them bearing the stamps and seals of the French custom service at Cherbourg, a fact that led him to surmise this had to be baggage from Dr. Franklin's nine-year sojourn in France as America's ambassador to the court of Louis the Sixteenth, from which he had just returned to Philadelphia. The odor of camphor which he found so pleasing emanated from one of the burlap bundles.

The remarkable silence in the house on a windy night and its unusual, uniform warmth led James to conclude that Dr. Franklin's dwelling was of quite tight construction and had some unusual means within it for the even distribution of heat.

James also inspected the two portraits in matching gilded frames above the dining room's mantelpiece. One of these portrayed a bespectacled Dr. Franklin, wearing an uncharacteristic wig, seated at a table reading a document held in his right hand while the fingers of his left hand were spread against his chest. The mate of this portrait depicted a portly, buxom woman with an intelligent, direct gaze, wearing a puckered cap of white muslin and a shiny-blue satin gown. James at once recognized this as a portrait of Dr. Franklin's dead wife, not only because of where it was hung but also because as a child, in accompanying his grandmother on her shopping in Market Street with Jane, Grandmère had sometimes encountered and chatted with this woman, and afterwards identified her as the wife of their grandfather's special friend. However, on those occasions Mrs. Franklin had never been attired in anything as splendid as the gown she wore in this portrait of her as the contented mistress of Franklin Court.

While engaged in scrutinizing the oil paintings hanging above the fireplace, James heard the footsteps and voices of two men descending the staircase to the foyer outside the dining room, followed by the sound of the opening and closing of the mansion-house's front door. A rather lengthy silence then ensued—the time, James supposed, it took Mr. Mahoney to escort the departing visitors out to the Market Street gates and return to the house, for almost immediately after he heard the front door open and close once more, Dr. Franklin's majordomo reappeared in the dining room to announce "He can see you now."

After extinguishing the candelabrum on the table, Mr. Mahoney conducted James upstairs to a large chamber on the second floor at the front of the house. It was ablaze with the light emanating from a single lamp suspended by a pulley in the center of the room's high ceiling. James surmised that this wonderful lamp had to be the one the people of Philadelphia were talking about, a gift to Dr. Franklin from its Swiss inventor, as everyone in Philadelphia had learned. The lamp's innovative cylindrical wick, according to the papers, produced a light equivalent to one hundred candles.

The same heavy blue drapes James had seen below in the dining room were also drawn across the windows of this apartment, which exhibited the same pleasing uniformity of warmth he had experienced there.

Books and papers were piled on every available surface of furniture and even on the floor. The room's furniture consisted of four wooden and two upholstered armchairs; a pair of finely wrought tables—the smaller one's top inlaid with ivory and ebony squares to form a chessboard; three tall bookcases; a pendulum clock; a cabinet with leaded glass doors above and wide drawers below; a viol on a stand; a ball harp; and, in one of the corners of the room farthest from the door, two glass apparatuses whose uses were not readily apparent. Four identical trunks were aligned along one wall and contained, judged by the contents visible in the two whose lids were raised, nothing but packets of papers tied in red tape.

The room's only wall ornament was a large, detailed map showing the boundaries of the United States from the Atlantic to the Mississippi and from the Great Lakes to Spanish Florida, an expanse of land larger than any country of Europe but Russia, whose metes and bounds Benjamin Franklin had negotiated at the Paris conference ending the war between Britain and the United States. As was known throughout America, the British negotiator had proposed that the United States be confined to the settled plain between the Atlantic coast and the crest of the Appalachian Mountains and that the much larger, unsettled wilderness to the west, between the mountains and the Mississippi River, be reserved as a perpetual habitation for the aboriginal tribes of America. But Benjamin Franklin had had a different concept of the boundaries of the United States, one firmly supported by his fellow negotiators, whom he led, and their American vision prevailed because Franklin's skills of negotiation far surpassed those of his British opponent, Mr. Oswald.

The room's principal interest for James, of course, was its occupant—whom he had seen as a boy but never met—seated behind a large, plain table of chestnut wood.

As soon as Franklin glanced up and saw James coming toward him, he put aside the quill he had been using and, aided by his cane, rose from his work table, smiling and extending his hand across the table to welcome James.

His first words were apologetic. "I regret having kept you so long below, Captain Jamison. The business of the two gentlemen who just left—Mr. Bullman Duffield and Mr. Nicholas Sproul from the Assembly—took longer than I expected. It appears a movement is afoot in the Assembly to elect me President of Pennsylvania. My friends, having long since consumed my flesh, now seem determined to make a dish of soup from my bones."

What impressed James most, besides Franklin's cheerfulness, was his large physical presence. Though slightly hunched by age, he was as tall in stature as General Washington, whom James had seen on more than one occasion during his years with the Continental Army; and though well past three score and ten, Dr. Franklin's massive calves and his firm, warm handshake indicated continued strength.

Benjamin Franklin directed Mr. Mahoney to remove the papers piled on one of the upholstered armchairs in front of his table and bade his visitor be seated. He remained standing until this was done. Once James had been seated, Franklin dismissed his servant with the admonition to remain close in case he was needed and himself sat down.

These preliminaries out of the way, and proper thanks having been rendered James for coming, the Man Who Tamed the Lightning From the Sky and Humbled a King made a speech, at the start of which he gestured expansively around his study, saying, "As you can see, Captain, I am writing the final report to Congress on my mission to France and the state of our relations with that important country. Almost everything you see here, including the books, pertains to some aspect of that subject. Other books and papers having no bearing on affairs of state are still in crates in the attic of my carriage house.

"I was obliged, you see, to bring many things back with me from the Eastern Continent because the British commander who lived at Franklin Court during the British occupation of Philadelphia in '77 and '78 took with him when he decamped the books, musical instruments, rugs, drapes, silver, china and porcelain my daughter and her husband had no time to gather up and take with them when they fled the city one jump ahead of the British occupiers. General Grey even looted a likeness of me that my daughter had to leave behind. The general seemed to feel, it appears, that if he could not lay hands on and hang an arch traitor to his king such as myself, he would at least take the traitor's image back to England with him and hang that."

Chapter 2

Dr. Franklin's genial way of addressing James instantly put him at ease. The great man's manner was replete with what Grandmère termed *"bonhomie,"* or cheerfulness. James's grandfather had often told him of Dr. Franklin's youth, when he was establishing himself as the foremost printer in the colonies. Samuel Jamison had witnessed his friend Benjamin Franklin doing printing jobs for some of the most important men in Pennsylvania, New Jersey, and Delaware—all of whom were much older than he was—and had seen him fraternize with these potentates on terms of respectful equality. Those stories of his grandfather now recurred to James as he experienced Franklin's easy politeness. Only now the situation was reversed. Dr. Franklin was the old, established potentate and James the promising young man. The effect, however, was the same.

Dr. Franklin's manner bridged the gulf of half a century in their ages and the still larger gulf in their attainments. Under the influence of Franklin's geniality, these immense gulfs were overcome, and James felt as if he and the much more accomplished, older man were renewing a friendship that had long existed between them which had been interrupted by an unexpected separation. Franklin's manner reminded James of the saying in *Poor Richard's Almanac:* "An old young man will a young old man make."

"You come from brave, intelligent stock, Captain Jamison. The papers on glassmaking your grandfather delivered before the Junto were among the most informed and useful ever presented for our club's edification. Did you know, Captain Jamison, that I once had the pleasure of conversing with your father?"

"No, sir, I never heard that you knew him."

"Our acquaintance was brief. We met at Braddock's encampment out by Lancaster in the spring of '55, when that British general was making ready to march to the Forks of the Ohio to confront the French and their Indian allies. Your father's Philadelphia militia company had been mustered, as you must know, to accompany Braddock on that ill-planned, foolishly executed expedition. I was in the camp in my capacity as the Assembly's agent to hire from the farmers around Lancaster the horses, oxen, wagons, and drivers needed to transport the expedition's mountain of camp furniture, fine viands, wines and other luxuries the British officers insisted on taking with them into the wilderness along with their necessary military supplies.

"Several of the American militia officers, including your father, wise in the ways of frontier warfare in America, counseled Braddock against taking so many superfluous supplies that could only impede the expedition and lessen its chances of success. But Braddock and his senior officers would not be counseled by colonials and proceeded to organize their foray into the wilderness of western Pennsylvania as if preparing for a campaign in Europe.

"Your father's death and the deaths of hundreds of other brave Pennsylvania and Virginia militiamen, as well as General

Braddock, might have been avoided had the British commander heeded the good advice he received from his American officers, instead of scorning it as coming from persons who lacked his aristocratic European breeding. I well recall the sorrow your grandparents experienced when the news came that their only child had perished in Braddock's defeat at the hands of the French and their Indian allies, a grief soon compounded by your dear mother's death in giving birth to you and your sister. My esteem for your family, Captain Jamison, and what I have learned of your own military service and your remarkably retentive memory are why I have invited you here tonight."

It did not seem proper to James to inquire into the nature of the subject Franklin wished to confer on, since he knew that his venerable host would reveal the purpose of their conference when it suited him.

Franklin continued by remarking, "I have been informed, sir, that you were among that stalwart company of men who transported, by ox and sledge, the cannons we took from the British at Ticonderoga, through hundreds of miles of ice and snow, to the coast of Massachusetts, which when placed on the heights of Dorchester, above Boston, enabled General Washington to force the British to abandon the city of my birth."

James acknowledged he had had a hand in that expedition under the command of General Knox, the head of the Continental Army's artillery corps, whose leadership, he said, had overcome every accident and obstacle encountered in traversing in the dead of winter the backcountry of northeastern New York and the breadth of Massachusetts.

Franklin continued, "I have also been told you served with distinction in Washington's maneuvers to keep the British from taking New York City and in the Army's subsequent touch-and-go retreat across the Hudson River and across New Jersey to safety on the Pennsylvania side of the Delaware. I have also learned, Captain Jamison, of your promptness during Washington's brilliant counterattacks at Trenton and Princeton, and that you likewise distinguished yourself in the good effect of your actions at Brandywine, Germantown, and Monmouth until rendered *hors de combat* by the wound you received in the battle at Monmouth."

James was flattered by the pains Dr. Franklin had evidently taken to inquire into his military service.

Franklin continued, "I've a question to put to you, sir, one which I have often pondered. As a participant in the battle of Monmouth, what is your opinion of the significance of that engagement?"

To this inquiry, James had a ready reply.

"I, too, Dr. Franklin, have often considered this question. What stands out in my mind the most, besides the loss of most of my left hand to a British cannonball, is the infernal heat on the day of the battle. Nearly as many men, on both sides, were prostrated by the sun's rays that day as were felled by musket and cannon fire. As you know, neither we nor the British gained a decisive victory at Monmouth or sustained a complete defeat. But if General Charles Lee had prosecuted General Washington's plan of attack as ordered, the result, I believe, would have been a victory over our foes so overwhelming that we would likely have taken the British commander and his entire army captive, as we did Burgoyne and his army at Saratoga, and the war might have ended then, instead of after our victory at Yorktown. Had we taken Clinton at Monmouth, as he withdrew with his army from Philadelphia and made his way across the New Jersey plains seeking the safety of the

British base at New York, we would have inflicted a blow so devastating—coming, as it would have, hard on the heels of the victory at Saratoga—that George the Third would probably have sued for peace then instead of three years later, after Yorktown. The victory at Monmouth that Lee lost cost us, I think, three more years of war."

Franklin agreed with this assessment of the importance of Monmouth, a coincidence of opinion which caused James a good deal of satisfaction.

"I understand that at Monmouth as you lay prostrate on the field of battle, after being wounded, you were captured," Franklin continued, "and were then taken to New York to have your hand operated on by a British military surgeon. Is that correct?"

"It is."

"And that while recovering from your wound you were approached by a young Tory woman you had once been engaged to in Philadelphia before she and her parents sought asylum in New York. I believe her name was Miriam Foreman. Is that right?"

This evidence of Dr. Franklin's assiduous inquiry into his service in the Continental Army was even more impressive to James because only his closest associates in the Army knew of the encounter with Miriam in New York.

"She offered, I understand, to arrange for you to pass military information to the British for pay after your exchange and return to our lines. Is this correct?"

"You have heard correctly, sir."

"But you resisted her blandishments, despite your previous connection to the lady and attraction to her charms?"

"The difference between the loyalty which Miriam and her parents felt toward the Crown and my allegiance to the

American cause of independence had already caused the rupture in our relationship, of which you have apparently been apprised."

"Captain Jamison, why, exactly, did you resist her offer of rewards?"

"Dr. Franklin, I was never conscious of a particular reason for not accepting Miriam's unseemly proposal, apart from its repugnance to my sense of honor and the oath I took when I donned the uniform of the Continental Army. Her attempts to get me to break that vow showed how unsuited we were to live together in the bond of holy matrimony. The proposal she made to me in New York erased all remaining doubt from my mind as to whether I had acted properly in breaking our engagement."

"Then your word is your bond?"

"Is it not for every gentleman?"

James saw at once how pleasing his reply was to Dr. Franklin, for his seventy-nine-year-old host leaned back in his chair and smiled. James then realized Dr. Franklin had been putting him to a test, which he had passed.

"Well said, Captain Jamison. Well said, indeed. Your sentiments do credit to your father and grandfather, as I had expected they would. But to have from you an affirmation of my expectations was necessary, to be certain. There were some officers in our Army during the war—Benedict Arnold, certainly; Charles Lee, probably—who considered themselves men of honor, and yet behaved knavishly. These men of false virtue persuaded themselves that they could betray the trust we placed in them and still be regarded as honorable men.

"If our country is ever subjected to ideas foreign to our way of life, it will, I assure you, be due to the influence of such consummate deceivers within our ranks. Reason is a wonderful thing, Captain Jamison, for it allows a man to find a reason for whatever he wishes to do."

James remembered, in listening to this disquisition, that Dr. Franklin's only son had been a Loyalist during the war. Before the war, Franklin's influence as Royal Postmaster General for the colonies had obtained for his son the lofty appointment of Royal Governor of New Jersey. But when the time came for every American to consider which side he would take in the conflict with the Crown, William Franklin had chosen to side with the king, despite the pleas of his father. Indeed, Franklin's only son had raised a troop of Loyalist cavalry and led it in battle, killing Americans as they fought for their independence and liberties.

James could not help but think that Dr. Franklin's approval of his faithfulness to the American cause when tempted to betray it was, at least in part, a reflection of his bitterness regarding his son William's conduct.

A thoughtful silence ensued as the two men recalled the immaterial losses the war had occasioned each of them and similar losses that friends and acquaintances of theirs had suffered.

Franklin resumed the conversation by asking, "What are your thoughts, Captain Jamison, on the affair being spoken of in Philadelphia these days as 'the Quaker Murders'?"

The question's abruptness, which seemed to James a complete departure from what they had been talking of, took him by surprise. He replied, "I read the reports of Mrs. Coons's death published in the city's papers with some interest because they concern a family to whom I have reason to be grateful. The son of the man who has been jailed on suspicion of strangling Mrs. Coons succored me at the battle of Monmouth. I would have bled to death from my wound, Doctor Franklin, had Sergeant John Maul not tarried with me, at the risk of his own capture, to stop the bleeding. He saved my life."

"Yes, I have been told you knew Jacob Maul's oldest son.'"

"I cannot say I knew him in the sense that we were associates or anything like that. I met John Maul for the first and only time on the battlefield at Monmouth shortly before I lost consciousness from loss of blood. I did not even know his name until later. We were taken prisoner together, and I learned his name from the surgeon who repaired my mangled hand, who had it from the Redcoats who brought me to him in New York. Doctor Campbell said that John Maul, in staunching the flow of my life's blood, had saved me from certain death. The British soldiers who transported him and me to New York from Monmouth as prisoners had made Maul carry me to Dr. Campbell."

"Your family, I suppose, knows what you've just related to me and feels the same obligation toward the Mauls because of Sergeant Maul's action in preserving your life?"

"Yes, they know I would not have survived had he not stayed behind with me out of Christian charity as I lay wounded and bleeding. My sister and my grandmother also know, as do I, that he paid for his charity with his life. For not being a commissioned officer, he was consigned to one of those dismasted derelict ships the British anchored in the East River and used as prisons, though it would have been nearer the truth to have called them floating hellholes. While Sergeant Maul was in one of those prison ships, he contracted a fever that went unattended and he died. I, on the other hand, being a commissioned officer, was humanely treated by our aristocratic foes and had my wound properly dressed and cared for by a military surgeon. John Maul perished because Britons put great consequence on social class."

"I have heard the death toll was indeed appalling among Americans incarcerated in those rat-infested hulks the British used for military prisons."

James's painful recollections pertaining to his survival and John Maul's death caused another interruption in the conversation as the older man, perceiving his guest's state of mind, suspended their talk until James regained sufficient composure to continue.

Dr. Franklin then asked James whether he had read the public notice published by the Quaker Elders Israel Godwin, Mrs. Rhymer and Samuel Thornhill, declaring the house of Jacob Maul a seat of disorder and expelling him, his son William, and William's wife from the Society of Friends.

James replied that he had read the notice and considered such action a disgrace, since Maul had not been formally arraigned and tried in a court of law. He expanded on his opinion by saying, "I do not see how the leaders of a congregation professing to be Christian can excommunicate an entire family for a wrong which one of them is thought to have committed. Mr. Maul, as I understand it, is being held in the Walnut Street Jail without bail because that is customary in cases of suspected murder, to make certain the suspect appears at his arraignment."

"You are right, Captain Jamison. Quite right."

"But may I inquire, Dr. Franklin, what your interest is in these matters?"

"You are wondering why I should take an interest in the affairs of a humble Quaker stonecutter? Years ago, when I built this house, in which we sit warm and snug tonight, I contracted with Jacob Maul for his skill and labor and saw much of him, day in and day out, during the course of several months as he laid the foundations for my house and its outbuildings, as well as the foundation for the high brick wall around Franklin Court that defines my property and separates it from the continuous rows of shops and houses of my neighbors. Jacob Maul also constructed my house's cellars, the curbing for my well, the cavity of my necessary, and the buried stone house I designed to keep ice through the summer. And it was he who executed the smooth stone pavements of my house's basement kitchen and subterranean storerooms, and the special hearths and chimneys I designed to heat my home.

"All of these demanding tasks he did well and on time, and for the agreed-upon price. I know Jacob Maul to be an honest workman and as fine an example of Quaker virtue as I have ever known—and I have known a great many Quakers during my many years in this principal center of their faith in America. Believe me, Captain Jamison, there is no better way of knowing a man's true character than to contract with him to perform a laborious task that takes much time and skill to complete.

"Murder is as alien to Jacob Maul's character as a lamb slaying a wolf, or a sparrow killing a sparrow hawk, or a fly murdering a wasp. Neither nature nor his upbringing has equipped Jacob to throttle a woman.

"But there is a further reason, Captain Jamison, for my interest in the plight of this humble stonecutter. The excommunication of an entire family on the suspicion that one of its members committed a terrible crime reminds me of Parliament's infamous Bills of Attainder, whereby Englishmen accused of treason against the Crown are deprived of the right to trial by jury and have their rights taken from them. The Elders of Jacob Maul's Weekly Meeting, in expelling the Mauls from their church and from the Society of Friends, as the Quaker community as a whole styles itself, have behaved in a similar fashion. In taking this action, they have deprived Jacob Maul of his most precious possession, his good name. For a man's possessions depend on his good name. No man of conscience who values his place in society ought to regard what has happened to Maul with indifference. The accusation against him should be answered. It must be rectified if possible.

"We Americans have just concluded a costly war with England which you and many others have fought at great personal sacrifice, Captain Jamison. And why? To rid America of the tyranny manifested in Bills of Attainder. If we in America tolerate acts like those of the Quaker Elders in expelling the Mauls from their church, I fear for the future of our independence and our republican virtue.

"A law of right and wrong exists which the Creator of all that is good and right—the God of Nature as we call Him—has put in place, and it is His law the Quaker Elders violated, a law which transcends the laws men make. We ignore God's moral law at our peril, Captain Jamison. It operates equally on all men, and its operation is as unerring as the laws which govern God's merely physical creations. As I have often said, no man is born booted and spurred to ride his fellows. Nor has any man been born with a saddle on his back to be ridden by other men.

"I have called you here tonight, sir, to enlist your aid in a campaign to undo the injustice being inflicted on Jacob Maul and his family. I want to get him released from jail. I want to reunite him with his son William.

"But these things I cannot accomplish alone. To prove who really killed Mrs. Coons and thus obtain Jacob's release from prison, I must have the assistance of an active, younger man, someone who shares my views and opinions. I am too old to ferret out the facts that must be ferreted out. You are that man, Captain, I believe. Will you help me in my pursuit of justice in this matter?"

After hearing this speech revealing why he had been called to Franklin Court, James Jamison hardly knew how to reply. The first thought which entered his mind was that Dr. Franklin's feelings were too involved in wanting to reunite Jacob Maul with his son William, who bore the same name as Franklin's own son, from whom he was unalterably alienated. That thought was instantly replaced by the knowledge that if he accepted Franklin's request he would be repaying the debt of life he owed Jacob Maul's son John, a debt he certainly wished he could repay.

The trouble was, James believed Jacob Maul *had* strangled his housekeeper, Mrs. Coons, and, years before, her sister to whom he was married. James had spoken with Grandmère of the case, as reported in the papers, and had concluded that, lamentable as it might be, all of the evidence pointed to the conclusion that the father of the man who had saved his life at the Battle of Monmouth was a murderer. The facts in the matter were quite clear to James.

Therefore, he answered Dr. Franklin's request for his assistance by saying, "Your sentiments do you great honor, sir, and nothing would please me more than to help you in a matter where I might be able to perform a service to you, someone for whom my family has the highest regard, while at the same time repaying my debt to Sergeant Maul. But I cannot in good conscience, Dr. Franklin, do what you ask of me. I believe the evidence against Jacob Maul that I have read in the papers is conclusive. My objections are as strong as your own to the highhanded ejection of Mr. Maul and his son William, and the son's wife, from the Society of Friends. But I have considered the case with all due seriousness. Allow me to explain myself by rehearsing those circumstances as I understand them.

"Two sisters, one of them Mr. Maul's wife and the other his housekeeper, have both died while living with him. Both bodies were discovered with bruise marks to their throats. The corpse of Maul's sister-in-law, Mrs. Coons, was found in a disused privy on his property but a week ago, wrapped in a canvas shroud, its feet and hands tied and the canvas tied around the body. The wife's corpse was found seven years ago next to Jacob Maul in the bed they shared. The deaths may have been separated in time, but their circumstances are similar—a close relation with Mr. Maul and living in his house; both bore the marks of being strangled; both corpses were discovered on his property. The talk which I have heard in the city's taverns, inns, ordinaries, and markets in the past week indicates that the great majority of people in Philadelphia— whether persons of quality or in the lower orders of society— are of my opinion, that he murdered these women.

"As every man should, Mr. Maul ought to have his day in court. But were I to be a member of the jury that will hear his case, I must tell you in all honesty, sir, I would be moved by the evidence, as I understand it, to cast a vote for his conviction on the charge of murder. Even my saintly grandmother, who is the soul of good sense and Christian purity, thinks as I do. I am not, I fear, the assistant you need to help you in this matter. I am sorry."

Having stated his views with complete frankness, it appeared to James that his refusal to be recruited by a man whose genius and accomplishments he so much revered, disconcerted him more than it did Benjamin Franklin, who listened to his statement with attentive silence and without any change to the genial expression on his face.

Upon James's conclusion of his summary concerning why he could not honor Dr. Franklin's request for help, the paunchy, elderly gentleman with brown eyes, perpetually serene face and balding pate merely remarked, "Such discourse as we are having, Captain, is dry work. I think it may be time to refresh ourselves with some cordials. Perhaps you would be so kind as to pull that cord hanging over there by the door to summon Mr. Mahoney."

Hardly had James finished giving the cord Dr. Franklin had indicated a tug than Mr. Mahoney appeared in the study's doorway.

"Francis, would you be so good as to bring up a bottle of the 1765 Chateau Ligneville for Captain Jamison? You will find it with the other Burgundy I had you put down in the cellar beneath the kitchen. And bring for me a bottle of Monsieur Le Vieillard's wine of nature."

(The reference to "wine of nature," James discovered, was Franklin's facetious way of referring to the bottled French spring water he had grown so fond of during his nine years in France that he had brought back twenty-two cases of it to Philadelphia.)

Mr. Mahoney, who understood perfectly his master's manner of expressing his wishes, acknowledged these orders with a nod of his head and departed.

"I see, Captain Jamison, by your repeated glances in their direction, that you are curious about my glass harmonica and the apparatus I purchased in Paris to study the circulation of the blood. Your interest, I suppose, arises from your family making its living from the fabrication of glass. Permit me to give you a closer look at these curiosities while we await Mr. Mahoney's return with our refreshments."

With that, he heaved himself to his feet by the aid of his gold-headed cane, as he had done on rising to greet James, and started off toward the corner of the room where the objects he referred to reposed, speaking as he went, James trailing after him.

"The glass harmonica, as the name suggests, is a musical instrument. It consists of hollow glass disks of varying sizes mounted on a spindle inside a wooden case. The spindle can be rotated by working a treadle, and as the disks are turning, musical notes of an agreeable warbling quality can be produced by pressing a moistened fingertip against the disk whose note you wish to hear, causing it to vibrate. The harmonica, which now incorporates some small improvements I suggested, is in use throughout Europe. The Continent's leading composers have written music for it. Allow me to demonstrate its sound by playing for you part of a little piece Mozart has composed for the glass harmonica."

Having said this, Dr. Franklin asked James to hold his cane, sat down on the stool drawn up before the instrument, started the treadle which put the glass disks in motion, and, having moistened his fingertips in the porcelain water cups attached to each side of the instrument's cabinet, began to play. For the next six minutes the extraordinary melodiousness of the harmonica filled Dr. Franklin's study.

When he finished, he smilingly looked at James and asked what he thought of the harmonica.

"Its sounds are ethereal, Dr. Franklin! The sort of music one imagines angels making! It surpasses anything I could imagine coming from a musical instrument. I never knew a wonder such as this existed. And you play it admirably, I must say."

"I'm glad you liked it. I thought you might."

"And this other machine? What does it do?"

"Ah, this instrument has a quite different purpose, pertaining to natural philosophy. It is an apparatus for studying the flow of blood which conveys the oxygen that we and other forms of animal life must have, as we see whenever the flow of blood is interrupted, as from strangulation or a grievous wound."

Dr. Franklin gestured for the return of his cane, rose from the stool in front of the glass harmonica, and took a few steps over to the table on which rested an intricate mass of glass tubing of varying sizes that was evidently connected in one continuous circuit. Some of the tubes were of such fine diameter that it astonished James, who had a good deal of practical insight into the fabrication of glass. At the center of this intricate maze was a vessel filled with a bright red fluid.

"This is a schematic display, Captain Jamison, of the vessels which convey blood throughout our bodies. The model was fabricated in Venice, which as you may know is a city renowned in Europe for its artisans skilled in glassmaking. The reservoir in the middle of the system represents the heart, and the tubes ramifying outward from it represent the vessels that carry the blood to the farthest extremes of our bodies and then return it to the heart by way of the lungs. This marvelous organ, the heart, which contracts and expands every instant of our lives, though we should live to a hundred, is the pump which furnishes the pressure for that ceaseless flow. Think, Captain Jamison, how many pumping performances that is in even a brief lifetime.

"Among the books General Grey stole from my library was the first English translation of William Harvey's 1628 Latin treatise on the blood's circulation. However, through an agent in Brussels, I have obtained a duplicate of that valuable tome. The mechanics of the blood have long interested me, especially as it pertains to the tiniest capillaries where the ruptures we call bruises occur."

"Might you put the machine in motion, Doctor Franklin, so I could see its operations?"

"I wish it were possible to humor your desire to see the machine in operation, Captain, but I'm afraid that cannot be, for the seal on the bellows which provides its impetus was damaged in shipping it across the Atlantic and the repair is still in progress.

"Let us return to our places. If you would be so kind, Captain, I would appreciate having the support of your arm."

After Dr. Franklin had eased himself once more onto the cushioned wooden armchair behind his work table, he said, "Thank you, sir. Movement worsens the discomfort I feel from the stones lodged in my organs. Sometimes I wish it were possible to suspend myself by silken cords from a petite version of the balloon Monsieur Montgolfier invented for transporting people through the air, which I saw demonstrated in Paris several years ago. I would then hire a boy to conduct me hither and yon by a cord attached to the balloon, and thus achieve a mobility that would not jar my afflicted organs.

"But I have had the good fortune of robust health during most of my life and have seldom been seriously ill, for which I am sincerely grateful. One cannot expect perfection always. The freedom which is necessary to life is not conducive to absolute perfection."

James smiled and nodded at these remarks, though he did not understand what Dr. Franklin meant by saying freedom and perfection are incompatible.

"If I remember aright, when we were discussing the case of Jacob Maul a moment ago, you mentioned the coincidence of two women dying on the same man's property with the same marks of presumptive violence on their throats, and that this coincidence convinced you of Jacob's guilt in their deaths?"

"That is so, yes. And perhaps you also recall that I mentioned one of the two corpses being found in Mr. Maul's bed. For me, these coincidences point to his probable guilt in the deaths of the women."

"But does it not seem to you, Captain," Dr. Franklin asked in his most reasonable, coaxing tone, "that there is another coincidence here which weighs perhaps more heavily in favor of Jacob Maul's innocence?"

"I do not see what that could be. The papers would surely have reported such a coincidence."

James's elderly host kept his eyes fixed on his hands, which were folded across the head of his cane; then, looking up, he remarked, "Ah, but the papers have reported it, James. They have reported it. Only, it is a coincidence easily overlooked by anyone who has made up his mind that Jacob Maul is guilty. Does it not strike you, my dear sir, as peculiar that no attempt was made to conceal either corpse? Is that not a coincidence as momentous as the bruising to the throats of the women and where their corpses were found?

"What sane man, I ask you, would strangle someone asleep beside him in his bed and then return to his slumbers as tranquilly as if nothing had happened? And I have it on good authority, from someone who attended the Coroner's inquest into the death of Jacob's wife seven years ago, that he had been in fact sound asleep when persons in his household discovered his wife stone cold dead. No. The coincidence which many people think proves Jacob's guilt, I see as evidence of his innocence.

"Then there is also this to consider. What reason did Jacob have for murdering his wife, or his sister-in-law? After all, he had married this wife not long before her death. And at the inquest into that death seven years ago, her sister, the now dead Mrs. Coons, whom he is also thought to have strangled, testified that Jacob and her sister lived in matrimonial harmony as befitted a man and a woman raised in the Quaker religion. Mrs. Coons was most emphatic on that point in giving her testimony at the Coroner's inquest into her sister's death. I have obtained and read the transcript of the inquest. The testimony of Mrs. Coons, we may be sure, influenced the Coroner in his finding that exculpated Jacob of any wrongdoing in the death of his wife.

"Jacob Maul benefited not one jot from either of these deaths, Captain Jamison, and no one has ever accused him of maniacal behavior, simply because no one could. On the contrary, his goodness and kindliness toward others have been a subject of comment by everyone who ever knew him."

Just as Dr. Franklin completed this remark, Mr. Mahoney reappeared in the room, bearing on a silver tray the bottled refreshments he had been sent to get, along with two goblets of cut glass and a plate of country cheese and home-baked crackers. His arrival with these cordials suspended all discourse on the Quaker stonecutter's guilt or innocence.

Chapter 3

Mr. Mahoney set the tray on Benjamin Franklin's work table, deftly uncorked the twenty-year-old Burgundy, poured a little of it into one of the goblets, and started to hand it to his master to see if the wine was still drinkable. But his master nodded toward his guest, and the servant gave the wine to Captain Jamison, who, after sipping some of it, drained his glass and praised the vintage.

"Never in my life, Doctor Franklin, have I tasted such wine. It savors of fresh cracked butternuts and at the same time has a hint of roast veal. It is a liquid that somehow partakes of the solid and chewable foods. I am again obliged to you for instructing me in the wonders of the world."

Having heard such high praise for his master's wine, Mr. Mahoney filled the guest's goblet with the Ligneville and placed the bottle within his reach. The recipient of this product of his grandmother's native country felt that a man might go to considerable lengths to have some of this extraordinary wine, and an entire bottle of it had just been opened for him.

"I'm pleased the elixir meets with your approval, Captain. The advice of several physicians keeps me from partaking of it with you. But I have savored its virtues in years past. Help yourself to as much of it as you care to have without further invitation."

When Mr. Mahoney had withdrawn from the company of the two men and each of them had had a bite of the cheese and crackers, Dr. Franklin proceeded with his discourse on the deaths of the Quaker sisters.

"I want to emphasize, Captain, that the Coroner's report on Mrs. Maul's death states as a matter of fact the entire absence of any animosity between Jacob Maul and his wife, and the further fact that he derived no benefit from her death. Moreover, his sister-in-law, Mrs. Coons, repeatedly said she did not believe he had any agency in the death of her sister. Her well-argued defense of Jacob appears to have influenced Mr. Constable, the same man now in the office of Coroner, to hold Jacob guiltless and to declare his wife's death to be A Visitation of God, which is to say having a cause beyond the present state of human knowledge to determine. Mr. Constable might have rendered the judgment of Murder by Manual Strangulation. But he did not.

"In reaching his conclusion, the Coroner may also have been influenced by the singular fact that in the century since William Penn founded this city as a refuge for Quakers not one person of the Quaker faith had ever been accused of any act of violence in a court of law, let alone accused of murdering a woman by manual strangulation. Witness after witness at the inquest into the death of Jacob's wife testified to his peaceable character, including every Elder of his Weekly Meeting. The Coroner may have asked himself, as I have, how such a man could have throttled his wife in the middle of the night and resumed his slumbers beside her corpse. Such a hypothesis was stranger than the facts which Mr. Constable was called upon to judge in finding her death A Visitation of God."

James naturally gave this long disquisition by Dr. Franklin respectful attention, then said, "I can see, sir, how the Coroner may have rendered the finding he did in the death of Mrs. Maul. But Mrs. Coons's recent death under the same circumstances—the bruises to the throat and her corpse being found on Maul's property, just as her sister's was—alters the situation considerably, I would say, and is a quite different matter from the circumstances Mr. Constable was called upon to judge seven years ago. As to Mr. Maul's impeccable reputation for goodness, it may have exonerated him once but hardly qualifies as a helpful piece of evidence after a second corpse is discovered on his property with bruise marks on the throat. I submit it is asking more than reason can allow to exonerate a man twice on the grounds that he has never been known to act violently, when evidence suggests that he may have acted violently twice. The second corpse establishes a pattern.

"History and our own experience tell us, I think, Dr. Franklin, that man is a being prone to violence and more than a little adept at deception. In regard to motives for such vile acts as strangulation, we may grant that Mr. Maul gained no tangible benefit from the deaths of these women, yet one may ask whether no vile act has ever been committed without benefit to the person who committed it. May we not observe that even persons of apparently spotless character have been known sometimes to do evil for its own sake, just as persons ordinarily do good for its own sake?"

Dr. Franklin responded to James's reasoning by saying, "Very well, sir. Then let us consider the matter in another light. There are only three possibilities. Either Mrs. Maul and her sister Mrs. Coons were both murdered, or one was murdered and the other one died of some natural but unknown cause, or they both died of natural causes. There are no other possibilities. And since Mrs. Coons was missing several days before her corpse turned up, week before last, in the old privy on Maul's property with its hands tied behind its back and feet tied together, rolled up in a piece of canvas which was also tied, we must rule out the possibility of a natural cause in both deaths. Therefore, we are left with only the possibilities that both sisters were murdered or one was murdered and the other died of a natural cause during sleep, conceivably involving spontaneous rupturing to the vessels in the throat which supply blood to the brain. Does the incompleteness of our knowledge of the flaws and diseases to which human flesh is heir justify ruling out the latter possibility? I would say not. The people talk of two murders because it is simpler and more in keeping with the common tendency to think ill of human nature. I prefer the hypothesis that seven years ago Mrs. Maul died in her sleep of some as yet undiscovered natural cause—the Coroner's finding of A Visitation of God—while Mrs. Coons, whose corpse was tied in a canvas shroud and deposited in the cavity of the old necessity on Jacob Maul's property, was murdered.

"Having ruled out the possibility that both women died natural deaths, which of the remaining two hypotheses, Captain, do you think we must believe to the exclusion of the other? Are you entirely unwilling to concede that the deaths of these two women could have different categories of causes, willful violence in the one case and natural lesion in the other? To rule out natural cause entirely in the death of Jacob's wife would be, it seems to me, unworthy of a man of experience and intellect. Why must the deaths of both women necessarily be attributed to manual strangulation? And if we accept the possibility that the wife's death could have been caused by some unknown weakness in her constitution while her sister's death was indubitably the result of violence at the hands of some unknown person, then the second murder hypothesis, the strongest reason for supposing Jacob Maul guilty of strangling Mrs. Coons, disappears.

"I have three reasons for my belief in Jacob Maul's innocence. One, as I have said, is his peaceable character, probably an inborn disposition which was further developed by his Quaker upbringing. My second reason is the absence of any motive for killing his wife or her sister. Third is the fact that no effort was made in either of these deaths to conceal the corpse, a peculiarity so conspicuous in the case of the wife as to point to some sort of madness, for which there is no supporting evidence."

James had to admit to himself in listening to Dr. Franklin's logic that his own belief in Maul's guilt did not take into account any of the matters Dr. Franklin had emphasized. However, it occurred to him, in the recent death of Mrs. Coons an effort had been made to conceal the corpse, and he was quick to point this out to Benjamin Franklin.

"You say, Doctor Franklin, that Mr. Maul made no attempt to dispose of either corpse. I will grant you that is eminently so in the case of the wife's death seven years ago. But was not the corpse of Mrs. Coons deposited in the cavity of a necessary on Maul's property, and was that not an attempt to conceal it?"

"Yes, but not a reasonable one. Anyone of mature years, sound mind, and common sense knows decaying flesh soon produces a telltale stench. Whoever murdered Mrs. Coons would have known that the whereabouts of her corpse would soon be revealed by its odor, which is exactly what happened. Why would Jacob Maul—supposing him to have been Mrs. Coons's assassin—have risked the discovery of her corpse on his property? If he took the trouble to tie up her corpse in a piece of canvas, why did he not take the additional step of including in the bundle a few stones, of which there was a ready supply at hand in his stoneyard, and then trundle the weighted bundle over to the Delaware—which was but a short distance away—to sink it in the river? Then, if the corpse ever surfaced, it could have no association with him.

"Yet in both deaths, the corpse *was* associated with Jacob Maul, and that association seems to me the primary feature of the mystery. If we regard Mrs. Maul and her sister Mrs. Coons as victims of strangulation by the same person, namely Jacob Maul, because the throats of both women exhibited bruising and both women lived in his house, and both of their corpses were found on his property, then we must conclude, I think, that Jacob Maul wanted to be found out for his deeds. But that presupposes some sort of mental aberration on his part, such as a desire for self-destruction, and no evidence exists in support of such a proposition. On the contrary, there is ample and consistent testimony that he was a conscientious, kindly man, an invariably sane workman, different from his fellow workers perhaps only in his extraordinary kindness toward others, the sort of conduct his son exhibited toward you on the battlefield at Monmouth. A man's character may change over the years, Captain. There is no doubt about that. But no man, I think, can conceal his true nature from everyone for as many years as Jacob Maul has lived."

Dr. Franklin's powers of analysis at last prevailed with James Jamison. Because of Franklin's gentle, methodical prodding, he had to admit to himself that he had made too much of where the corpses had been discovered and nothing at all of their non-concealment.

He reached for the opened bottle of Ligneville in front of him, poured his glass full of the delectable wine, savored an ample draught of it, and said to his host, "What would you have me do, Doctor Franklin?"

The good Doctor gave a nod of his head in acknowledgment of this delayed consent and said, "The first thing we must do, James, is adopt a method of inquiry. No puzzle of any sort can be solved without a procedure for addressing it. To attempt to make an inquiry without a method would be as little to the purpose as proposing to get rich without a plan for doing so. Our method in this instance, I think, should be to separate the deaths of these two women, Maul's wife and her sister, Mrs. Coons. We should assume they had distinct causes, one violent and one natural, and make that the basis for our inquiries. The violent, recent death of Mrs. Coons is our chief concern. Perhaps in the end we will discover that the two deaths are in some particular way related. But for the purpose of our investigation, we should treat them as discrete and unrelated events. Whatever happened in Mrs. Maul's death seven years ago, that track is now cold, and ought not to distract us from our main purpose, which is to discover who killed Mrs. Coons in order that we may lift the cloud of suspicion from Jacob Maul. As Poor Richard says, 'The man who pursues two hares at the same time will catch neither.'

"Our first step," Dr. Franklin continued, "should be, I think, to gather as many facts as we can about Mrs. Coons's history and her relations with other persons to discover who may have benefited from her death. Your first order of business therefore should be to visit William Maul and his wife at the Maul stoneyard on Dock Street, for they are the likeliest source of what we most need, information on Mrs. Coons's behavior in the days leading up to her disappearance and knowledge of her character and who her acquaintances were.

You can use your obligation to John Maul for saving your life at Monmouth as your reason for your interest in the matter which has so affected the Maul family."

"But, Dr. Franklin, wouldn't it be better if the people I talk to knew of your interest in Mrs. Coons's death and regarded me as your agent? That, it seems to me, would incline them to be more forthcoming."

This observation caused an abrupt change in Dr. Franklin's demeanor. His speech, which had hitherto been mild and affable, became suddenly peremptory and stern.

"James, you must never let it be known that you and I are acquainted! Under no circumstance must anyone know of our association. Not even your grandmother, your sister, or your sister's husband is to know of our alliance. No one! You only are to bear public responsibility for the investigation. Do you understand what I am saying?"

James solemnly nodded his understanding of this fiat. Franklin, seeing the effect his words had had on his ally, whose help and loyal cooperation he needed, reverted to his habitual tone of gentle, Socratic persuasion.

"You may think me harsh, James, in taking this view. But I do not want to acquire in my old age a character for being willing to untangle the affairs of my neighbors. Were I to acquire such a character, my remaining years of life, whether few or many, would be intolerably vexed by constant requests for such assistance. My life would then be at the mercy of all sorts of demands. Whether you and I succeed or fail in our endeavor to discover who killed Mrs. Coons, you alone must be responsible for the result. Do you agree to this stipulation that you are never to reveal my connection to our inquiry into what the town is calling the Quaker Murders?"

"I do. I give you my word, Dr. Franklin. Your part in the matter shall remain a closely kept secret with me. I understand I am to bear entire responsibility before others for whatever result we shall obtain. I make this pledge to you on my honor."

"I expected nothing less, James, from the grandson of Samuel Jamison."

Having reached this understanding, James naturally wanted to know everything Dr. Franklin knew of Jacob Maul's history, and his director agreed the information was needed to conduct his inquiries intelligently.

The History of the Quaker Stonecutter Jacob Maul

As immigrants poured into Philadelphia in the 1730s and 40s, the trade of stonecutting became highly profitable because the rapid increase in population produced an increasing need for houses and other buildings. Maul was apprenticed during these years to an unmarried brother of his father, who owned a stoneyard on Dock Creek, not far from the river. As an apprentice stonecutter, Jacob Maul showed a natural aptitude for the work and soon qualified as a journeyman stonecutter. Upon his uncle's death, and in the absence of a will or any closer heir than Jacob's father, who wanted his son to inherit the stoneyard, Jacob became the proprietor of an established, thriving enterprise.

He prospered as owner of the yard, and on the strength of his proprietorship married the daughter of one of the founders of Philadelphia's guild of carpenters, a marriage made in accordance with the Quaker discipline of obtaining the permission of the Elders of both the bride's and the groom's Weekly Meeting. Three sons were born of this union—John, William, and Robert—all of whom survived into manhood and came to work for their father in his business. It was at this time, at the height of Jacob Maul's prosperity, that Benjamin Franklin had known and employed him in the building of Franklin Court.

The War for Independence which commenced in 1775 was the beginning of schisms in the Quaker community, which heretofore had dominated the economy and government of Pennsylvania, and marked the start of Jacob Maul's decline.

In the autumn of that year, Maul's eldest son left Philadelphia to enlist in the Continental Army being mustered outside Boston under the command of General Washington. John Maul's enlistment in the army was of course a violation of the defining doctrine of Quaker discipline—nonviolence— and his action had severe, immediate consequences.

John Maul had not consulted either his father or his mother about his intention to leave home to join the American effort to throw off monarchical rule, for he knew his parents would never consent to what he wanted to do. The teachings of Maul's religion strictly forbade members of the Society of Friends from having anything to do with warfare, even if it was only making shoes for soldiers to wear or selling blankets for their use. Whoever departed from these teachings was excommunicated from the Society in a formal denunciation known as "separation" and Quakers in good standing in the Society were to shun those who had been excommunicated from that moment on. For his violation of Quaker discipline, John Maul was "separated" before the congregation of his Weekly Meeting, including his father, mother, and two brothers.

The shame of his son's expulsion from his church and the father's duty, as a devout Quaker, to shun him were heavy blows to a man of Jacob Maul's religious sensibilities, though his son's apostasy was by no means an uncommon occurrence. Several prominent Quakers of Pennsylvania, such as Thomas Mifflin and Samuel Wetherill, as well as a goodly number of ordinary Quakers, supported the War for Independence and were expelled from their Weekly Meetings and read out of the Society of Friends. The Elders of the Quaker churches throughout the colonies tirelessly preached loyalty to the king and denounced support of the war. Those Quakers who refused to remain obedient subjects of the king and to eschew violence were excommunicated just as John Maul had been. The theme of Quaker preaching in America was that whoever joined the uprising against the Crown or supported it in any way desecrated "the Truth of the Inner Light" on which the Quaker religion was established. Quaker congregations were told over and over that such persons were not being expelled from the Society of Friends but rather were expelling themselves by their rejection of the Inner Light.

The winter following John Maul's enlistment in the Continental Army, a far heavier blow befell Jacob Maul. The companion of his life, his wife, the mother of his sons and helpmate, slipped on the ice while crossing Market Street and slid under a passing dray cart, whose heavy iron-rimmed wheels crushed the bones in both of her thighs. These tremendous compound fractures soon became infected and brought on a lingering agony in which Jacob Maul shared as he kept steadfast vigil, day and night, at her bedside until her death.

A year after his wife's death, Jacob Maul married the nurse who had attended her, one Margaret Gilbert, a woman the same age as his eldest son. Again, he married according to Quaker discipline by obtaining the permission of the Elders of his Weekly Meeting, which, in this instance was the same Weekly Meeting his intended wife attended.

Margaret Gilbert combined with her maidenly virtues of tenderness and compassion the courage, strength, and prudence of a much older woman. There was iron in her nature along with kindness. Her lanky body, elongated hands, feet, arms, and legs and her general appearance of gauntness suited the mood of melancholy which possessed Jacob Maul after his first wife's death. It was this woman, Margaret Gilbert, whose corpse was found in the Quaker stonecutter's bed less than a year after he married her.

Maul received the news of his oldest son's death in the British prison ship the year following the death of his second wife.

But his troubles were not over. The deaths of his wives and his eldest son were followed by yet another blow. His youngest son ran away from home to join the Continental Army, saying in the note he left behind for his father that he wanted to replace his brother John in the fight against Britain. Whether young Robert Maul failed in his intention to join the Army or lay buried in some nameless grave with other Americans fallen in battle, no one could say. But in any event, he had not returned home in the two years since the end of the war.

Robert's leaving home without being transferred to the discipline of another Weekly Meeting was in itself sufficient cause for excommunication, whether he succeeded in joining the Army or not, and so he, too, had been denounced by the Elders of his family's Weekly Meeting in the presence of his father and his brother William and separated from the Society of Friends, as his brother John had been.

Dr. Franklin had also learned from his informants that during the British occupation of Philadelphia a pair of Hessian soldiers had been billeted in Jacob Maul's house on Dock Street. This was no small matter since the stonecutter was at that time supporting his sons William and Robert, his new wife and the wife's widowed sister, Mrs. Coons, and her young daughter, an indentured maidservant, and a hostler who slept in a lean-to attached to the stable and looked after the six horses Jacob Maul kept for hauling stone.

Furnishing board and room for two robust soldiers in addition to his seven dependents and himself strained the Quaker stonecutter's resources since he had lost many of his customers because of his refusal to perform any of the stone work on the military fortifications being constructed to defend the city against the expected British invasion. As the war dragged on, the hearts of many Americans were hardened toward anyone who would not support the struggle or were slack in their support, or, as in the case of Quakers, categorically opposed warfare and rebellion.

The strain from Maul's loss of business became so burdensome that, finally, he had to sell two of his three teams of horses and get rid of his hostler, whose services were no longer needed to care for just two horses. Maul's straitened circumstances also forced him to sell his maidservant's indenture.

Now, with his imprisonment on suspicion of having murdered Mrs. Coons, the ruination of this once flourishing Quaker stonecutter and his family seemed complete.

Chapter 4

Having given James the history of Jacob Maul, Benjamin Franklin now addressed the practical matter of how they were to communicate without revealing their acquaintance.

"To receive messages from you," he told James, "and for you to deliver to me daily written reports of everything you have learned in making your inquiries, we must establish a post. You will also have to come to Franklin Court to confer with me each week, say every Tuesday and Saturday at eleven, the same hour at which you came earlier tonight, if that is agreeable to you. I sleep but little—usually four or five hours a night—so eleven is an agreeable hour for me if it is not too late for you, James. I do much of my work while other men slumber."

James assured his director that he, too, was often up late writing in his journal and on other matters during the quiet hours of the night while everyone else was abed. He had thought perhaps Dr. Franklin might inquire of him what sort of things he wrote, but he didn't.

"Mr. Mahoney will show you a more convenient way, both for you and for him, to enter Franklin Court on your visits than the way you came tonight. He will also show you the post where you are to leave your written reports, and will explain how we can convey any urgent messages or questions we might have for each other in regard to unexpected developments.

"As an aid to gathering the information we need, I want you to publish in the Philadelphia papers an announcement saying that you're looking into the death of Mrs. Coons, giving as your reason your debt to Sergeant John Maul. The advertisement, which I will write and give you the money to publish, will offer ten Spanish dollars for information regarding Mrs. Coons's death. Long ago I found out, James, in the promotion of various projects for the improvement of our city, that the most effective way to recruit people's interest and support is to give them a clear statement of your purpose and the reason for it. Arousing the sensibilities of the people is always beneficial in any undertaking, no matter what it may be.

"To make the most of the advertisement, I will have 200 handbills of it run off on my printing press, which my grandson Benny is operating in the attic of my carriage house. He accompanied me on my mission to France and is as perfectly habituated to keeping my secrets as Mr. Mahoney, even from his mother, my daughter Sally. He will deliver the handbills to your house tomorrow night for placement throughout the town day after tomorrow. They will supplement the utility of the newspaper advertisement.

"Please help yourself to more of the wine, James, while I compose the ad. Where should I say the information should be delivered to you? Surely not to your home."

"I usually take my meals at the City Tavern when not at home, and often conduct business there."

"Very well, then. The City Tavern. That's an excellent place for our purpose because everyone knows where it is, even if they do not patronize it."

After writing the announcement and handing it to James to read, Dr. Franklin left the room by a door James had not noticed because it had been constructed to appear to be part of a wall. He returned in a few moments with a small leather pouch.

"Here is the money you will need, James, to pay for the ad and have someone put up the handbills, and to reward anyone who gives you useful information. I will provide you with more money if this proves insufficient. What do you think of our advertisement?"

"It is admirably clear and succinct, Dr. Franklin. I would only suggest we add that Sergeant Maul died in one of those pestilential hulks the British used as prisons. I think that would arouse more sympathy for our efforts to aid his incarcerated father." Franklin agreed and made the changes to include this detail.

In handing the corrected ad back to James, Dr. Franklin advised him to take the notice around to the papers in person rather than hire someone to do it. That way, even before the appearance of the advertisement, the hands who worked in each shop would hear what he said to the publishers of the newspapers and would spread the news of James's investigation into the death of Mrs. Coons as the latest gossip on the Quaker Murders.

"Word of mouth, James, is always the most productive form of advertising."

Franklin also advised James to speak as soon as he could with the Coroner and Dr. Phineas Finley who, he understood, had both examined the corpse of Mrs. Coons. The first order of business for James, however, he said, should be to find out all that he could from William Maul and his wife about Mrs.

Coons. He should also, as soon as possible, visit the Walnut Street Jail and talk with Jacob Maul.

Franklin then summoned Mr. Mahoney by the same means as before and told him to escort James from Franklin Court "by the door in the west boundary wall" and "give him the usual instructions." James's director then stood up behind his worktable, shook James's hand, and bade him good night, thanking him for agreeing to aid him. He also said he had complete confidence in James's abilities to get the information that would be needed. The final thing Dr. Franklin said was that he was glad James had finished the Ligneville, for once a bottle of wine was opened it should not be re-corked.

Before escorting James from Dr. Franklin's mansion-house, Mr. Mahoney lit James's lantern and returned it to him. He then led him through a sitting room and a smaller room to a back door of the house and outside. From there they went past a large brick necessary and another outbuilding behind the carriage house to a small portal in the ten-foot-high brick wall topped with jagged pieces of broken glass that surrounded Franklin Court. After unlocking this door, Mr. Mahoney handed James the key to it.

"Take care not to lose this, Captain Jamison," Mr. Mahoney said, "for without it you will not be able to enter this hidden door to Franklin Court, which is always kept locked. It leads to a passage next to the Indian Queen and out onto Fourth Street. On future visits come down this passage and enter the grounds of Franklin Court by this door, then come to the back door of the house we just used and knock on it like this."

He demonstrated the signal, a little rhythm of one knock, pause, four knocks, pause, and two concluding raps in rapid succession; then he had James practice the rhythmic knock.

"I shall be waiting by that door at the appointed time to admit you when I hear that signal. On the other side of this portal, you'll find a holly bush, and behind the bush, in the fourth course of bricks from the ground, there is a loose brick. By removing it, which is easily done, you will find behind it a small cavity containing a sealskin pouch. Put your written reports for Dr. Franklin and any other messages you have for him in the pouch. When he has a message for you, it will be deposited in the pouch, and you'll know of its presence by the peephole in the carriage gates on Market Street being left open.

"I'll check the pouch each morning and evening, and you are to do the same to see if the peephole has been left open. Do you have any questions, Captain Jamison?"

James had nothing to ask. He was astonished that Dr. Franklin's taciturn majordomo could make such a detailed speech.

After bidding Mr. Mahoney goodnight, going through the postern, and locking it behind him, James looked for and found the cavity behind the holly bush and the sealskin pouch.

The passageway which ran out to the street beside the Indian Queen Tavern, he discovered, was barely wide enough to admit a man through it without moving sideways. He also discovered that it made a right-angle turn near the space where the holly bush grew, so that from Fourth Street all anyone would see was the appearance of a high brick wall rather than the door or the holly bush. This discovery explained why Mr. Mahoney called this postern hidden.

As James went down the constricted passage, the odor of urine became stronger and stronger the closer he got to Fourth Street. By the light of his lantern and the smell of excrement, he also found that he had to be careful where he stepped.

As he emerged into Fourth Street, a shapeless figure muffled in quilts, asleep next to a doorstep, was the only person visible by the light of the whale oil lamps illuminating the silent street. The wind, which had been so blustery when he'd entered Franklin Court, had died away and been replaced by a very slight breeze. The air was noticeably colder and quite refreshing after his hours in Franklin Court. His grandmother's word for such air was "brisky."

When James arrived home, he saw the glow of a candle in his grandmother's bedchamber window and decided to pay her his devoir. In softly cracking open the door to her room, he spied her alertly looking at the door. She wore a flannel nightcap and lamb's wool shawl and her petite figure was propped up in bed by pillows. She held in palm-gloved hands one of her books on Catholic history and thought, which a French bookseller in Tours sent to her each June, and which she methodically read during the course of the ensuing year at the rate of one a month. Her native France seemed to have an endless supply of such books, and her appetite for them seemed likewise inexhaustible.

James opened the door and, going over to his dear Grandmère, he saluted her the French way, as she had taught him to do as a boy, kissing her on both of her smooth, rosy cheeks. She in turn asked him, as she always did when he came home from one of his outings, if he was hungry. He said no, he'd had some refreshments in town. She did not ask him where he had been because she was opposed to what she called "meddling." She would ask him questions only on subjects he introduced or if she had sent him on some errand of family business regarding the glassworks her husband had bequeathed to her. Neither James nor her grandson-in-law, Lawrence, who assisted her in running the glassworks, had noticed any decline in its management since she had become the owner.

Despite her cheerfulness toward him, James knew she worried about him. That he was not eating enough. That he was too conscious of his maimed hand. That he was avoiding the company of women because of the hand's grotesqueness. She had been the one who had suggested he have a glover sew a specially made black glove of the softest kid for his mutilated hand to lessen its raw appearance, a glove he now habitually wore, except in bed.

Her chief concern seemed to be that he would never marry and have children, as his sister Jane had done, which Grandmère regarded as a sacred obligation of all good Christians.

By way of suggesting what he had been up to and getting her approval for spending time on Dr. Franklin's project away from his usual duties at the Jamison Glassworks, James told her he had decided to take an interest in the arrest of Sergeant John Maul's father.

To this she said nothing at first; then, "*Très bien*. But why? We discussed the affair and decided the man was probably guilty of what he is suspected of doing. Was that not so?"

"Yes. But I've been thinking. Why would a man who has always lived an exemplary life kill two women and make no attempt to conceal his crimes? That puzzles me, Grandmère. The death of the wife seven years ago is too far in the past to discover much about that. But perhaps it might be possible to find out if the housekeeper had an enemy who wanted her dead. If I could prove Mr. Maul innocent of her death and obtain his release from prison, it would be for me as if I had paid the debt I owe his son for saving my life at Monmouth. It would be nice of you to allow me to do this. Lawrence and Mr.

Bartlett can do whatever I might have to neglect at the glassworks in the next few weeks."

"Very well, Jamie. You were always a generous boy. Generous and bright. Your grandfather and I often said that about you while you were growing up. If anyone can find out something new in this affair, you will. *Que Dieu bénisse ton entreprise.* It is time for you now to rest, *mon cher*. Livy has kept a fire for you in your chamber to warm you when you arrive."

Having heard these words of dismissal, James bent over and kissed his grandmother's snow-white nightcap and went upstairs to his bedchamber, where he found his Franklin stove radiating heat into the room. Next to the stove was a fresh scuttle of coal that Livy had lugged upstairs.

He removed his officer's greatcoat and hung it in his armoire, then took from his waistcoat the key to the door to Franklin Court and the advertisement Dr. Franklin had written for him to put in the papers. Depositing in the drawer of his escritoire these proofs that he had not imagined what had befallen him, that it was not all a dream and he had actually become a confidant of one of the greatest men of the Age, he dressed for bed, said the prayers he had been taught to say as a child, and went to sleep.

Chapter 5

James awoke from his few hours of deep slumber much refreshed and eager to perform the tasks he had promised Dr. Franklin he would perform. Looking from his chamber windows to the east and north, he saw the day was gray but dry, and windless, since the trees and bushes were all quite still.

To take the chill off his room, he put a scoop of coal in the Franklin stove and with his bellows got it burning. He brought in from the hall the pitcher of warm water, wrapped in a towel, that Livy had placed outside his door, washed his face, and shaved.

Grandmère and her maid were chatting in the kitchen when James came down for breakfast. He kissed his grandparent and thanked the comely maidservant for keeping the fire going in his room the night before.

Livy smiled and said in return, "That's all right. I've brewed a pot of chocolate. There's also salted mackerel, oatmeal with brown sugar and milk, bacon, baked eggs, toasted wheat bread with butter, and jam. What would you like?"

"I'll have everything you have, Livy, as quick as you can get it ready," James replied. "My innards are starving—I could eat a bear!"

It was clear from Livy's face that the joviality of James's hearty response pleased her, and Grandmère listened approvingly to this conversation between her grandson and Livy.

While his breakfast was being prepared James sat down next to the fire, where his grandmother was busy knitting a coverlet for the new baby of Jane and Lawrence, which was on its way and due any week now.

"Grandmère, I have to tell Lawrence and Mr. Bartlett that I'll not be at the glasshouse for a while, as I mentioned to you last night."

"*Très bien.*"

"I think I'll ride Cheval rather than walk to the Northern Liberties, because after I talk with Lawrence and Mr. Bartlett I have some other things to attend to. Shouldn't we look to buy a new horse, Grandmère? We won't be able to ride Cheval much longer, he's so old."

"He'll do for a while yet. If we got a new horse to do his job, Cheval's feelings would be hurt, *n'est-ce pas*? Old horses like to be useful. Besides, he was your grandfather's favorite. There's no reason to spend money on new horses with Jane's baby on the way, and more perhaps to come in the next few years."

Going down Market Street on Cheval a bit later, James went by the entrance to Franklin Court and looked to see whether the peephole in the carriage gates was open, less in expectation that it would be than to get into the habit of seeing if Dr. Franklin might have left him a message.

This morning the events of yesterday night appeared a long time in the past. It seemed to James he had always been a collaborator of Benjamin Franklin, the most famous man in America after General Washington. As he passed among the pedestrians, carts, wagons, horsemen, and post-chaises of

Market Street in all their morning hustle and bustle, it suddenly occurred to James how difficult Dr. Franklin's proposal was. To find one man—the man guilty of killing Mrs. Coons, who was now walking these streets—among the tens of thousands of persons in the city. Thinking of that dissipated the lighthearted mood he had enjoyed since getting out of bed and having his breakfast feast. The task would have to be accomplished, he decided, the way he and his fellow soldiers had fought the war, one battle at a time, never giving up faith that the enemy would in the end be vanquished, no matter how remote final victory might seem or how many battles were lost.

The Northern Liberties, where the Jamisons' glasshouse was located, was a district of small manufactories at the north edge of the city. It had been James's home for the first sixteen years of his life, until his grandparents built the bigger house in the western suburbs and moved there with him and his sister Jane, five years before the war.

The glassworks was the size of a barn and built of brick. Its large, square chimney billowed smoke as James tied Cheval's reins to the metal hitching post in front of his boyhood home next to the works, where Jane and Lawrence now lived with their little twin boys. The glassworks' door was ample enough to admit a farm wagon, and its two halves were wide-open since the furnace for making glass was operating full blast. Only on winter's coldest days was the door ever completely shut. Large, open windows at both ends of the building's eaves, high up near the peak of the roof, also dissipated the heat. Little cheeping birds swooped in and out of these unobstructed openings to the shelter of the beamed trusses in the building's lofty interior.

The first person James saw as he entered the factory was
Lawrence in his leather apron, shoveling sand, soda, lime, and
cullet into a big wheelbarrow for making a new batch of glass.
Stephen Lunt, the oldest boy in the glasshouse, was using a
thick wooden paddle to mix the ingredients as Lawrence
measured them a shovelful at a time into the barrow.

The house's four glassblowers were grouped around a
semicircular, iron-topped table, each with a pot of molten glass
beside him. They were blowing green bottles. James paused to
watch Mr. Tift, one of the glassblowers, as he twirled a gob of
molten glass from his pot onto the end of his long metal
blowpipe and rolled it on the table's smooth metal until it had
the shape he wanted. Then he quickly reheated the gob to the
right viscosity in the fire beneath his pot of molten glass before
placing it in the mold, which the boy who assisted him then
swiftly locked, and the glassblower, his cheeks bulging with air,
blew the molten glass into a bottle inside the mold. James
never tired of watching the process and the skill it required at
each step.

After the bottle had been blown, the boy cut the still
malleable glass loose from the blowpipe with a pair of shears,
unlocked the mold, and carefully lifted the red-hot bottle out
by the neck with tongs, setting it on a mesh of stiff wire above a
bed of coals, while the glassblower knocked the cullet, or bit of
congealed waste glass, off the end of his iron blowpipe against
the table. Small boys kept the table free of broken cullet by
sweeping it into a bin under the straight edge of the table, and
other boys had the job of using tongs to move the just-made
bottles as they cooled to higher and higher steps of mesh above
the coals. They were then moved over to one of the clean brick
pavements on either side of the door, where they were left to
cool to air temperature before being packed in sawdust and

wood shavings in lightweight wooden boxes. Except for these pavements for cooling the ware, the floor of the glassworks was dirt.

When Philip Bartlett, the oldest of the four glassblowers, noticed James, he laid aside his blowpipe and came over to shake hands. He had been part of the Jamison glassworks from the beginning, having helped Samuel Jamison construct his furnace and been the first glassblower he had hired. For several years, Mr. Bartlett and Samuel Jamison had blown all the ware the house had produced. After James went into the Army during the war and Samuel had died, Mr. Bartlett and Lawrence had overseen the glassworks.

"We don't see you as often as we used to, James," Mr. Bartlett said as they shook hands.

"Getting customers for our ware takes more time than you might think, Philip. That's why you don't see me. But the business does better with me beating the brush for customers than it would with me working here alongside you and Lawrence and the others. It looks like you're coming along well with the order from the Pennsylvania Hospital."

"Yes. One more batch of green glass should do it. Lawrence is mixing it up now."

"So I see. Here he comes to say hello."

The Revolutionary War veteran and bachelor gave a warm embrace to his brother-in-law, whom he had seen only the night before, in that other life before he had become Benjamin Franklin's confidant.

"Lawrence, I want you and Mr. Bartlett to know I'll be doing some other work in the next few weeks. There are enough orders on hand to occupy you, I think, and I'll bring you any new ones that come in. I just won't be active in drumming up new custom. There's a big order for glass from Lancaster we might get."

"Oh, you're not leaving town, I hope," Lawrence said. "Jane's lying-in is almost any day now."

"No, I'll be here for that. It's something else. The man who saved my life at the battle of Monmouth was a son of the Quaker who's been arrested on suspicion of murder. I think the man could be innocent. It strikes me as odd he should murder two women and do nothing to get rid of either body. The man is not insane. He ought to have sunk the corpses in the river, as he could easily have done. If I can help the father, I will repay the debt I owe the son."

Neither James's brother-in-law nor the old glassblower said anything to this. The idea of James clearing up a life-and-death mystery was too strange to them to be immediately comprehended or commented on.

"I'm going to run an advertisement in the papers appealing for information, and put up a handbill around town making the same appeal. Do you think you could spare Stephen Lunt to help me do that tomorrow? Putting up the handbills, I mean. I'll pay him for it out of my own pocket."

"Sure, that would be all right with me. What do you think, Mr. Bartlett?"

"Anything James needs is fine with me. We can get along without Stephen for one day. It's a big thing you're going to be doing, James. I've known Jacob Maul a long time. He's a good Quaker."

"So I've heard."

Before leaving the glasshouse, James had a friendly word with the other three glassblowers. He also spoke to Stephen Lunt about the job of putting up the handbills around town, telling him the hour he should come to his house to get them, and what he would be paid for the job.

From the Northern Liberties James rode back into the center of town to the City Tavern. But every hitching post along Second Street by the tavern was taken, so he rode Cheval to Walnut Street and tied him there.

As he returned on foot to the City Tavern, he fell in with Richard Erlong, a fellow officer in the Army, now a partner in one of Philadelphia's counting houses. Richard said he was on his way to the Tavern to take a bowl of sangaree and invited James, who accepted the invitation, to drink it with him.

As they entered the City Tavern, the sociable hubbub of many conversations going on at the same time flowed out of the taproom, and they were greeted by the head clerk of the popular establishment, Peter Procter.

"Captain Erlong. Captain Jamison. Glad to see you. May I conduct you to a private room to dine? We have the freshest oysters in town today. Just in. Also the finest venison and the choicest turtle soup."

"No, thank you, Mr. Procter," Richard Erlong replied. "James and I are bound for your taproom to drink some of your first-rate sangaree."

"Of course. As you wish," the manager replied. "Perhaps later you may desire to take something to eat."

James said, "You go ahead, Richard, and order the bowls. I'll be along right away. I have business with Mr. Procter."

"Good. Don't tarry. I have news for you."

Richard Erlong disappeared into the buzzing taproom, leaving James at the desk by the tavern's entrance.

"Mr. Procter, I hope you will grant me a favor."

"Of course. As you wish, Captain Jamison. Always glad to oblige a good customer. If I can do what you ask, I will."

"Well, I would like to mention the City Tavern in an announcement I am going to put in the papers today."

"Certainly. That would be perfectly fine, I'm sure. We are always happy to be noticed in the papers. What, if I may ask, does the announcement concern?"

"The Quaker Murders. You see, I think the man who is going to be arraigned may be innocent, and I want to solicit information on the murdered woman from the public. I need a place to leave the information that may come in answer to the ad."

"Innocent? I thought the case against this—what is he? I forget—this stonecutter, was very strong. Wasn't the woman's body found in his necessary?"

"Yes. But as a Quaker notably obedient to his faith, his character raises a serious doubt about whether he is capable of such violence. I would like to help the man, if I can, to repay the family for the aid the man's oldest son rendered me during the war. He saved my life at the cost of his own."

"I see. But wasn't there also another woman he was supposed to have killed, some years ago? His wife, I believe. Found strangled in his bed, they say. That was before I came to Philadelphia. But I've heard the talk about it, along with the talk of the woman found in the necessary a week ago."

"The Coroner's finding in that earlier case, Mr. Procter, was A Visitation of God," James said, "because the man had no reason to want to kill his wife and was on good terms with her, according to interested persons who lived in the house with them at the time."

"I see," Mr. Procter said, still somewhat skeptical. "How exactly does the City Tavern figure in what you wish to do?"

"Here—let me show you the announcement I want to put in the papers. It explains everything."

James took from his pocket the ad Benjamin Franklin had written, which the tavern manager read attentively.

"This seems reasonable, Captain Jamison. Your wanting to be of service to the father of your dead benefactor certainly does you credit. And, may I say, you show considerable talent in writing this ad. I see no objection to the City Tavern serving as your depository of information. I'll apprise Mr. Morley, the night clerk, so he will know of our arrangement. One of us is always here, day and night. The City Tavern never closes. If any information comes for you as a result of your advertisement, I will see that you get it."

"Thank you, Mr. Procter," James said. "Thank you very much. I'm truly obliged for your courtesy in this matter."

"The City Tavern wants to be of service to people of quality," the head clerk replied, "especially when, like yourself, Captain Jamison, they've served in the war for American independence and been wounded."

When James joined his companion, Richard Erlong said, "That was a lot of business, James. Here's your sangaree. There's more nutmeg there if you want it. What were you and Procter discussing?"

James told him.

"So you think old Maul did *not* strangle those women?"

"Not unless Dr. Rush or some other competent authority on illnesses of the mind certifies to me that Jacob Maul is insane. No sane man would have failed to take steps to prevent his association with apparent murder. Instead, we find both corpses on Maul's property, and—in the one instance—in his very bed."

"That's a theory I never thought of! The worst evidence against a man proves his innocence! No one else of my acquaintance, James, is reasoning this way, though I've been hearing plenty about the Quaker Murders. You're a highly original thinker, I must say, old friend. It'll be interesting to see what information your appeal in the papers turns up."

"You mentioned you had some news for me, Richard. What is it?"

Erlong took a draught of the sangaree before answering.

"I saw Miriam Foreman, now Hyatt, two days ago in New York. She was walking in Broadway with her little girl when we encountered each other and spoke."

Unsure whether he'd done the right thing in telling James about having spoken with Miriam, Richard took another drink and remarked *sotto voce*, "This really is excellent sangaree."

James said nothing in response to Richard's news of the woman he'd been engaged to marry before their clashing loyalties in the war had separated them. He had thought of Miriam Foreman less and less often since that rupture in their affections eight years before, but the memory of it, aggravated by her marriage to a Tory named Daniel Hyatt, still rankled.

"She asked about you," Richard added softly.

"What did she ask?"

"How you were. Whether you were married. I told her you were well and didn't seem interested in marrying. That seemed to sadden her. She has an exquisite little girl."

James passed a moment in solemn silence, then asked, "How did she look?"

"She is as radiant in appearance as ever she was, I would say. But her husband's loss of his property, along with her parents' loss of theirs, has been hard for her. She no longer wears beautiful clothes to show off her figure and complexion, though her little girl, who much resembles her momma, was well turned out. Her parents returned to England last year to live with a relative of her mother—a baronet, I believe she said.

It seems Miriam's husband is trying—without much success, apparently—to obtain compensation for the confiscation of his property. She said he had just left for London to present his case before the Loyalists Claims Commission. They did not have enough money to permit her to accompany him. She and the child are living in New York for the time being with an elderly aunt of Miriam's."

"We have all suffered losses in the war," James commented. "Some beyond any power of compensation to remedy. The Foremans and the Hyatts cannot expect to be immune to that suffering."

The same somber remembrances as had come up in his conference with Dr. Franklin the night before muted for a time James's conversation with his comrade and friend.

After dining with Richard Erlong on oysters and rye bread in the boisterous taproom, James went round to Philadelphia's half-dozen newspapers to place his ad. Everywhere he went he did as Benjamin Franklin had directed him to do and explained in the presence of the journeyman printers and apprentices in each shop the interest behind his investigation. He noted that their attention to his argument for the innocence of Jacob Maul seemed to be keen.

As he left the last of the newspaper publishers, James estimated that there was still enough time for him to speak with William Maul and his wife.

Although he had never been to the stoneyard of the Mauls, he knew where Dock Street was and had no trouble locating the yard. James's knock was answered by a soft-spoken young woman in somber Quaker garb cradling a babe in her arms. When asked, she affirmed that she was William Maul's wife and, in reply to James's inquiry, informed him that William was in the stable, currying a horse.

William Maul proved to be a muscular, intelligent-looking Quaker. After shaking hands with James, he begged leave to finish currying his horse, saying the day's work had just ended and he was almost done with his necessary attention to the animal.

He asked, as he continued to clean the horse with firm, long strokes of his brush, how he could be of service to James, who stated his desire to help William's father. In explanation of his interest in helping a man he didn't know, he told William—as Dr. Franklin had instructed him to do—that his brother John had saved his life during the war.

"John always was a charitable man," William said, as he finished currying the horse. "More like Father than Robert or me."

Placing the brush in a dry bucket, he gestured toward the house and said, "If thee would come inside, Captain, we can speak more comfortably and have some tea."

When they came in, Rebecca Maul was rocking her infant's cradle and singing to the baby, who was cozily asleep.

"Becky," her husband said, "this gentleman is Captain Jamison. He knew John in the war and believes in Father's innocence. Please prepare some tea for the three of us. The Captain would like to ask us some questions."

Turning a chair at one end of the kitchen's long, scarred table toward the fire, the young Quaker invited James to sit.

While the tea was being prepared, James asked the son of Jacob Maul to tell him about the woman his father was suspected of killing.

"Lizzy, as we all called her, was married to a drover who took his cattle to market at New Ark in East Jersey. He died of the speckled fever and left her with a little girl to raise. A few months after that, she came to live with us."

"Whose idea was that?" James asked. "Your father's or your stepmother's?"

"I suppose it must have been Margaret's idea. I really don't know, Captain Jamison. But I can tell thee for certain that Father agreed to the arrangement. We all did—Margaret, myself, Father, and my younger brother Robert, who was to become a pet of Lizzy's. Rebecca had not yet come into our family."

William Maul ceased speaking, and James encouraged him to continue.

"When Lizzy came to live with us, we were still grieving my mother's death. Lizzie was a ray of light in our gloom, especially for Margaret, her sister, who as mother's nurse had taken her death almost as hard as Father, Robert, and I had. She was very devoted to Mother. Lizzy's presence was good for Margaret, Father, Robert and me. Her cheerfulness was a tonic for us all."

"She was very kind," Rebecca Maul said, as she set down the teapot and cups on the table where the men were seated. "Lizzy had a knack for keeping the house in good trim. She was very likable."

"I understand, William, that your mother's fatal injury caused your father much anguish," James said.

Before William could reply, his wife began saying a blessing over the tea; then she asked James whether he wished sugar in his tea.

While the tea was being drunk, William answered that his father had suffered terribly. It had been a blessing, he said, when Margaret Gilbert volunteered to nurse his dying mother, something she often did for families in their Meeting with members who were gravely ill.

"Margaret and Father often sat up with Mother all night. We would find them in the morning asleep in chairs on either side of her bed. Margaret became very attached to Mother, and Father came to depend on her support. It seemed to me he married her mainly for that reason. Another thing you need to know—Lizzy became almost as devoted to Father as Margaret was because he had given her and her child shelter when they needed it."

Rebecca Maul interrupted her husband's narrative with the observation, "When William and I married, and I came into the family, Lizzy showed me such consideration as I shall never forget. My own sister could not have shown me more kindness. She had a way about her. She made everyone feel more comfortable. Why, once she even. . . ."

The memory of her dead friend's affection overwhelmed Rebecca Maul, and she could not finish saying what she had wanted to say and began sobbing into her apron.

In an attempt to distract his wife from her grief, William said, "Lizzy was the best witness in defense of Father at the inquest into Margaret's death. She told the Coroner over and over, as she often told our neighbors, that God had taken Margaret, and Father was not answerable for her death."

In the presence of Rebecca's weeping, James, too, thought to change the subject, and asked William, "What did Mrs. Coons say about your brother Robert running away?"

"She thought Robert would return one day. She said we should not give up hope of seeing him again. She was quite sure of it. Lizzy was especially fond of Robert, and he of her. She showed special affection for him in many little ways."

James then brought the conversation back to the death of Mrs. Coons.

"Tell me, did anything out of the ordinary happen in the days before the disappearance of Mrs. Coons? Particularly the day she went missing."

"Nothing that I recall. Father and I went up to bed directly after supper that night, the night she disappeared. I had a job to do at first light the next morning, and Father was spending more hours asleep than he was awake, something he had never done before. He had always been the most active of us."

Rebecca, who had regained control of her feelings, disagreed with her husband on this point.

"William, does thee not recall that Lizzy dropped the green bowl while she was washing it and made no apology for breaking so precious an article? That was not like her. Does thee not recall that? She also went out to the necessary that last day more often than was her wont, and when I asked her if anything was wrong, she became cross with me. She was never cross."

"That was not the necessary where her body was found, was it?" James asked.

"No," Rebecca said, "it was the new one she went to. None of us used the old one."

"The body," William explained, "was found in the old necessary."

"After William and your father-in-law went up to bed, did you spend the evening in Mrs. Coons's company, Mrs. Maul?" James asked.

"We sat by the fire mending clothes and talking."

"What did she say?"

"Oh, we spoke of the usual things. The baby. Lizzy's little girl. What had been said at Meeting. Goings-on in the neighborhood. Our sewing. The washing we had to do the next day on Wash Day. The last thing we spoke of was which of us would make the porridge in the morning, and she said she would. But when I came down the next morning, there was no fire in the hearth and no porridge. So I built a fire and made it, thinking she had stepped out of the house and would be back soon to eat it with me. William had already left for his job, and Father Maul was still in his room.

"When Lizzie didn't appear, I ate my share of the porridge to keep it from getting cold, and when she still didn't come, I went to her room to see if she was sick. But the room was empty, and the bed looked like she hadn't slept in it." Rebecca's eyes began to glisten, but she held back the tears.

"Did you see anything out of place that morning as you left the house?" James asked William Maul.

"Nothing. Everything was quiet and as it always was."

"Did you see your father that morning?"

Having recovered herself, Rebecca Maul answered this question, "He was still in bed when William left. After I found Lizzy gone, I went to his door and rapped on it and told him Lizzy wasn't in the house."

"What did he say?"

"He said perhaps she had gone on an errand and would return soon. But I said I had been up for over an hour, and I hadn't seen her and that she had promised to make the fire."

"What did he say to that?"

"He said he would get up and help me look for her. He asked if I had been to the stables and the lean-to, and looked in the necessary, and I told him I had not."

"Did you look in both necessaries?"

"No, we looked only in the new one because no one ever goes to the old necessary. We use it only for putting things that are no longer of use. It did not occur to me or to Father Maul to look for Lizzy in the old necessary."

"Please tell me what you found in Mrs. Coons's room. You said it didn't look as though she had slept in the bed?"

"It looked as if she had lain on top of the covers, which were all bunched up. Lizzy was always particular about smoothing her bed and making it neat after she got up. All her clothes were in her closet, except for the ones she had on when she went up to bed—and her cloak. Her porcelain-faced doll in the blue dress was the only thing missing."

"A doll?"

William answered this query. "It was a childhood gift from her father, the most precious thing she owned. It was from France, and she often boasted of how much money it had cost her father."

It was past suppertime and dark by the time James left the home of William and Rebecca Maul, having arranged with them to return the next afternoon to inspect the grounds of the stoneyard and the necessary where Mrs. Coons's body had been discovered.

Chapter 6

On Tuesday morning Livy showed James the bundle of handbills she had found outside the kitchen door when she'd gone out to the well to get a bucket of water.

Stephen Lunt appeared half an hour later and received from James his instructions for distributing the handbills. He was given a wheelbarrow to carry them around to the city's markets, inns, taverns, coffee houses, and ordinaries, and a bag of tacks and a hammer to affix them to walls.

Having started the boy on his all-day errand and having had some of Livy's griddle cakes and butter for breakfast, James saddled Cheval and set off for the house of Dr. Phineas Finley on Fourth Street. He found the physician and his lady at breakfast and was invited to join them in a cup of tea.

Dr. Finley was a quiet, lean man with a continuously benevolent expression. Both he and his wife, a plump, bright-eyed woman with a florid complexion, had heard of James's investigation.

"My dear Captain Jamison, it would be so nice if you could help this poor Quaker," Mrs. Finley said as soon as James was seated with them at their breakfast table. "But I really don't see how you can. Mrs. Leighton was saying to me only yesterday when she told me of what you plan to do, that she and her husband are sure of the man's guilt. They don't understand why he wasn't hanged years ago when he strangled his poor wife. The whole thing is a scandal! The Coroner ought to be put out of office now that the sister of that poor woman has been strangled!"

"Now, Catherine," Dr. Finley remarked, "the Coroner's no fool. We may be sure Mr. Constable had reasons for declaring Maul blameless in his wife's death. His finding in the wife's death of A Visitation of God means that in his judgment no one could determine the actual cause of the wife's death. Such things happen."

"A visitation of God, indeed! That's only the fiddle-faddle of freethinkers! God does not strangle innocent women!"

"Well, Mrs. Finley," James said, "though I agree with you about God not strangling women, no one in his right mind would strangle a woman and go to sleep beside her corpse to await discovery of his crime. And Mr. Maul is not being accused of insanity."

"That may be, Captain Jamison. That may be, as you say. But facts is facts, and there's no denying he was found asleep beside that poor, strangled woman."

"Supposing she was murdered," James mildly observed.

"Supposing? How else but murder would you explain the bruises to her throat, and her stone-cold dead? I do declare, Captain Jamison, putting your sympathies aside, facts is facts. What do you say, Dr. Finley? You are a physician. I'd like to know, do bruises on a woman's throat appear for no reason? Could that Mrs. Maul have died in any way other than strangulation? Pray give us your opinion."

"My opinion, my dear, is that we are not letting the good Captain ask the questions he came here to ask me, if you will forgive me for saying so. What is it you wish to know of me, Captain Jamison?"

"I want to know what you saw as a medical man when you examined the corpse of Mrs. Coons."

"I saw a woman's body in an advanced stage of bloating and decay, with the livid marks of strangulation on her throat. She seemed to me to have been dead three or four days, which, I was told after I had given that as my opinion, was the number of days she had been missing from her home."

"So it was your opinion that she was killed the night she disappeared?"

Dr. Finley replied, "It appeared so, judged by the color of the body and its state of deterioration. It's not possible to be precise in one's judgments on such matters. The bruises to the throat were quite pronounced and deep."

"Did you unwrap the corpse?"

"Before I arrived, the Coroner, Mr. Constable, had cut away the canvas from the body with a pair of shears."

"Did you also cut off the woman's clothing to examine the condition of her torso in addition to her exposed face, neck, and hands?"

"We did not. The circumstances did not seem to require it. After the Mauls—the father and the son—identified the body as that of their housekeeper Mrs. Coons, the Sheriff was mainly interested, it appeared, in knowing when she'd died. It seemed obvious how she had died. Neither Mr. Constable nor I liked handling such a decayed corpse any more than necessary. We concurred that manual strangulation had been the cause of death. He and I also agreed that death had probably taken place three or four days before."

"Did you see anything out of the ordinary?" James asked.

"Yes, there was something odd. The woman's shoes were on the wrong feet."

"Were the shoelaces tied?"

"Oh, yes."

"Did you observe any marks besides the bruises to the throat?"

"Well, the extremities were bloated, as was the rest of her body, and because of this swelling the cords tying her hands and ankles had cut rather deeply into her flesh. We, of course, cut the cords binding the hands, arms, and feet. Then, too, the vermin had chewed through the canvas and fed on the corpse's nose, lips, and ear lobes, causing considerable damage to those parts of the body."

"Oh, how dreadful!" Mrs. Finley exclaimed.

Having gotten all the information he could from Dr. Finley, James took his leave of the doctor and his wife after thanking them for answering his questions and for their hospitality.

James's conversation with the Coroner, Mr. Paulus Constable, confirmed Dr. Finley's account of the general condition of Mrs. Coons's corpse and produced the same answers to the questions he had asked the physician.

Mr. Constable volunteered the additional information that Jacob Maul had seemed to him to have shown no particular sensibility when the Sheriff required him and his son to make a formal identification of the corpse. The Coroner particularly wanted James to know that he had not been influenced in his finding of Manual Strangulation as the cause of death in this instance by the circumstances of Maul's wife seven years before.

"The two cases presented quite different circumstances," Mr. Constable insisted. "In the case of Mrs. Coons, all the circumstances were consistent with violence. The deep bruises to the throat. The tying of the hands behind the back. The pinning of the arms to the sides of her body with cord. All of those things point to ruthless violence. There was none of the strange inconsistency in this death as was evident in the death of her sister seven years before, between where the woman's body was found and the superficial bruising to her throat—which, as I recall, was not nearly as distinct as the bruises on the throat of Mrs. Coons—and her husband's sterling character. The circumstances under which that body had been discovered were also distinct. The dead woman was in her bed, and her husband had been asleep beside her when he arose from the bed to answer the knocks at the door to the chamber, whereas this corpse had been thrown into a pit."

"Are you telling me, then, Mr. Constable, that Jacob Maul did not strangle his wife?" James inquired.

"What I'm saying, Captain Jamison, is that as the Coroner I decide the cause of each death that comes before me for judgment according to the facts presented in each case. In Mrs. Maul's death seven years ago, I had grounds for a reasonable doubt as to whether a violent assault had been the cause of death, whereas the facts in the death of Mrs. Coons left no such room for doubt. It was the Sheriff's judgment, not mine, that Maul should be arrested and imprisoned on suspicion of murder in this death. I only concluded what the facts in the case indicated. Manual strangulation."

Upon leaving the Coroner's office at Market and Front streets, James rode over to the Walnut Street Jail to speak with Jacob Maul and dropped off his report for Dr. Franklin.

The prison occupied the half of the square between Prune and Walnut streets not occupied by the State House with its imposing cupola, where John Adams, Benjamin Franklin, Thomas Jefferson, George Washington and the other brave patriots of 1776 had, at the risk of their lives, declared America's independence from Britain.

As he approached the prison, James thought that never had two edifices so near to one another presented so great a contrast: one the epitome of man's noblest aspirations, the other everything most reprehensible in human nature. Appropriately, the jail occupied the part of the square behind, not in front of, the State House.

James had often passed the Walnut Street Jail and been assaulted by the drunken rants of those of its inmates who could afford to buy liquor from the jailer or otherwise obtain it. These inebriates amused themselves by pressing their drink-inflamed faces against the barred windows of the prison and, with their arms outstretched, screaming obscenities at passersby in the street. It had never occurred to him he would ever have reason to enter the precincts of this dismal place of incarceration.

In mounting the long flight of stone steps that led to the jail's main entrance on the second floor, James passed the flimsy dwellings the warders had built for their families against both sides of the stairway. As he mounted the stairs, he could see off to his right the Potter's Field on Sixth Street. During the nine months the British had used the Walnut Street Jail as their army's provost prison, it had been commonplace for British soldiers to bump corpses down these steps and drag the bodies across the pavement to the ditch beside the Potter's Field, where they were left for whomever might care to bury them. Otherwise, the crows, seagulls, vultures, rats and dogs disposed of them. The families and friends of prisoners in the Walnut Street Jail had formed the habit of visiting the grisly ditch every day to see if their loved one's corpse was in it, to give it decent burial. Other people of good will had also interred strangers, but not every corpse was attended to because some eighty American prisoners a week died in the

Walnut Street Jail during the British occupation of Philadelphia.

The inmates of the Jail during that time had considered rats a delicacy. Some of the emaciated corpses dumped in the ditch next to the Potter's Field even had splinters of wood and grains of mortar in their mouths, in token of the desperate hunger that drove them to gnaw wood and eat mortar.

But even under American rule and even in times of peace, James knew this notorious prison was the scene of outrages against humanity. Deaths from sickness, cold, and hunger were normal because the jailer made his living by selling necessities—food, clothing, blankets, and medicine—to the inmates. Those prisoners without money went without those necessities unless friends or family could supply their needs.

When he reached the top of the stairway James stated his business to a turnkey who stood on the other side of a grate of flat iron bars spanning a huge archway. After paying the gratuity this man demanded for James's admission to the Walnut Street Jail, the iron door was opened for him.

A vaulted corridor now confronted James, at the end of which were two other grates of flat iron bars. Another turnkey presided over these inner barriers, the tallest, brawniest man James had ever seen, whose glaring scowl came perhaps from years of squinting down from his elevated height at shorter men.

After a parley and the customary payment, this giant warder unlocked his outer door, then locked it behind James before unlocking the innermost grate to give James access to the main part of the jail, where the inmates roamed at will. The turnkey, who remained safely between his two iron grates, ordered a lackey on the other side of the inner barrier to "bring the Quaker murderer to this gentleman."

While waiting for Jacob Maul to be brought, James felt the chill emanating from the prison's massive stone walls, which had absorbed the cold of the night before and were still releasing it. The combination of the cold and the peculiar odor of the jail's atmosphere made James wish he were somewhere else. The smell, he thought, was the essence of all the squalor, despair, incontinence, drunkenness, vice, and debauchery the jail had contained during its history, the aroma of an establishment that made no attempt to regulate the conduct of its inmates or any provision to separate the different categories of people being held there. Those being held merely to give testimony in a trial from those who were serving sentences for crimes. Convicted criminals from those awaiting trial. Those guilty of heinous acts from those guilty of misdemeanors. Those green in misdeeds from those grown hoary in repeated violations of the law. Or even the men from the women, some of whom had small children with them.

When the turnkey's lackey brought Jacob Maul to where James awaited, a respectably dressed Negro, broad-shouldered and of middling years, accompanied him. Maul's clothing was disheveled, his matted gray hair contained pieces of straw, and a large welt reddened one of the points of his forehead, as if it had recently been struck a hard blow. Maul stood passively by while his Negro companion identified himself to James as a free man named Robert Cash.

Cash explained that he had, years before, worked for Maul in his stoneyard in Dock Street. He wanted James to understand he was not a criminal or under any suspicion of crime. He was in the prison merely because he had to give testimony in a criminal case that was to come before the Quarter Session and had been unable to post the necessary bond to assure his presence in court.

"Fur watchin' over Mr. Jacob an' keepin' him safe," Cash said, "Mr. Jacob's son William, he brings me my grub ebry mornin' when he brings his Daddy his. 'Cause I don' have nobody on de outside to do fur me, an' I don' have no money to buy fur myself. An' believe me, dey's dem in here wud rip po' Mr. Jacob's clothes right offen his back an' steal his grub, an' beat him somethin' fearsome jes' 'cause dey think he kilt dem wimmen. But he never did. Mr. Jacob, he de nicest man eber was. He alus treated me an' all his hands good when I wuk'd fur him at de stoneyard. He paid his wuk'rs equal fur what we dun fur him, an' warn't never late wit de money neder."

Seeing the dazed condition Maul seemed to be in, James naturally addressed himself to Cash rather than to the Quaker.

"Will he speak with me?"

"Le's step ober yonder," Cash said, indicating an empty alcove overlooking one of the prison's courtyards.

"Mr. Jacob," Cash said in a kind tone to his former employer, "dis yere gentlemun wants teh talk wid yuh. He come special jes' fur a talk."

Maul gave Cash a blank stare and turned his head slowly away from him without saying a word.

James tried to penetrate the air of indifference that enveloped Maul by saying, "Mr. Maul, listen. I knew your son John in the army. He saved my life. I want to help you if you will answer some questions for me."

"John?" the old stonecutter asked, showing a responsive interest for the first time. "Is John here? I'd like to see him. He and Robert went away to the war."

It was a pitiable sight.

"Is he this way all the time?"

"Purty much. Mos'ly he don' say anythin'. Sumtimes he talk crazy."

"What does he say?"

"It's allus sumthin' it wudn't be right teh do—like he was arguin' wid a woman named Margaret. I can't make out clear what he sayin' when he gets all excited like."

"Has he ever been violent with you or anyone else, Mr. Cash?"

"Mr. Jacob? Na'sir, he don' never get violent 'ceptin' wid hisself. He wudn't hurt nobudy, not him. He's jes' real unhappy, das all. But sum of de peoples in here, like I said, dey's wantin' teh git violent wid him. Yas'sir, dey is. Dey calls him names like 'stranglin' man' an' 'wimmen killer' an' 'hangman's bait,' an' things wus den dat. I's sometimes 'fraid fur him, an' fur myself, 'cause I's tryin' teh take care o' him."

"Did one of the other inmates or one of the warders give him that bump on his forehead?" James asked.

"He done dat to hisself. We wuz going down de hall teh de jakes yesterday, an' all of a sudden he banged his head against de wall, hard—on purpose, like—fo' I cud catch him. Das de way he come by dat mark teh his head."

"Besides violence to himself and talking crazy, has he ever done anything else that seemed strange to you, Mr. Cash? You're with him all the time, I take it."

"Yas'sir, I's wid him all de time. Well, anytime he hears one o' dem heavy wagons goin' by in de street, de kind wat has dem big wheels, it bothers him consid'rable. De soun' o' dem big wheels on de stones seems teh make him jumpy. It sets him moanin' sumtimes."

Having asked Cash everything he could think of to ask, and there being no chance of eliciting information directly from Maul, James wished the Quaker's Negro protector good luck and left the jail.

In saying goodbye to Cash, James gave him a Spanish dollar, not in payment for information, but in recognition of the charity he was showing his former employer.

In James's estimation Cash's benevolence exceeded that of the Good Samaritan in the Lord's parable. For the Samaritan had dispensed his charity in the safety of a wayside inn, while Cash's protection of his suffering neighbor exposed him to the risk of assault.

Chapter 7

James left the Walnut Street Jail feeling grim. But he was also glad to be breathing the clean, free air of the street again after his brief sojourn behind prison walls. He wondered how Dr. Franklin would receive his report on Maul's mental state.

He rode over to the City Tavern, where he had a quick meal of turtle soup and fresh-baked oatmeal bread, and made some notes for Dr. Franklin on his conversation with Robert Cash and the condition of Jacob Maul. Then he went on to Dock Street to talk again, as agreed, with the young Mauls and to see the place where the corpse of Elizabeth Coons had been found.

After an exchange of greetings, James told William Maul, "I have just seen your father and had a talk with Robert Cash. How long has your father been in this condition?"

"Father began to withdraw into himself after mother died," William answered. "Marrying Margaret lessened his hypos, and Lizzy coming to live with us cheered his spirits a good deal. But then Margaret and Lizzy both died mysteriously. On the day Lizzy's body was discovered, I noticed, his spirits took a considerable downward turn. Being arrested and put in the Walnut Street Jail touched Father to the quick. Since then, he has been in the state you saw. Now he does not always know who I am when I take him his food and try to speak with him.

Thank God Mr. Cash is looking after him. I remember him as one of my father's workers from when I was a boy."

"The Coroner told me this morning that your father showed no feeling when you and he were asked to identify Mrs. Coons's body," James said.

William Maul replied, "I would say he was confused. Perhaps afraid. The presence of Sheriff Tuttleton intimidated both of us. We Quakers are not accustomed to dealings with officers of the law. No Sheriff had ever come to our house before. The discovery of Lizzy's body on his property affected Father very much, I know, whatever impression the Coroner may have had. To see the marks of great violence on her corpse and the way it had been chewed by vermin was a terrible thing for both of us."

This conversation took place in the Mauls' kitchen, with Rebecca preparing supper, and she now interrupted the conversation she was hearing.

"As William has told thee, Captain Jamison, it was very trying for us. I never cried as hard as I did that day, not even when my own mother died. Who could have wanted to treat such a good person as Lizzy in that shameful way? It still makes me heartsick to think of it."

"Who actually discovered the corpse?" James asked. "Was it one of you or your father?"

"Some boys had been sporting on the empty ground behind our place," William said. "They were the ones who found Lizzy. They said they smelled something and traced it to the necessary, and when they looked down the hole they saw the canvas bundle and came running to our house to tell us what they had seen. It was the hand of Providence that I was not away from home that afternoon. Had Rebecca gone out to the necessary, I'm not sure she could have stood what I saw."

"What exactly did you see?"

"Well, just as the boys had told us, the door into the necessary and its seat had been torn off, and the refuse inside it—old demijohns and such—was scattered around on the ground. Whoever put Lizzy in the necessary's hole must have done that. I could see from the shape of the bundle in the cavity that it was probably a body, and I had a presentiment it was Lizzy. So I sent the oldest boy off to bring the Sheriff, and the next oldest to the upper end of Dock Street to tell a friend of mine I needed him. I thought he might help me take the bundle out of the necessary. Then I went back to the house to tell Becky and Father to stay there. I didn't want them going out to the necessary and seeing what I had seen."

"Did your Father say anything to you? Did he want to go to the necessary to see what you had seen?"

"No, he didn't say anything. I told him to stay with Becky, and that I would tell them more when I knew more. Then I went back to the necessary to wait for the Sheriff and my friend from the shambles to come. When I got there, I found more boys as well as several men and a few women from the neighborhood standing around. One of the men said he thought there was a body down in the pit, and offered to bring it up. But I told him we ought to wait for the Sheriff to arrive. By the time he came, more onlookers had gathered, for many people in Southwark knew of Lizzy's disappearance, and the youngest boy had apparently spread the news that something had been found and I had sent for the Sheriff."

"What did the Sheriff do when he got there?"

"He ordered the bundle brought up and carried into the stable, which was done using the door that had been ripped off the necessary as a stretcher. So many men were eager to do this that I did not have to touch the bundle myself, for which I was very glad.

"The Sheriff had the bundle laid in an unused stall in the stable. But the smell of it upset the horses so much he had the men put it in the lean-to attached to the stable, where our hostler lived when we had one. There's a door connecting the lean-to and the stable that can be closed. The Sheriff then sent men to bring the Coroner and Dr. Finley, and ordered everyone out of the lean-to and stable except his deputy and me. The Sheriff said he wanted to open the wrappings on the bundle with medical authorities present."

"Was there anything unusual about the canvas used to wrap the body that might identify where it came from?"

"It was faded and old," William answered. "It looked like it might have been part of an old sail because it looked bleached by the sun. Old sailcloth is common, of course, in a great seaport like Philadelphia, with many ships coming and going and being outfitted in fresh rigging."

"What did the Sheriff say to you and your father after you identified the body as being Mrs. Coons, a member of your family?"

"He asked when Lizzy had gone missing and which—"

James interrupted William's narrative, "Excuse me, didn't he already know she was missing from your household?"

"No. We hadn't reported that to the authorities. We kept hoping she would return."

"What else did the Sheriff want to know?"

"He wanted the names of everyone who lived in our house. I told him there was only myself and my wife, our baby, and Father."

"But didn't Mrs. Coons have a child?"

"Yes, but some years back she went to live with a relative of Lizzy's, a Mrs. Merkle, a cousin who keeps a vegetable stand in the Jersey Market in Market Street."

"You had already been to see if Mrs. Coons had gone to her cousin, I suppose."

Rebecca Maul answered this question. "Yes, I went there looking for Lizzy the morning she went missing and asked Mrs. Merkle if she had seen Lizzy. But she hadn't."

"Did the Sheriff have any other questions for you, William?"

"He wanted to know where Father and I had been when Lizzy disappeared."

"Please tell me what you saw when the canvas shroud wrapping Mrs. Coons's corpse was cut away."

"The Coroner was the first to arrive, and the Sheriff said he wanted Father present when the bundle was opened and sent me to bring him to the lean-to. Mr. Constable then proceeded to cut the cord tying off the canvas at the head-end of the bundle, and he slit the canvas down to the shoulders, revealing Lizzy's face and neck."

"What did he use to do this? A knife?"

"No. He used a pair of shears he had in a little leather bag he brought with him."

"What else did you see?"

"The face was so discolored and swollen it didn't look much like Lizzy, and the rats had chewed on her face. One of the eyes was open and the other one closed. But I knew it was Lizzy from the hair and her dress. I told the Sheriff who it was, and he asked Father if he agreed. Father just nodded and left the lean-to."

"Were her clothes ripped or torn?"

"No."

"Was there anything at all peculiar about her garb that you noticed?"

"When they cut away all of the canvas, exposing her whole body, I noticed she had her shoes on the wrong feet and was not wearing stockings. Lizzy always wore stockings."

"Was there anything else that was odd?"

"Not that I noticed," William Maul replied.

"What happened next?"

"I asked the Sheriff's permission to leave and send a message to my Weekly Meeting to prepare a grave, and then told him that I wanted to tell my wife what we had found. He said I could go, but that I was to come right back because he had some things he wanted to ask me.

"I found Father weeping in the kitchen, sitting at this very table, with Becky trying to comfort him. He had not told her what he had seen, and when I told her she was very upset and cried, too. I cried myself. Mrs. Cleaver and her husband, who are our closest neighbors, and two other neighbor women were also in the kitchen. I asked Peter Cleaver to take a note to Israel Godwin, our Meeting's oldest Elder, about getting a grave dug. As soon as Becky could speak, she said we should send for Philomen Lyons so she and Philomen could wash Lizzy for burial."

"Who is Philomen Lyons?" James inquired.

"She's the Negro washerwoman who helps us clean house every spring," William said.

"And did she come and help to wash the body?"

"Yes. But she did it herself. I did not want Becky to touch or see Lizzy's corpse."

James asked where he could find Philomen Lyons, for it was obvious he would have to speak with her as the only person who had complete, direct knowledge of the dead woman's corpse, for she had removed Mrs. Coons's clothes to clean the corpse for burial; and he was given directions to the washerwoman's house.

"What did the Sheriff ask you when you went back to the lean-to?"

"He wanted to know why we hadn't reported that Lizzy had gone missing, and I told him what I have told thee, Captain Jamison. He also wanted to know her history and if Lizzy had any relatives or particular friends in Philadelphia. I gave him the names of her cousin Mrs. Merkle and Mrs. Cleaver, and the names of the servants we once had, who lived with us when Lizzy first joined our family. Susan Love and Solomon Lort."

William seemed tentative in making this last statement, and James, sensing his hesitation, asked, "Were there names of other acquaintances of hers that you might have given the Sheriff, but didn't?"

William hesitated again.

"Well, there were the two Hessian soldiers billeted on us during the British occupation of Philadelphia. She knew them. They were a corporal and a sergeant, and I have heard one of them is in German Town working for an uncle of his named Polzer who owns a farm there."

"But, William," Rebecca Maul said, "what would they have to do with Lizzy? They are foreigners and have not lived in Philadelphia for seven years."

"Yes, but they saw Lizzy every day for almost a year, and they were very forward with her, especially the sergeant, August Weber. And he is rumored to be the one living in German Town only a few miles away. The corporal, whose name was Schmidt, Diedreich Schmidt, also seemed interested in Lizzy. The way they looked at her made Robert angry. He said it was as if they wanted to 'eat her up,' and that they laughed and spoke to each other in German in a way Robert thought was about her when she was with them in the kitchen doing her housework. Once he almost came to blows with Weber and Schmidt over it."

"But," James said, "it's only a rumor that this August Weber is in German Town on his uncle's farm."

"Yes," William answered, "it's only a rumor. But a good many of the Hessians did stay on in Pennsylvania after the war, you know."

"Where could I find your former servants, Susan Love and Solomon Lort?" James asked. "I will have to speak with them."

"Father sold Susan's indenture when our custom began to fall off and he could no longer afford to keep her. Peter Odell bought the indenture. He has a rope walk in Race Street near the river. Father let Solomon, our hostler, go at about the same time. He's now taking care of the horses at the shambles by the tannery in the upper part of Dock Street."

Dusk was coming on and James still had to inspect the grounds of the stoneyard and the place where Elizabeth Coons's body had been found.

"Is there anything else you would like to tell me?" James asked. "About your father, or anything else?"

"Well, a couple of years ago, Father spoke in Meeting. That was not like him. He is among the many Friends who are pious and upright but never speak in Meeting. In my whole life, I have never known my father to be moved by the Spirit to speak in Meeting, except that one time"

"What did he say?"

"Something about suffering. He seemed unable to express his thought clearly and soon sat down. But that often happens. The Spirit will move a person to stand up in Meeting, but they cannot find the words to say what is clear to them, and so their speech is not clear to others, or they say something that is only commonplace, no matter how hard they try to say what is in their hearts. What was unusual in Father's case was his standing up at all."

Rebecca, hearing this, turned from her cooking and said, "That brings to mind the time Father Maul and I were alone here in the kitchen, and he asked me whether I thought it was right to end someone's suffering if they were in pain and could not get well. And I said I didn't know, I'd never thought about it."

"Is there anything else?" James prompted.

"Our Meeting," William said, "turned down my request to bury Lizzy in its burying ground. Thee may not know, Captain Jamison, but it is our custom in the Society of Friends to bury our dead as soon as they die, and not to mark the grave with the dead person's name. But Elder Godwin refused permission to use our Meeting's burial ground to bury Lizzy. When Mr. Cleaver brought me word of this, I was very distraught and told the Sheriff I would bury Lizzy on our property. While he was trying to persuade me not to do that, a Quaker I'd never seen, named Fithian, overheard my dispute with the Sheriff, and spoke to me, offering to have a grave prepared in the burial ground of the meeting house he belonged to, the Free Quakers on Fifth Street. That is the Meeting organized by the Quakers who supported the war for American independence.

"I accepted his offer, and when Philomen Lyons had finished washing and shrouding Lizzy's body to make it decent for burial later that night, Friend Fithian and I drove it to the Free Quakers' burial ground and interred it in the grave that had been dug there."

After hearing William out, James asked to be shown the stoneyard and its buildings, particularly the old necessary.

The Mauls' property occupied about an acre of ground on the north side of Dock Street. The house was right by the street, along with a six-stall stable and a large shed for keeping the Mauls' heavy wagon and sledges for transporting stone. On this wide, deep lot, the yard for sorting, cutting, and storing stone occupied most of the property, and the entrance to the yard separated the house from the outbuildings. The two necessaries, the old one and the new one, were as far from the house as they could be, the old one farther away than the new one. Both were outside the high fence of vertical boards surrounding the yard, so it was impossible to see either of them from the house.

A mound of horse dung next to the lean-to attached to the stable showed the slowness of the Mauls' commerce of late, for it was covered all over with bright green sprouts of grass, not having been added to much in recent years. Across the rear of the property, adjacent to the necessaries, lay an open ground overgrown with sumac, goldenrod, Queen Ann's lace, and other weeds. The houses of the Mauls' nearest neighbors on either side were, like theirs, next to the street, and the high board fence around the stoneyard prevented them from seeing either of the necessaries.

James's tour of the property with William convinced him that Mrs. Coons's death probably had occurred the night of her disappearance rather than on the following day, for her body could not have been dumped in the old necessary in the light of day without someone seeing it done from the houses behind the waste ground at the rear of the Mauls' property. And the body could only have been maneuvered into the old necessary's pit while it was still somewhat supple, before its limbs had stiffened. James, from having been in charge of more than one burial squad after a battle, knew something about the stiffness of dead bodies and how long it took for them to get stiff.

He also concluded that the closer the place of her death had been to the necessary, and therefore the less time needed to carry her body to it, the nearer the hour of her death could have been to dawn the morning following her death. The lean-to built against the side of the stable, where James had noticed a cot when William was showing him the outbuildings, was less than a minute from the necessary where Elizabeth Coons's body had been found.

Chapter 8

Night had arrived by the time James took his leave of the little Quaker family, William and Rebecca Maul and their baby, and rode home through Market Street to the western suburbs.

He put Cheval in the stable, rubbed him down, and watered him. The old horse now had the stable all to himself because Grandmère, who as an indentured servant in her youth had known poverty, had sold the other three horses owned by her husband when he died, keeping only his favorite, Cheval, for James's use.

James took his supper with Livy and Grandmère in the kitchen—eating there during cold weather saved fuel by avoiding the need to build a second fire in the dining room. There was no general conversation during the meal. James was visibly preoccupied with his thoughts, and the mistress of the house and her maidservant spoke in lowered voices of commonplace topics.

After supper, James went to his room and wrote up what Rebecca and William Maul had told him, as well as his other interviews of the day. He decided he would not ride Cheval into the city. To leave him tethered in the street in the vicinity of Dr. Franklin's mansion-house for several hours two nights a week might make the City Watch inquisitive about the horse's owner and his purpose in being in the city at such regular intervals in the middle of the night. It would perhaps also expose the horse to thieves. James lay down and rested for an hour and a half and then set out on foot to keep his scheduled conference at Franklin Court.

As before, Benjamin Franklin received James in his study, which was as brilliantly lighted and as pleasantly warm, and as cluttered, as it had been two days before, though the books and papers were now in somewhat better order. An empty chair was already drawn up for him beside Dr. Franklin's worktable, and next to the chair, on a silver platter, were two crystal wine glasses, a plate of wine biscuits and cheese, and a bottle of the Chateau Ligneville he had enjoyed so much on his previous visit, along with a bottle of Monsieur Le Vieillard's spring water.

"Welcome, Captain Jamison," Franklin said, shaking hands across the table and motioning to him to have a seat. "What news of our investigation do you have to report?"

"I have been to see the Mauls—once to talk with Maul himself in the Walnut Street Jail and twice to talk with his son and the son's wife in Dock Street, and to inspect their stoneyard. I've spoken with Dr. Finley and Mr. Constable, and have had the handbills you sent to me distributed. I've also placed our advertisement with the newspapers."

"Mr. Mahoney has told me he has seen the handbill all over town, and I myself read the ad on the front page of *The Columbian Advertiser and Chronicler* this evening. I applaud your energy.

"Francis, pour Captain Jamison some of his wine and a glass of the French water for me. Then you may leave us. I will summon you if I need anything more."

After the servant's departure Dr. Franklin asked, "What reaction have you received, James, to your effort on Maul's behalf? Has it been positive?"

"It has been generally favorable," James said. "Only one person I have spoken with has taken a negative view of my undertaking. Dr. Finley's wife insisted Mr. Maul must be guilty of murder."

Dr. Franklin laughed, a sort of subdued, snickering laugh.

"I have been acquainted with Catherine Finley many years. She likes to croak. Her opinions derive from a dismal view of human nature—excluding her own, of course. But the men of affairs you have spoken with, and the journeyman printers in the shops of the newspaper publishers, what has been their opinion of your proposal? Did they seem to approve it?"

"They seemed to."

"Then all is well. We may yet convince the people of the justice of our cause and receive useful information from them."

"I'm afraid, though," James said, "that I have something to report concerning Jacob Maul that may cause you to doubt your judgment of your friend's innocence."

"Oh? And what might that be?"

"I found him deranged in his mind."

"How so, James? In what way did he seem to you mentally deranged?"

"Dr. Franklin, he is no longer of this world. He's not in his right mind. I have written down the particulars of my visit with him, and with other persons I have spoken to, so you can understand what my inquiries have uncovered since my first report."

James removed from a pocket of his coat the narrative of his various interviews and handed it to his host who received the pages with interest and read them rapidly, with a concentration such as James had never before observed.

"You are to be commended, James," Dr. Franklin said when he had finished reading. "These are exceedingly detailed descriptions of the conversations you have had with your informants. They also display considerable skill in questioning them. I especially appreciate your asking William Maul to tell you what kind of instrument Mr. Constable used to cut the canvas from the corpse of Mrs. Coons, by which I understand you were testing whether his account of what he saw when her body was unwrapped coincided with the particulars of Dr. Finley's account."

James was gratified to have his efforts appreciated.

"You must not think, however," Dr. Franklin continued, "that Jacob's mental condition means he could have killed Mrs. Coons two weeks ago. Even the insane—and I would not classify him as insane—have their motives, and he never had one for murdering Mrs. Coons. According to his son's testimony, his present distraught condition dates from his incarceration in the Walnut Street Jail. Before Mrs. Coons was killed and he was locked up in that loathsome prison, he was in possession of his faculties, and to use your language, 'of this world.' He has suffered in recent years the torments of which I told you. The agonizing death of his lifelong companion and mother of his sons. The loss of two of those sons under to him shameful circumstances. The forfeit of his former livelihood because of his religious convictions. The mysterious death of his second wife who had been a comfort to him during his first wife's suffering and death. The brutal slaying of his devoted housekeeper and staunch defender, Mrs. Coons. And, finally, the humiliation of his imprisonment on suspicion of having murdered her. Each of these disasters sapped his mind and spirit. Is there much wonder, then, that he has finally withdrawn from so cruel a world?"

"Tell me, Dr. Franklin, what you think," James asked, "of Mr. Maul's Negro friend, Robert Cash."

"As you mention in your report, he is a sort of Good Samaritan, a selfless protector of a downtrodden neighbor. The food he receives from William Maul might be viewed by some as motivating his actions. But apparently he began protecting his former employer before William included him in the daily rations he takes to his father. And any recompense he has received is outweighed by the danger he exposes himself to in aiding a man generally thought to have killed two defenseless women.

"It is interesting, is it not, that even the inmates of a school for vice such as the Walnut Street Jail make moral judgments. That seems to be part of our nature, even when we ourselves have done wrong."

"That irony also struck me, Dr. Franklin," James said. "I've been thinking of a couple of things Cash said, such as his remark that sometimes Maul speaks as if addressing a woman named Margaret, telling her it would not be right to do something, and that the sound of heavy dray carts passing by in the street outside the jail disturbs him."

"His first wife, you recall, James, was fatally injured by the wheels of a dray cart. I suspect the sound of such carts on the cobblestones in front of the Walnut Street Jail reminds him of his wife's suffering from her injuries. Margaret was the name of his wife's nurse. He and Margaret kept vigil together many nights beside the dying wife's bed. It would be natural under those circumstances, in the long hours of such vigils, to talk of many things, and it would appear that Maul and the nurse sometimes spoke of something he thought it would not be right to do in regard to the suffering wife, though he may have considered doing it. What that might have been is suggested by the question he asked his daughter-in-law regarding suffering. Maul's striking his head against a stone wall, as if in punishment of himself, is also suggestive."

"If I understand you," James said, "you are saying Maul and the woman who became his second wife may have done something to shorten the suffering of Maul's first wife."

Benjamin Franklin replied to this observation, "The possibility does appear that the nurse, or the two of them together, discussed shortening the dying Mrs. Maul's suffering. It would have been easy to have administered to her a lethal dose of the laudanum she was probably taking to alleviate her pain."

"But, Dr. Franklin, doesn't this raise the question, especially in light of Jacob Maul's violence against himself, that he could have killed his second wife to eliminate the only other person who knew about such a mercy killing of his first wife?"

"That question assumes too many things, James. It assumes that there indeed was a mercy killing and that the two of them, Jacob Maul and the nurse who later became his second wife, acted together in effecting it. It is possible they discussed doing this but Maul resisted the idea. Remember, Cash reported he said when he was 'excited' something like, 'it wouldn't be right to do that.' It's possible the nurse, unable to stand seeing Mrs. Maul suffer any longer, went ahead on her own to carry out a mercy killing and that Maul knew she did. But we do not know that as a fact. It would be worth finding out from Rebecca Maul whether it was before or after the death of Maul's second wife that he asked her whether ending someone's suffering would be right if you knew the person could not get well. I suspect it was afterwards."

"I will do that."

"You have, I think, accomplished a great deal, James," Franklin continued. "The information you have obtained begins to give us a picture of Mrs. Coons's character. I would also congratulate you for establishing a basis for surmising why she may have left the house that night, for it is unlikely that an abductor entered the house and forced her to go away with him. It seems from what you have found out that her departure from the house was unplanned but voluntary, and you have given us a notion of how she went. She left, it seems, thinking she would return."

James wondered what part of the information he had provided had led Dr. Franklin to these conclusions.

"Let us consider Mrs. Coons's character," the master of Franklin Court said. "The wife of William Maul gives us an adequate sketch of that, and his opinion supports his wife's judgments. First of all, Mrs. Coons was evidently an orderly person who liked good housekeeping. That tells us that she was a woman who cared about appearances and the opinions of others. Secondly, by temperament she also appears to have been a cheerful soul, someone who by nature preferred to look on the positive side of things, a characteristic that would likewise have made her attractive to others. By the way—and I say this, James, not to reproach you, for your efforts have been impressive—something is missing from your report, don't you think? What did Mrs. Coons look like? Was she tall and lank, like her sister, the second Mrs. Maul? What color of eyes and hair did she have? How old was she? Physical appearance, in conjunction with character, has much to do with one's relationships with other persons.

"It would appear that Elizabeth Coons, or Lizzy as everyone called her, was an attractive woman both in her character and her physical appearance. In the days to come, as you talk with her neighbors and her cousin, the market woman, you will have opportunities to find out how she impressed others physically."

James was embarrassed by his failure to obtain such basic information on the living woman, though he had obtained descriptions from several persons of her grotesque corpse. He apologized to his director for this omission.

"No, no, James! There is nothing to apologize for! In fact, I would say it is just as well that you did not ask the people she lived with, Rebecca and William Maul, for a physical description of her. Being persons who felt great affection for her, they might not have given you accurate information on the impression she generally made. When it comes to physical charms, or the lack of them, it is best *not* to ask persons who love the person whose physical description you seek. We may assume that she did not make a repulsive figure in the world, because according to William Maul the Hessian soldiers found her attractive, though their attraction does not tell us much. A soldier garrisoned in a foreign city during a war, far from home, is likely to find any female he associates with attractive, I think. Mrs. Coons, whatever her appearance, was sufficiently appealing to arouse jealousy, for William Maul has testified that his brother Robert, who was still in his minority at the time, almost came to blows with the Germans over their attentions to the lady. I will return to the question of that interesting young man, Robert Maul, in a moment.

"Let us now consider the circumstances of Mrs. Coons's disappearance. We have reason to believe that she left the house of her own free will. One of the most telling details you have collected, James, proves it was not a planned departure. For she told Rebecca Maul before they went up to bed that she would light the fire in the morning and make the porridge, a promise she was not in the house the next morning to keep.

"As to what caused her to leave the house, we may assume it had something to do with her health—an ailment she did not want to reveal to her companion Rebecca Maul. I base this deduction on several pieces of information you gathered, James. The extraordinary number of visits she made to the necessary that day and her snappish response to Rebecca asking her if she was not feeling well. Her breaking a valuable bowl without apology likewise shows her mind was preoccupied with something more important to her than ordinary household matters. Evidently, by that evening she must have felt some improvement, for she participated with Rebecca in one of their household tasks—mending clothes— and talked with her about ordinary domestic concerns. But Mrs. Coons did not feel well enough to sleep when she went up to her room. Rather, she lay atop her bedclothes. We have Rebecca's testimony to that. And sometime during the night, whether early or late, as the Mauls slept, she stole from the house.

"That she evidently expected to return is indicated by her not taking any of her clothes with her, not even hose or a change of small clothes. Apart from her cloak she took only one thing. The doll which was, from what William Maul told you, her most valuable possession."

Chapter 9

"I wondered about the doll," James said. "Why would she take that and leave all her clothes?"

"I think we'll have to wait until further information comes to us before we can understand this part of the puzzle," Dr. Franklin replied.

"Might the absence of the doll signify she did not expect to return?" James asked. "She could, after all, obtain other clothes, but not a childhood token of her father's love."

"Perhaps. But her offer to start the fire the next morning and make breakfast rather indicates an unplanned departure from the house, wouldn't you say? I can't imagine why she would suddenly conceive in the middle of the night of leaving the only home she had with the intention of never coming back. I rather think I see in this precipitous action the possibility of some health problem she didn't want her family to know of suddenly becoming acute and motivating her to leave the house quickly to seek aid. Though why she would not want to ask her family for help is unclear at present.

"When you interview her cousin, Mistress Merkle, the market woman, you must ask her whether Mrs. Coons had any health problem known to her. If we knew the nature of the ailment that seems to have sent her hurrying from her house in the dead of night, we would be a long ways toward knowing the person she went to for aid that night. It occurs to me you might consider asking Rebecca Maul, the next time you see her, if Mrs. Coons consulted a physician, apothecary, or folk healer when she felt poorly, and obtain the name of that person. I'm afraid I am burdening you with many questions to find answers to, James."

"But they must be answered," James replied. "I see the sense of your questions, and it is becoming intriguing work to find answers to them. Besides the debt of life I owe to Jacob Maul's son John, I am now curious to find out the truth about Mrs. Coons's death."

"It is like an experiment in natural philosophy," Dr. Franklin agreed. "If you want to learn more about some natural phenomenon—say electricity—you begin with systematic observations of it and make a record of them. Then you study your observations, looking for a pattern. Finally, you formulate a hypothesis about what you have studied—say the hypothesis 'Lightning is a form of electricity'—and construct an experiment to test it, even if the experiment involves a degree of danger.

"The question before us is 'Who killed Mrs. Coons?' Once we have made enough observations, we will formulate a hypothesis about that question—the identity of her killer—and test it by confronting the man. I would not want simply to turn over a name to the Sheriff with our reasons for thinking that man was Mrs. Coons's murderer, without being ourselves absolutely certain beyond any doubt whatever that we had proved our hypothesis. We want to offer the Sheriff absolute proof because he has jailed the man he thinks committed the murder and will thus be loath to admit he has imprisoned an innocent man, especially a pious Quaker, particularly considering that no Quaker has ever been arraigned for any crime of violence in Philadelphia."

"Why do you think the Sheriff arrested Maul?" James asked. "Does he have evidence we do not?"

"I doubt it. I have heard he strongly disagreed with the Coroner calling the death of Maul's second wife A Visitation of God. So when another woman's body with bruise marks on her throat was found on Maul's property, he had Maul arrested. Many people in Philadelphia do not like the Quakers, James. They are heavily involved in banking, and moneylenders are never popular. But more than that, the strong opposition of the Quakers to the recent war has brought them into disrepute, as has their strong stand against slavery. And their custom of marrying only among themselves has led many people in Philadelphia to believe they consider themselves superior to other people, which is something Americans generally dislike when they encounter it in others.

"The arrest of a Quaker for murder has therefore met with more approval than if Maul had been a Methodist or a Baptist, I think. And because the Sheriff's office is elective, he must have a high regard for popular opinion if he wants to retain his office. In the long term, of course, the judgment of the people is trustworthy. Majority rule is, after all, the first principle of republican government. But in matters of justice, I have on occasion wondered whether the people are sufficiently wise and reliable."

James paid close heed to these remarks. Both Dr. Franklin's views and the mild way in which he advanced them engaged the younger man's full attention. He felt himself in the presence of someone who had distilled in the alembic of his mind the experiences of a long life without letting any memory diminish his joy at being alive or his faith in human nature.

"I was struck, Dr. Franklin," James said, "by the Quaker custom of burying their dead in unmarked graves the day they die. I didn't know they did that."

"They think gravestones are a sign of vanity," Franklin responded, "and that the Creator frowns on vanity. Through immediate, unmarked burial they believe they conform to the biblical view that man is dust and hasten the process expressed by the scriptural text 'dust to dust.' In this matter they resemble the Jews of old."

The conversation paused at this point while Dr. Franklin refilled his glass, ate a cracker and some cheese, and invited James to partake of the same.

"What do you intend to have me do, Dr. Franklin," James asked, "in regard to the Hessians billeted in the Maul household during the British occupation of Philadelphia? If we are to believe William Maul, both of them paid attention to Mrs. Coons when they lived with the Mauls, and one of them may be nearby in German Town. Whether that is true or not, it is certain that of the tens of thousands of German mercenaries who served in America during the war, thousands of them did stay behind in Pennsylvania, either with the permission of their superiors or as deserters, when the Hessian troops returned to Europe at the end of the war."

Dr. Franklin, in replying to this inquiry, said, "It is too soon to go scouring around German Town looking for the farm of a German named Polzer, to see if a nephew of his named Weber may be there. What would we question him about in regard to his connection with Elizabeth Coons? Whether he knew her? We already know that. Whether he felt some amorous attraction to her? We may be fairly sure, on general grounds, that he well may have. Whether he actually did have an affair with her and continued to see her after he left service in the British army is quite another matter. We need some indication that he did—don't you think?—before we try to track him down."

Dr. Franklin's observations made sense to James, but did not satisfy his curiosity.

"But don't you think it possible he may have had a liaison with Mrs. Coons and could have been involved in her death? During their military service in America, the Hessians had a reputation for cruelty."

"I would say this, James, that when it comes to affairs of the heart, practically anything is possible. And nothing increases a passion more than proximity to its object over a long period of time without an opportunity to consummate it. Delights that burn only in the imagination have an intensity that actual amours seldom attain. The memory of such an encounter can smolder for years in a man's memory, like an ember in seemingly dead ashes. It is certainly possible the former Hessian mercenary Sergeant Weber could have conceived a passion for Elizabeth Coons while living in the Mauls' household. It is also possible that if he is still in the vicinity of Philadelphia he could have seen her by chance—say on a trip into the city to buy at the market houses—and that his old passion for her could have flared up again. But all of this is conjecture only. Even if these suppositions are true, it would still not be clear what they might have to do with the death of Mrs. Coons. If every man who ever had a liaison with a woman who disappeared were suspected of murder, where would the justice in that be? We are far from formulating our hypothesis of who killed Elizabeth Coons."

"You mentioned," James said, "that you found Robert Maul 'an interesting young man'—I think that was your phrase—and said that you would return to that subject. I am curious, Dr. Franklin, what you meant."

"Robert Maul seems to have been a casualty of the war, having apparently gone off to enlist in the American army to fight the British, whom he held responsible for the death of his imprisoned brother. But whether he did die in the war or survived and for some reason chose not to return home is unknown. All that is known is that he was a passionate young man not averse to violence, as shown by his declared intention to join in the fight against England and his almost coming to blows with two Hessians. We also know, again from his brother William's testimony, that he was a favorite of Elizabeth Coons, and that she showed a partiality for him that manifested in her favors to him. I believe in your report you said William remarked that his brother Robert was her 'pet.' We know from Robert's reaction to the attentions the two German soldiers paid Mrs. Coons, as reported by his brother, that he reciprocated her attentions, enough to be moved to jealousy.

"Another detail in your report which drew my attention, James, was Elizabeth Coons telling William that she was sure Robert would one day come home. Was Robert writing letters to her perhaps? I would advise you to return to Dock Street and ask Rebecca Maul to show you any letters or other papers Elizabeth Coons may have left behind when she disappeared. I should have thought to tell you the first time we spoke, when you agreed to aid me in this investigation, to ask to see any papers Mrs. Coons left behind."

"I had better also ask Rebecca whether Mrs. Coons had any other relatives besides her cousin who keeps the vegetable stand in the market," James said.

"Inquire likewise if Mrs. Coons ever had occasion to leave the city," Dr. Franklin said, "and if so, for what reason and where she went."

Again Dr. Franklin filled his glass and took a bit of cheese and cracker. James did likewise.

"In addition to the questions you put to Rebecca Maul, talk as soon as you can, James, with the Negro washerwoman, Philomen Lyons. Also the neighbor Mrs. Cleaver and as many other neighbors as you can, especially those who live nearest the Mauls. And don't forget to question the former servants of the Mauls, the hostler named Lort and the indentured maidservant named Love. Discover their impressions of her character, and in talking with the neighbors inquire into any change in her conduct in the days and weeks before her disappearance.

"In questioning Mrs. Lyons, get her to tell you every detail of what she saw in washing the corpse of Mrs. Coons for burial. She will also be an important source of information about the character of Elizabeth Coons. For as I have always said, there is no truer way to find out a person's true character than doing heavy work for them, such as spring housecleaning, for pay. The maidservant, Susan Love, will also be a good source of information in that regard, too. She should also be able to tell you something about the rest of the Maul household.

"From the cousin who runs the stall in the Jersey Market find out all you can about Mrs. Coons's family history and, as I said, any medical problems she may have had. I am particularly interested, James, in finding out why Mrs. Coons sent her child to live with the cousin instead of keeping the child with her at the Mauls. Find out from the hostler and the maid what they may have seen of the relations between Mrs. Coons and the Hessians, and what they thought of her relations with Jacob Maul and his sons. It might also—"

The clanging of a nearby bell interrupted Dr. Franklin's statement, and was almost immediately amplified by other alarms being sounded.

"That sounds like a fire," the master of Franklin Court said as he rose, and by the aid of his cane started off as hurriedly as he could toward the windows of his study.

James also got up and went to the window. Dr. Franklin was already drawing aside the drapes. A point of orange light was visible through the window over the housetops to the north, toward the river. The light visibly wavered.

Francis Mahoney, unbidden, came into the room.

"Your Honor, should I go in front to see what I can find out?" he asked.

"Yes, by all means, Francis," his master replied, "see what you can find out."

Having been commissioned, Mr. Mahoney departed.

"It seems to be above Arch Street," Franklin said to James as they watched the pulsing orange light, "somewhere in the vicinity of Bread Street or Elfreth's Alley, it appears. Thank goodness it is a windless night. Perhaps you should step into my bedchamber, through that door, Captain. My daughter and her husband will likely come here to talk about the fire, and it would not do to have them see us together. No one will go into my bedroom, you may be sure, and you can see things just as well from there as through this window."

"Certainly," James said. "As you think best."

Dr. Franklin's rectangular bedroom was much smaller than his square study, with only one window instead of two. There were, however, two doors into it, the small one from the study that James had used and another from the hallway. There was also a closet door next to the bed. James could not see much of the room's furnishings until he drew aside the drapes and let in the street light, revealing a half-round table, an upholstered chair, and a highboy. A small fireplace was angled into one corner of the room. The room's walls were wainscoted. A little tapestry, three feet by two feet, of St. George slaying the dragon hung above the half-round table opposite the hall door.

James had been in the room only a few minutes, watching the orange glow above the northern rooftops, which seemed to be expanding, when he heard, audible above the still-clanging but diminishing fire alarms, the voices of a woman and a man in the next room along with Dr. Franklin's deeper tones. The conversation lasted some time, and then James heard another male voice, which sounded to him like that of Mr. Mahoney.

Not long after the alarms and the talk from the next room ceased, there was a knock, and Dr. Franklin opened the door from the study and said, without entering, "You may return now, James. I hope you were not discommoded by being put in my closet."

Dr. Franklin informed James that, according to what Francis Mahoney had found out, a house in Elfreth's Alley was on fire, and the Sun Fire Company, the Union Fire Company, and other bands of volunteer firemen were fighting it effectively. Mahoney had run up to Elfreth's Alley to see the blaze, so he could give his master a fuller report.

Dr. Franklin related this while standing by the window, gazing at the orange light of the fire, which was now noticeably diminished. As the proposer and organizer, half a century before, of the Union Fire Company, the first volunteer fire company in Philadelphia, Franklin had a great interest in fire suppression. He enjoyed boasting that Philadelphia had the best fire protection of any city in the world, though he never boasted that his initiatives had made it so.

Before James left Franklin Court by the concealed door in the west side of the property, Dr. Franklin told him he had sent letters to illustrious medical friends of his in Austria, England, France, Italy, and Germany, describing the peculiar circumstances of the death of Jacob Maul's wife Margaret Gilbert and asking if any of his correspondents, in their experiences in the large, cosmopolitan populations of Europe, had ever encountered such a death. One of these eminent physicians, he said, was his longtime Dutch correspondent Jan Ingenousz, the court physician to the empress-queen of the Austrian empire; another was the distinguished London doctor Sir Charles Fauxhall.

Chapter 10

On Wednesday morning James debated in his mind whether to go first to see the cousin of Mrs. Coons or the Negro washerwoman who had prepared her corpse for burial. He decided to see Philomen Lyons first because the market houses where Mistress Merkle kept her vegetable stand were usually crowded in the mornings, and it would be better to try to talk with Mrs. Merkle at some other time.

He rode rather than walked to the Negro washerwoman's house because it was on the outskirts of the city, where the Southwark District of Philadelphia met the woods and fields nearest the city to the south.

It was a modest house set on six big stones, with two steps up to the simple porch built across half of its front. Both it and the smaller wash house next to it had an air of long-established residence. Both buildings had chimneys, and the smaller structure, which was lower to the ground, had, as James could see through its open door, a brick floor. It was clear from what he saw, and from the fact that Mrs. Lyons had her own business, that she descended from the numerous class of free Negroes in the city William Penn had founded and dedicated to the idea of Brotherly Love. The Society of Friends had been the first religious body in America, generations before, whose leaders had preached and published tracts against slavery and in token of their sincerity had freed the slaves they owned.

As James dismounted in the yard of Mistress Lyons's house, she was busy at her kettles in the yard, assisted by two good-looking, lively boys. The boys were busy under her watchful eye, hanging wet clothing and linen to dry on lines strung between trees in the yard and spreading the smaller, lighter pieces of laundry on bushes and tall grass. These lads, he soon learned from the washerwoman, were her grandsons.

Mrs. Lyons looked up from her kettles as he entered her yard but kept on feeding the fires under them, stirring the boiling clothing and bed linen with her wooden paddle made pale by many years of use in hot water.

When he had introduced himself and said he wanted to talk with her about Mrs. Coons in order to help the Mauls, Philomen Lyons sent one of her grandsons scurrying into the house to bring her visitor a stool. But she did not stop her work on his account. Every little while as they talked, she lifted with her paddle from her big iron kettles a heavy load of water-soaked laundry and deposited it to drain in one of the strong wicker baskets set on nearby trestles. There the laundry steamed in the chilly morning air until it was cool enough for the boys to hang it up on the lines to dry or spread it out on the bushes and tall grass. Once it was dry they would carry it into the brick-floored wash house, where their grandmother would later iron it.

Mrs. Lyons was quite willing to talk with James about the Mauls because of his declared intention to help a family for whom she expressed great fondness and loyalty.

"De Mauls is good peoples," she said, "startin' wid ol' Mr. Jacob. John Maul I knowed from when he wuz a boy. He wuz jes like his Daddy. Quiet an' nice. Good worker. I he'p'd de wife o' his bruddah, Mr. William, in her birthin' a few munts back. It be a shame John didn't live to have chil'ren born to him."

James silently agreed with these sentiments about the dead John Maul, and it pleased him to hear Mrs. Lyons express such positive opinions of John and his afflicted father. But he was there to carry out Dr. Franklin's directive to obtain information from the washerwoman.

"I understand, Mrs. Lyons," James said, "that you washed Mrs. Coons's body and put the shroud on her for burial. I need to know what you saw while removing the clothing from her corpse. Knowing that might help me to find the man who killed her."

"Dat's right, I washed her. Yassuh."

"And what did you see? Were there any marks on her besides the bruises to her throat?"

"It wuz mighty ugly, I tell you. De way she died an' all. De rats chewed on her face somethin' awful, po' ting. An' she wuz terrible bloaty—her han's, an' feet, an' belly—de way a lady wuz I done fur once dat drownded in de river. An' dere was an awful strong smell. It wuz bad work, makin' Miz Lizzy decent. Ise sorry fur Miz Rebecca. Dem two wuz good fr'en's. Miz Lizzy wuz a fine, lovin' soul."

"But what about marks on her? Were there any marks?"

"Well, suh, dey wuz marks on her t'roat, four of 'em. Dey wuz crossways, like dem marks on de Dutch bread. You might say dey wuz different from de marks on Mr. Jacob's wife. Not de furs' one dat died frum de acciden' but de secon' one. I dun fur her, too, an' fur Mr. Jacob's firs' wife. I dun fur all tree o' dem wimmins da's passed on in dat fambly."

Philomen Lyons's statement that she had washed the corpses of both sisters found dead on Maul's property with bruises on their throats interested James much more than her saying there had been four bruises on Mrs. Coons's throat like the baker's marks on a loaf of Dutch bread. He was speaking with probably the only person who could compare the bruises on the throats of the two sisters whose deaths had put Jacob Maul under suspicion of murder.

"How were Mrs. Coons's bruises different from the bruises on the throat of her sister, Mr. Maul's second wife?" James asked.

"It's been years 'n' years since Mr. Jacob's wife passed. I'm not rightly sure I recall how dey wuz diff'rent. But dey sure warn't de same. You could see dem four marks on Miz Lizzy's t'roat jes as plain as you please, like de marks on de Dutch bread, like I said, one 'bove t'udder. De hurts on Miz Marg'ret seemed more scattery-like, as I rec'lect."

"Did you notice any other marks on Mrs. Coons's body? Any other bruises, for instance?"

"'Side frum what de rats done 'round her mout' an' nose an' all?"

"Yes. Besides those marks."

"Well, suh, dey wuz de marks de cords dun made, dat was dug sometin' fierce into her po' flesh counta de swellin'."

"But no wounds or bruises of any kind?"

"Dey wuz sum marks on her belly. Tiny little lines, dey wuz. But dey warn't no bruises. Dey wuz mo' like pinched up skin. Mo' like little welts, kinda, de same color as her skin. Dey wuz reg'lar like, back 'n' fo't' 'cross her belly."

This pattern of fine welts on the skin of Elizabeth Coons's belly puzzled James. But what Mrs. Lyons said next astonished him. She leaned forward toward him and, glancing over at her two grandsons, who were absorbed in their tasks, confided to James in a lowered voice, "She wuzn't wearin' no stockin's a'tall. An' dere wuz sum blood on her shif', an' her petticoat wuz on backwards. I never tol' a soul 'bout dis eber befo'. I wud'n've tol' you, neider, 'ceptin' yuz a gentleman da's tryin' tuh he'p a fambly da's had mo'n its share o' de suff'rin'. Nudder t'ing wuz her shoes. She had 'em on de wrong feets. But de mos' stranges' t'ing wuz her shif'. It wuz on ober her petticoat, 'stead o' t'udder way 'round like it ought tuh've been."

"But how could there have been blood on her clothing if there were no wounds? Didn't you tell me there were no wounds?"

"Das what I said. Yassuh. But dey wuz blood on dat petticoat an' on her shif', sho 'nuf, an' de petticoat wuz on under 'stead o' ober her shif'."

"And you're certain the petticoat was on backwards?"

Mrs. Lyons laughed heartily at this, and her grandsons left off what they were doing and stared at her.

"You git back tuh work ober dere!" she called out with authority, then, turning to James, said, "Nah, suh, no woman puts her petticoat on backwards. She'd feel de wrong o' it. Miz Lizzy never done dat her own self. Sumon' else musta dressed her. An' I tell you, dey wuz no cuts on her. I'll tell you sumpin else, too, now dat I'se talkin' free like. It seems to me like Miz Lizzy might o' had herself a chil' befo' she died. Yassuh, da's my notion."

Naturally, James pressed Mrs. Lyons for particulars on such a momentous statement as this. But he could not get the washerwoman to state as a fact that Elizabeth Coons had given birth before she died. She would only say that it was her "notion" that she had.

When questioned further about the blood on the petticoat, however, she was absolutely positive. She gave it as the judgment of someone with long experience in washing women's undergarments stained with blood.

"I knows blood on clo's when I sees it," she said. "Lord amighty, I'se washed 'nough o' it outa de small clo's o' de ladies in ma life to know blood when I sees it."

She was just as positive that there had been no sign of blood anywhere on Mrs. Coons's outer clothes.

Having received these wonderful pieces of intelligence, it seemed certain to James that Elizabeth Coons had been disrobed the night she was killed, and that someone must have put her shoes and shift on her incorrectly. And probably omitted putting on her stockings. This could only have been done before her arms, wrists, and ankles had been tied with cord.

But why would a murderer have bothered to put her clothes back on her before subjecting her corpse to the indignity of dumping it in an old necessary?

The last thing Philomen Lyons said to James was to repeat her opinion of how good a woman Lizzy Coons was—"as good as de day is long, suh," was how she put it—and in saying this, she repeated her previous judgment of the entire Maul family that the Mauls were "good peoples."

When James left Mrs. Lyons, he tried to give her a token of his appreciation for taking the time to speak with him and providing such valuable information. But she refused his money. When he tried to give the coin to her grandsons, who appeared eager to have it, she forbade them taking it, saying, "It ain't right tuh take money fur tellin' de trut' 'bout a po' lady what dun had her life taken by wicked mens, de way Miz Lizzy's wuz."

And no attempt at persuasion by James or look of disappointment on the faces of her grandsons could alter her mind.

When James swung into the saddle and turned Cheval back toward the city, he headed for Dock Street to speak with the Mauls and interview their neighbors.

Rebecca was alone, her husband having gone off to do one of the occasional jobs of stonework that still came his way even though his father and he, as steadfast Quakers, had opposed the war.

She invited James into the kitchen and, as on his previous visits, asked if he would like a cup of tea. But he refused the invitation, saying he had several places to go after talking with her and did not have time to stay long.

"Mrs. Maul, what physician, apothecary, or healer did your friend Elizabeth Coons go to when she wasn't feeling well?"

"I never knew Lizzy to be sick a day in her life. She was healthy as a little horse."

"Were there any papers—particularly letters—among the things Mrs. Coons left behind?"

"I'm sorry to tell thee, Captain Jamison, there were none. No papers of any sort."

James next asked whether her friend had any relatives other than her cousin the vegetable seller in Market Street.

"None that are known to me. I never heard her speak of any relative but her cousin who has the stall in Market Street."

"What about trips? Did she ever leave the city to travel to some other place for a visit?"

"She never left town since I've been in the family."

"The last time we spoke, Mrs. Maul, you told me of a conversation you had with your father-in-law. Do you recall?

He wanted your opinion on whether it would be right to help a person die who was suffering, if you knew the person could not get well."

"Yes, of course, I recall."

"When was it you had that conversation with him? Was it before or after his second wife's death?"

"Oh, after. Sometime in the past four or five months."

After speaking with Rebecca Maul, James made a tour of the Mauls' neighbors, starting with Mrs. Cleaver and Mrs. Nash, the neighbors who lived on either side of the stoneyard.

Everywhere he went, he encountered the same response. Elizabeth Coons had been a good, respectable woman, and the Mauls were kind, hardworking, honest neighbors who had suffered many misfortunes in recent years but had borne their adversity without complaint. More than one of their neighbors expressed the view that Lizzy Coons had been "pretty" and a heartfelt regret that Jacob Maul had been arrested and put in jail on suspicion of having killed her. Several volunteered the opinion that Jacob Maul could never have committed such a crime. No one had seen or heard anything amiss the night Elizabeth Coons had disappeared or noticed anything strange in her behavior in the weeks before her disappearance and death.

In the early afternoon James went to the nearby Blue Anchor Tavern at the foot of Dock Street to have some of its famous fish stew. As he approached the tavern, the sight of its sign brought to mind what his grandfather had told him about the place—that over a hundred years earlier, this same sign with the blue anchor painted on it had greeted William Penn when there was no other building in the vicinity of what would become Philadelphia. On Penn's first sail up the Delaware River, he had come ashore in his boat right here, where the sandbar at the mouth of Dock Creek had made an easy landing place. At that time this tavern that served watermen going up and down the Delaware had only recently been erected.

But the tavern Penn had seen was no more, James reflected. Since that time its logs had been clapboarded over, the boards painted, and dormers built into the tavern's roof. The Blue Anchor had become a thoroughly modern establishment. Similarly, the creek that had emptied into the Delaware at this site, which for decades had been a convenient sewer for the offal of the tanneries and shambles along its banks, had recently been filled in and paved over; so Dock Creek was now Dock Street. And the sandbar at the mouth of the creek had become a boat basin of dressed stone. The Tavern was still, however, the haven for watermen it had always been. Pilots bringing ships up the river from Delaware Bay especially liked to use it as a place to rest and eat before heading back down the river to pick up another ship to pilot.

When James entered the Blue Anchor, he saw four of the handbills regarding his investigation tacked to the wall just by the entrance. When he sat down for his meal, the proprietor of the tavern approached him and got his name, which he recognized as that of the person who'd had the handbills put up and placed the advertisement in the papers he had read. The tavern keeper told James his name was Josiah Cratty and said he had heard gossip about James's visit to the Mauls the day before.

He wanted to know what James had found out. James told him only that he had been to see Jacob Maul in the Walnut Street Jail and had found him distracted.

"Aye," Mr. Cratty agreed, "Maul's not been himself for some time past. And what think ye of the Quaker Murders, Captain Jamison? Who d'ye think killed Lizzy Coons? I used to see her, most every day, go by my windows. She was as trig a woman as I ever saw. I wish ye luck in findin' the man what treated a spruce lady like her so cruelly."

"It's far too soon to tell who's guilty of her death, Mr. Cratty," James replied. "I still must gather a lot of information. So you think Mrs. Coons was an attractive woman?"

"Aye, she made a fine figure, she did. And she was always a cheerful one. Always had a kind word if I was standin' in the door when she passed. Well, one thing's certain. A sailor's mixed up in this somewheres. I seen them bring poor Lizzy's body out of the necessary and the canvas and cord it was tied up with. It was a piece of old sail and the cord was marline, the kind used on ships. That says sailor to me or I didn't spend years on ships. If I was you, Captain Jamison, I'd look amongst the sailors of this town, though there's a mighty good chance the man what done Lizzy Coons in is long gone from Philadelphia, bound for some far-off heathen ocean where the laws of civilized men can't lay a hand on him. Jacob Maul never harmed a hair on the head of Lizzy Coons."

Chapter 11

After eating his fill of the Blue Anchor's famous fish stew, James asked Mr. Cratty for pen and ink and wrote a report for Dr. Franklin on the astonishing information he had obtained from Philomen Lyons. He also summarized the answers Rebecca Maul had given to his questions and the opinions of the Mauls' neighbors, as well as Mr. Cratty's statements. Having completed his report, he rode to the Indian Queen Hotel to deposit it in the post for Dr. Franklin.

In the hotel's taproom he had a glass of Madeira, then exited by the Fourth Street door and went down the narrow passage that ran along the south side of the Indian Queen. After he put his report to Dr. Franklin behind the loose brick concealed by the holly bush at the end of the passage, he retrieved his horse and rode over to the City Tavern to see what responses, if any, there were to his newspaper and handbill advertisements.

He found three communications waiting for him. Two of them were hostile to his enterprise, and one of these threatened to do him bodily harm if he persisted, saying that if he continued to "defend the Quaker Tory" he would have "a short life." Neither missive was signed. The third communication was a note written on the back of a receipt for the purchase of a cow. It was signed and read:

Capt. Jamison,

To find who killed the woman ask Anthony Scull what William Maul said about her the morning she disappeared when he was building Scull's lay stall. He lives in the third house to the right above Vine on Front.

Bring my ten Spanish dollars to No. 3 Appletree St.

Joseph Ayles

James asked the hotel manager to describe the persons who had left these missives, and was told that two of them had been left at the desk when the manager was escorting guests to private dining rooms. The other had been brought by "a man in his middle years with a limp," who did not have the appearance or address of a gentleman. Mr. Morley said he was the one who had written the note on the back of the bill of sale.

James did not linger at the City Tavern, but went on his way to find Peter Odell's rope walk on Race Street near the river, to inquire after Susan Love, the former indentured servant of the Mauls. There were more than a dozen factories for making rope and cord in Philadelphia, most of whose products went into the rigging of the ships built in the city's several shipyards. Three of these rope walks were on Race Street.

James finally found the one belonging to Mr. Odell, but discovered that Susan Love's indenture had been bought a year after Odell had acquired it by a fuller named Peter Hannah, who wanted to make Susan his wife.

Mr. Odell directed James to look for the Hannahs in a brick tenement, one of the first substantial buildings erected by the Quaker settlers of Philadelphia, which had long since fallen into disrepair and been divided into apartments for hire.

James found the former maidservant of the Mauls at her cooking. The smell of cabbage and meat filled the apartment. Her four-year-old daughter was following a busy little red-haired toddler around the room, keeping him from doing harm to himself and the modest furnishings of the household.

Mrs. Hannah, a robust young woman, redheaded and freckled, had worked for the Mauls, she said, for four years. Her manners were those of a simple country girl who desired to please others. She wanted James to know that she had come to America from the Protestant part of Ireland, not the Catholic part.

She had nothing to say about the Mauls except to sing their praises for their kind treatment of her. She was grateful to Jacob Maul for buying her contract and affording "a lass from a poor country" the chance to come to America to seek her fortune and, she said, "find the happiness I've had in my marriage."

In speaking of the three mistresses she had had in the Maul household—Elizabeth Coons and the two wives of the owner of her indenture—she was particularly generous in her praise of Mrs. Coons.

She had been in the Mauls' household only one year when the first Mrs. Maul died. She recounted in detail the agony the woman had suffered from her broken legs and how she wouldn't let them cut her legs off to save her life after they started to "mortify and smell." She also recalled the morning Maul's second wife, whom she referred to as "poor Mrs. Maul," was found dead in her bed with "them terr'ble marks on her neck."

James did not interrupt this rambling speech, even though he wanted Mrs. Hannah to give him information on Elizabeth Coons. He had learned in his interview with Philomen Lyons that useful information can sometimes be obtained simply by being a respectful, patient listener.

"Miss Elizabeth sent me," the former indentured servant told James, "to see why the master an' the mistress was layin' abed so long, an' to tell 'em to get up and come down to breakfast. I knocked on their door but didn't hear nothin', so I went downstairs an' told Miss Elizabeth.

"'Well, they must be sleepin' pretty sound,' she says, 'or else you didn't knock loud enough, Susan.' So she ups an' leaves the table to go herself to knock on their door. An' one of them Germans, on a sudden, said he'd wake 'em up, certain. An' when he left the table, Solomon followed him, though he didn't say nothin', being a quiet sort of man, not much for talkin'. So everybody finally was goin' upstairs with Miss Elizabeth except that other German. He stayed at the table, eatin'. The boys, Robert an' William, had already left the house. They wasn't there.

"Miss Elizabeth was at the head of the parade, just about at the door of the master's chamber, when the German sort of went on by her an' banged on the door hisself, an' him a-shoutin' in his big German way o' talkin' for the master to get up, as if he had a right to be bellerin' like that and orderin' his betters about!

"Well, the master he opened the door to ask what was the matter. I never heard him unbolt it. With all the racket that German was makin' it was a wonder a body could hear anythin'! Behind the master, in the bed, you could see the mistress layin' with her back to the door, an' Miss Lizzy she went in to see why her sister wasn't movin' an' let out a big holler when she found her dead. We all went in then, an' seen her stone-cold, starin' dead, with them big bruises on the front of her neck. It was the horriblest sight I ever did see! I don't understand still how Mr. Jacob could o' done it, him being so sweet in all his ways. They asked my opinion of him at the hearing, an' that's what I told 'em."

What she had seen that morning, seven years before, was still vivid enough in her memory to cause Mrs. Hannah to wipe the beginning of tears from her eyes with the back of her wrist.

"Tell me, Mrs. Hannah," James said, "what sort of men were the Hessians?"

"Lord o' mercy, sir, they was foreigners!"

"Yes, but did they get along with the Mauls? Did they show any interest in Mrs. Coons? Was either one of them ever forward with her?"

"They was bossy, they was. Least ways the one that went upstairs with us that morning, the sergeant of the pair, was. They was thick as thieves, them two Germans. Always talkin' in German 'n' laughin' between 'em. A body got the feelin' they was laughin' at us, as if they was the lords o' the earth an' we was the peasants. An' Lord o' mercy could they eat! Allus complainin' 'bout the grub an' allus callin' me to bring 'em more of it! That's the sort o' men they was.

"I never put no stock in their foreign ways. I had as little truck with 'em as I might. I served 'em at table, like I was supposed to, but that was all. Robert, he didn't like 'em none, neither. Told me so many's the time. Him an' me felt the same about 'em."

"But you never saw them insult Mrs. Coons in any way?" James persisted.

After a short pause, she said, apparently remembering her feelings, "I never liked the looks o' that smart German."

"You mean the sergeant? His name was Weber, I believe."

"No, t'other one. His friend. The one who never said much. They called him a corporal. Oh, he had a sly look about him, that one, always grinnin' at a body. The devil was in that one, believe you me."

"What sort of man was Solomon Lort, the hostler?"

"Solomon? Like I said, he was a kind of quiet man, not much for talkin'. He was allus remarkable clean for a man that worked in the muck takin' care of horses. He only come into the house for meals. Other times he was busy in the stables or haulin' loads of stone to wherever the master told him to go. He slept out in the shed by the stables."

"Was Solomon or either of the Hessians ever forward with you?"

She blushed at this question and exclaimed, "Good gracious, no! No, sir. Nothing like that ever happened to me!"

Whether this reply was more of a testament to the chasteness of the males she had once lived among before assuming her rightful place as a wife and mother, or whether it bore witness to her modest claim to comeliness was beyond James's ability to judge.

As he said goodbye to the former indentured servant who was now the mistress of her own household, she assured James with touching sincerity that everyone in the Maul family, but most particularly Mrs. Coons, was free of any sort of moral blemish. With this assurance of the moral perfection of the Mauls in his ears, James went to find the quiet, cleanly hostler who had also once worked for Jacob Maul.

When he found Solomon Lort at the slaughterhouse where he now took care of dray horses and drove them, James discovered a man of ordinary stature and clean-cut features whose clothing was, as Susan Hannah had told him, remarkably neat. He was, as she had also said, a man of few words, and the work he was engaged in—harnessing a team of

huge dray horses to drive a load of split beeves to market—
required the greatest part of his attention.

In putting the horses in their heavy gear, he exhibited
uncommon strength and dexterity. The horses had immense
haunches and chests, higher than the hostler was tall, and
hooves as big as his head. The ease with which he dominated
this pair of powerful creatures was wonderful to behold and
fascinating to watch.

He spoke to them in a low, soft voice that was both cajoling
and commanding in tone, calling them by their names. He
accompanied his confident, firm commands with strong,
maneuvering pushes against their massive bodies.

Lort was not very informative. He appeared to be
unaccustomed to conversing with people.

When James asked whether during his time at the Mauls'
stoneyard he had ever seen an amorous word, look, or gesture
pass between Elizabeth Coons and the Hessian soldiers
billeted in the house, Lort answered with an unemotional,
emphatic "no" that foreclosed further discussion of the topic.

When James asked his opinion of Mrs. Coons, Lort
answered rather impertinently, "Maul didn't pay me to have
opinions."

Since the tone in which he spoke Maul's name contained a
touch of dislike for his former employer, James asked what he
thought of Jacob Maul.

"The Hessian who went upstairs the morning the Quaker's
wife was strangled," Lort said, "was of the same mind as me.
Maul ought to have stood trial for killing her. The woman was
in his bed. The door was bolted from the inside."

In a flat, unemotional voice, he added, "I hope he goes up
the rope for what he did."

With that remark, Solomon Lort completed his gearing up of the horses, hitched them to the dray wagon loaded with beef carcasses, got up on the wagon seat and drove off without another word.

It was getting on towards evening before James found the vegetable stall rented by Mrs. Coons's cousin, Mrs. Merkle, in the Jersey Market. It was the closest to the river of the four identical market houses built end-to-end down the middle of Philadelphia's broadest street, which had given the street its name, Market Street, and made it the city's bustling center for buying meat and vegetables, both fresh and processed. The ground floor of each market house had two rows of stalls facing each other across a central aisle. A few stalls sold baskets and other goods. An active, pretty little girl of about twelve was helping customers at Mrs. Merkle's stall. James surmised that this was probably Mrs. Coons's daughter.

"What may I get for you, sir?" the girl asked James as he approached the stall and came within speaking distance. "We have fine cabbage today," she added.

"I need to talk with your mistress, thank you."

Mrs. Merkle, who had been conversing with a heavy-set woman at the next stand, heard James say this to the girl and, leaving her colleague, came over to James.

"Yes, sir, what is it you wish to say to me?" inquired the burly woman whose otherwise plain face exhibited a harelip.

"I believe you are a cousin of Elizabeth Coons," James stated. "I am making inquiries into her death because I do not believe Jacob Maul killed her. You may have read my advertisement." He gestured toward two of his handbills tacked on a nearby wall. "My name is Jamison. Captain James Jamison."

Mrs. Merkle nodded her head several times as James spoke, and when he finished she said, "It would be best if you came back at the close of business, Captain. An hour from now. Then we can talk."

James offered the market woman his hand, which she took and pumped once before releasing it. He nodded respectfully to the girl, who was wiping tears from her eyes with the edge of the apron she wore. As he took his leave, the woman, who had also noticed the tears, was embracing her small helper and comforting her.

Before exiting the market house, he turned and looked back to observe the operation of the vegetable stand he had just left. The girl, who had recovered from her crying, appeared to be quick-witted with the customers. She did most of the talking and selling. The woman handled the money and kept the display tables in good order and well stocked with vegetables. The arrangement worked well. The girl's prettiness and quickness offset the woman's harelip. As he watched the woman and the girl working together James thought the saying "Harelip, harebrained" certainly wasn't the case here.

Since he had an hour to spare, James decided to ride over to Vine and Front streets to find Anthony Scull and talk to him about the note he had received from Joseph Ayles regarding William Maul.

When James rode up to the Scull residence, Anthony Scull and his adolescent son were just bringing six milk cows down Front Street and into the cowshed behind their house. James dismounted and Mr. Scull asked his son to take charge of the cows, then turned and addressed the muscular, clear-eyed gentleman with the peculiar black glove on his left hand. Mistaking James for a potential customer, he explained that he pastured the cows in a field above Margaretta Street and was just bringing them down to be milked. He wouldn't have milk for sale until he'd finished his milking.

James clarified his errand and introduced himself. Mr. Scull knew about the Quaker Murders as everyone in Philadelphia did and said he had seen James's handbill which had been put up all over the city.

James showed him the note he had received from Joseph Ayles which referred to the dairyman. Scull was not surprised, he said, that Ayles had applied for James's reward for information on Mrs. Coons since the man had no regular occupation and got by doing occasional jobs. He added that Ayles was forever talking of ways to make money.

"I would like to know, Mr. Scull, if I may," James said, "your connection with William Maul."

"He built a new laystall for me here at my cowshed two weeks ago, as Ayles says in his note."

"And is it true William Maul made a remark to you about Mrs. Coons the morning she disappeared?"

"William arrived before sunup that day to finish the job for me. Said he had to start another job that morning, repairing the wharf at Austin's Ferry, and because his custom had fallen off, he was glad to have two pieces of work in one day. Maul said, as I recall—Joseph Ayles was here at the time—that he had left home so early that morning that he had not eaten breakfast and would have to get something at the market houses on his way to Austin's Ferry."

"But what did he say about Mrs. Coons?"

"Only that he wished she had been up to prepare the breakfast at his house before he left home because he liked the way she fixed the porridge."

"That's all he said?"

"That was all. He didn't mention her by name. He called her his father's housekeeper. He liked the way his father's housekeeper made porridge, but she hadn't been up yet when he left home that morning."

"So why did Ayles think I should know this?"

"I would guess because he's always looking to make a shilling."

Dusk was coming on when James got back to Mrs. Merkle's stall. The market woman was settling her accounts for the day with her suppliers who had come to collect their baskets and receive her orders for the next day's market. The girl was sweeping up the vegetable trimmings from the floor of the stall and the aisle in front of it.

A few minutes later, Merkle—her scales clutched in one hand, her money-box tucked under that arm, and holding the child's hand with the other—readily accepted James's invitation to go to a nearby tavern for their conversation. She proposed the Hen and Rooster, which, she said, was a favorite resort of workers in the Jersey Market.

The barman at the Hen and Rooster cheerily hailed Mistress Merkle as "Kate," and she was similarly welcomed as she led the way to the far end of the tavern's noisy taproom to a table by the fire, which had just become available and that James indicated as his preference.

He ordered a flip for himself, a bowl of sangaree for the market woman, and a sweet English beer for her ward. While they waited for their drinks, James asked Katherine Merkle if the girl was the daughter of her cousin Elizabeth Coons and was told that she was, and he was also told that the child's given name was Sarah.

"I'm curious to learn," James said, "why your cousin would be willing to part with her only child."

Before the market woman could answer, the child herself spoke up, "My momma said I was a likely girl who could be a help to Kate, who would teach me to be useful. I like working in the market."

"You are a likely girl, my pretty Sarah," Kate Merkle said, smiling at the child and stroking her hair, "and you have been a big help to me." Then, turning to James, she said, "Lizzy told me the Mauls' house got too crowded when the Hessians were billeted there and she asked if I would take Sarah. She said Sarah would be company for me and when she got older could help me in the stall. And so she has. The child has been a great comfort to me, Captain Jamison. My business has improved since she's been with me. I don't know what I'd do without her now."

The girl piped up again proudly, "Kate says we are in business together. When I grow up, I'm going to have my own stall in the market."

Just then the child sprang from the table and ran over to a man and woman and a girl her own age who were just entering the Hen and Rooster. Mistress Merkle explained to James that the other child was Sarah's only friend among the children who worked at the market.

"The rest of them have teased Sarah nearly to death about her mother being strangled, God rest poor Lizzy's soul!"

"Can you tell me, Mrs. Merkle," James asked, "did Elizabeth Coons have any male acquaintances?"

"There's not much I can tell you," the market woman said. "Lizzy knew the three men in the Maul family, of course. The youngest one, after he ran away and joined the army, wrote letters to her, addressed to me. I have one of them that came for her last week, after Lizzy died. I never opened it. Then there was the Hessian soldiers who were billeted where she lived. That's all I know."

This information pleased James very much. Dr. Franklin's guess of a secret correspondence between Mrs. Coons and Robert Maul had been right. The letters she had received from Robert through Kate Merkle were doubtless why Mrs. Coons had told the Mauls so confidently that she believed Robert was alive and would return home one day.

"Could I see the letter?" James asked.

"I suppose it would be all right, since you're trying to help the Mauls and find out who killed Lizzy. It certainly wasn't Jacob. I have the letter in my room above the Jersey Market. I'll get it for you when we leave here."

Just then Sarah returned to the table to get her sweet English beer and announce to her guardian that she was going to sit with her friend Martha.

"As I was about to say, Captain, Lizzy and her child, who was then only four, came to Philadelphia a few months before the British took over the city. They stayed with me for a few days before going to live with Margaret, who had married into the Maul family."

"Did Mrs. Coons spend much time with her daughter Sarah after Sarah came to live with you?" James inquired.

"On Sundays she'd come by and take her to Meeting and keep her for the day. She used to come by every Sunday, but in the last year or so, we haven't seen her that regular. I hadn't seen Lizzy to talk to for the better part of a month before I saw the news of her murder in the papers. Whenever she came to buy vegetables from me, she always asked if she had a letter from Robert or her sister in New Jersey, who also sent her letters through me. My cousin was a kindhearted person who had a cheery word for one and all, but she was not much of a one for gossip. That's about all I can tell you about her."

James was making discovery after discovery. Here was another secret correspondent of Lizzy Coons the Mauls did not know of, a sister who wrote to her in care of Mrs. Merkle.

"What is this sister's name and where does she live?" James inquired.

"Her name is Mary. She's married to a Baptist preacher named Leet who has a farm and a church in Hopewell, in East Jersey, near Princeton."

"Why didn't Mrs. Coons take Sarah back to live at the Mauls' after the Hessians were no longer there?"

"Because," Mrs. Merkle said, "when Lizzy proposed to take her back, I begged her not to. I had grown used to having Sarah with me, and said my keeping her would ease the burden on the Mauls whose business was not doing well. Lizzy finally saw the sense of that and agreed to my keeping Sarah until Jacob Maul's business picked up."

"Did Mrs. Coons have other relatives besides her sister Mrs. Leet in Hopewell?"

"There's an aunt named Elizabeth Rundell in Princeton. Lizzy's father named her for this sister."

"Did Mrs. Coons ever say anything to you, Mrs. Merkle, about the Hessian soldiers living with the Mauls?"

"No, she wasn't much for gossip, like I told you. Come to think on it, though, she did say something once. She was buying an odd-shaped turnip from me and said it reminded her of one of the Germans living with her people in Dock Street. She said it reminded her of the shape of his head. She said he was moonstruck on her. I remember now. She laughed in saying it."

Chapter 12

It was full dark when James left the Hen and Rooster with Sarah and Mistress Merkle and went with them to get Robert Maul's letter to Elizabeth Coons. The room Katherine Merkle rented above the Jersey Market was of modest dimensions and furnishings. Sarah had her own bed.

Having gotten the letter, he took his leave of the market woman and her charge and headed for the Indian Queen two blocks away to read the letter. As he walked Cheval toward the hotel he passed the carriage gates into Franklin Court and saw the peephole open, signaling he had a communiqué from Dr. Franklin.

Seated at a table near the entrance of the Indian Queen, he discovered that Robert Maul, in his letter, repeatedly expressed his desire to marry Lizzy Coons, a desire he evidently was not expressing for the first time, and he assured her he would soon have enough money to return to Philadelphia and make her his wife. He proposed moving to Virginia after their marriage, which he said was a state with plenty of opportunities for a man to get ahead. He said there was no reason a man of twenty-four should not marry a woman of thirty-six; nor any reason why a good Quaker woman shouldn't marry a man who had been read out of the Society of Friends, if he loved her and she loved him.

Hastily folding up the letter and putting it in his wallet, James borrowed a lantern from the hotel desk and went to the mail drop behind the holly bush. In the sealskin pouch was the message "Philo. L.'s information requires consultation. Come tonight (Wed.) at eleven if possible, otherwise tomorrow at that time."

James put in the pouch the communications he had received in response to his advertisement as well as Robert Maul's letter to Mrs. Coons, on which he had written at the Indian Queen, "You were right. R. M. did write to E. C."

Benjamin Franklin's words of greeting to James later that night were, "Congratulations on your successes, Captain! Your activeness is moving our investigation along more rapidly than I had expected."

The usual refreshments were at hand, and the master of Franklin Court invited James to help himself to the Chateau Ligneville '65, to which he was growing pleasantly accustomed, as well as to the excellent homemade crackers.

Dr. Franklin began their colloquy with a request.

"Your last report was of great interest to me, James. But before discussing anything in it, perhaps you should tell me what you learned from the former maidservant and the hostler of the Mauls, and also from the cousin of Mrs. Coons who gave you Robert Maul's letter. That information could change, or confirm, the deductions I have tentatively reached from the information you collected from the worthy Philomen Lyons, the proprietor of the Blue Anchor, Elizabeth Coons's neighbors, and Rebecca Maul, which Robert Maul's letter that you have brought to light tends to corroborate."

James informed Dr. Franklin of what his latest interviews had turned up, along with his impressions of the character and manners of each person. In absorbing this verbal report, Franklin again manifested talent for absolute concentration.

After James finished reporting, Dr. Franklin said, "What you have just said strengthens the surmises I've made. An idea of Mrs. Coons's situation is forming, which suggests that at the time she died she was involved in an affair of the heart. Every indication points in that direction. I think I must ask you to go to German Town to find out whether the Hessian August Weber who was billeted on the Mauls is indeed living there, and to speak with him if possible.

"But first, I would have you find and talk with Mrs. Coons's sister in Hopewell to discover what she knows. Mrs. Coons evidently corresponded with her sister, but did not save her sister's letters to her—just as she apparently did not keep the letters from her other clandestine correspondent, Robert Maul. The sister, however, may have saved the letters she received from Mrs. Coons, and I would like to read those if possible. She may be willing to lend them to us so we may study their contents. And since you have discovered that there is an aunt of Mrs. Coons who lives near where the sister lives, you ought to talk to her as well. You could get whatever information the aunt in Princeton may have before going to Hopewell and then return to Philadelphia by way of German Town. Would this circuit be convenient for you?"

James answered, "I am more than willing to undertake the expedition you propose, Dr. Franklin. However my sister will be giving birth to a child a week or so from now, they say, and I have promised to wait with my brother-in-law while she does."

"I do not see any reason why that ought to affect your journey to New Jersey and German Town, which will not, I suppose, take more than four, five days at the most, depending on your luck at German Town in looking for the Hessian. The baby might come three weeks from now as well as tonight. The arrival of babies is not as predictable as when the sun will rise tomorrow."

"There is another consideration, however, Dr. Franklin," James said. "I'm not sure my horse can stand such a trip, he's so old."

"Oh, I see. Well, there's an easy solution to that," Dr. Franklin responded. "We'll get you a new and stronger horse. You can travel to Princeton by coach—at my expense, of course, since you are my agent in this matter—and buy a good horse there, which I will also pay for. Then you can make your journey to Hopewell and German Town and come back to Philadelphia by horseback. A better horse would also be useful in making inquiries here. If you have as good an eye for horseflesh as your grandfather did, you might make a good bargain out of purchasing a horse in a country town like Princeton and selling it in Philadelphia's weekly horse market when we're finished with our investigation."

James agreed that a horse and saddle bought in Princeton might be profitably sold at the Wednesday horse auction in Philadelphia. And he also agreed with what Dr. Franklin said about the unpredictability of when Jane might have her baby. He liked the plan of taking the stage to Princeton, proceeding by horseback from there to Hopewell and German Town, and riding back to Philadelphia.

"I won't be able to leave until day after tomorrow, though," James remarked. "The stage to New York that goes through Princeton leaves Philadelphia early in the morning, and while it is all the same to me whether I take it this morning—a few hours from now—or tomorrow, I ought not to leave town without speaking with my grandmother first, and she is not an early riser. She will still be in bed a few hours from now when the coach for New York goes out today."

"I quite agree your dear grandmother should not be worried by waking up and finding her only grandson gone. Starting your trip tomorrow morning instead of today will not adversely affect our purpose."

Dr. Franklin then said, "In Hopewell you must inquire of Mrs. Leet what connections her sister had with men. It is of the highest importance that you obtain any letters Mrs. Coons may have written to her, particularly any written during the time the Hessian soldiers were living with the Mauls. If you obtain such letters, post them to me from Trenton on your return into Pennsylvania from Hopewell, along with your written report. That will leave only the results of your inquiries at German Town to report after you get back to the city."

"What do you think, Dr. Franklin, of the opinion of Philomen Lyons that Mrs. Coons gave birth to a child the night she left Jacob Maul's house?"

Tilting his head down and looking at James over the top of his spectacles, Benjamin Franklin said, "The pattern of evidence points to that conclusion. There's a saying in my native Boston that I've always admired for its perspicacity. It says, 'Some circumstantial evidence, such as a trout in the milk, is very strong.' And this milk has more than one trout in it."

James did not understand the saying, and his incomprehension registered on his face, as it always had since he was a boy in school. Seeing this, Dr. Franklin explained that farmers kept their milk fresh in crocks set in cold, springhouse water and that sometimes such water had fingerling trout in it. So if a person who bought milk from a farmer found a fingerling trout in the milk after he got home, only one conclusion was possible, though the evidence was merely circumstantial. The farmer had diluted his milk with water while it was in his springhouse.

"Are the little welts Philomen Lyons saw on the belly of Mrs. Coons circumstantial evidence, Dr. Franklin?"

"They are. A piece of circumstantial evidence as clear as a trout in milk."

"I do not understand their significance, though."

"Let us review the evidence you have collected, James," replied the famous researcher into the mystery of electricity. "It is the congruence of details in this mystery that is significant, as it always is, not one piece of evidence by itself.

"First, there is William Maul's testimony that the two Hessians were attracted to Mrs. Coons. The remarks of the Blue Anchor proprietor, a man of some worldly experience, indicate that she had a certain appeal for him as well. The jealousy that Robert Maul manifested toward the Hessians shows that he, too, thought Mrs. Coons attractive, and the letter you have uncovered from that interesting young man fully corroborates his passionate attachment to her, to the extent of him wanting to marry her. Then there are the details Rebecca Maul furnished that suggest that on the day Elizabeth Coons vanished she was coping with some physical ailment she did not want Rebecca to know of. Such an indisposition is indicated by her frequent trips to the necessary that day. The testimony of Philomen Lyons points to the conclusion that the indisposition was related to impending childbirth.

"Let us consider exactly what the estimable Mrs. Lyons said. First, we notice the washerwoman's fondness for Mrs. Coons. And, by the way, James, one of the most interesting patterns in the information you have gathered on Mrs. Coons's character is its consistency. Men and women of every condition liked her. The Negro washerwoman who did heavy work for Mrs. Coons while she was in charge of Jacob Maul's house. Her female companions in the Maul household, Rebecca Maul and the maidservant Susan Love, now Mrs. Peter Hannah. Her female neighbors. The male members of her adopted family, and the proprietor of the Blue Anchor, Mr. Cratty. Not to mention the market woman, Mistress Merkle, a blood relative to Mrs. Coons. All of them found her to be an attractive person. That is a large array of diverse evidence.

"It was Mrs. Lyons's fondness for Mrs. Coons that caused her to insist that it was only her 'notion' that Lizzy Coons had given birth before she was killed. And Mrs. Lyons would not have shared her opinion with you except for your evident sincerity in wanting to help the afflicted Maul family. As befitted a woman speaking on a matter that seriously touched the honor of another woman of whom she was fond, Philomen Lyons would not state as a fact that Elizabeth Coons had given birth to a child out of wedlock but only that it was her 'notion' that she had, from the condition of her body, probably a reference to a distention of the birth canal's opening. The fact that Mrs. Lyons is an experienced midwife gives her opinion a very considerable weight.

"But how, we may ask, does the theory of Mrs. Coons's good character comport with her having a lover who got her with child? Perhaps in this wise: if an attractive, good-hearted Quaker woman thinks her virtue makes her safe, she is exposing herself to a contest of wills with whatever patient, determined seducer she may encounter. The fact that none of the persons with whom you have spoken have said Mrs. Coons was having an affair must be balanced against the fact that clandestine love can perform prodigies of concealment.

Indeed, a reputation for virtue can serve to mask an amour if the woman is also discreet and careful.

"Given the violent manner of this good woman's death, and the way her corpse was abusively disposed of in the cavity of an old privy, we are compelled to conclude that her life, however respectable it may have appeared, contained some irregularity. Perhaps the violence she was subjected to that night was not the first time she had fallen prey to force. Perhaps on some earlier occasion her virtue had been assaulted, and she was ashamed to have anyone know her honor had been compromised. It is also possible that a patient seducer finally succeeded in making her his willing paramour.

"Which brings us to the little welts on Mrs. Coons's belly. These, James, are the chief evidence that this likable, attractive woman was indeed with child the night she died. For these strange marks are the sort left by the bandages which some women tightly bind across their bellies when they want to preserve their usual female shape and conceal the swelling of the womb during a pregnancy."

"I've never heard of such a thing!" James exclaimed.

"I assure you, James, some women resort to this unnatural practice, despite its unhealthiness. A woman such as Elizabeth Coons, living in a respectable Quaker household and finding herself with child out of wedlock, might well resort to binding her womb to preserve her respectability."

James responded to this revelation by saying, "I see now how the blood on Mrs. Coons's underclothing that Mrs. Lyons told me of and the absence of wounds on her body are consistent facts. Mrs. Coons bled from the birth canal. But before her delivery, her petticoat—a garment Mrs. Lyons says is worn over the shift—as well as the shift itself, had to be removed, then later put back on her by another person who mistakenly put the shift over—instead of under—the petticoat."

"Your reasoning duplicates my own, James," Dr. Franklin said. "The shoes being on the wrong feet is likewise consistent with the view that she was disrobed and then dressed by someone else. Another deduction is also possible. The child she gave birth to had to have been delivered before she was killed, for the strenuous muscular contractions needed to push a child out of the womb require life in a woman's body."

"But why," James asked, "if Mrs. Coons was great with child, didn't Rebecca Maul tell me?"

"It is not likely that she knew. In some women, the outward signs of pregnancy are slight. I have known of women 'in the state,' as midwives call being pregnant, who take no measures whatever to conceal their pregnant condition yet arrive at their lying-in without manifesting any outward signs of their pregnancy to inexperienced eyes. Besides, in Mrs. Coons's case the little welts across her belly indicate that she had tightly bandaged her pregnancy to conceal it.

"Several unanswered questions remain, James. Where did Elizabeth Coons go to give birth? Who assisted her in her labor? And why was she strangled after giving birth? We must consider the connection between the birth and the murder. Was it her lover who strangled her? Also, what became of the newborn child? When you return from your journey into New Jersey, you must make inquiries among the midwives of Southwark to find out if any of them assisted in or has any knowledge of a lying-in around the time of Mrs. Coons's disappearance."

With these words, Dr. Franklin produced a slip of paper on which he had written five questions. He handed it to James with the observation that he had always found it helpful in investigating a mystery of nature to write down the most important questions pertaining to it, and had thought the same would be useful in this instance regarding the points to be addressed.

1. Who assisted Mrs. Coons in giving birth and where did the birth occur?
2. What connection was there between the birth and the murder?
3. Why were her hands tied behind her body *and* her arms tied to her sides?
4. Why did she take the porcelain-faced doll with her?
5. In what way did the bruises on Mrs. Coons's throat resemble "the marks on Dutch bread"?

In connection with the last question, Dr. Franklin had drawn a little sketch of the round loaves of bread baked by the Pennsylvania Dutch.

Chapter 13

Seeing the drawing with its four parallel marks on the crust, James realized suddenly that in saying the bruises on Mrs. Coons's throat resembled "the marks on Dutch bread" the washerwoman had been referring to the number and arrangement of the bruises, not the vividness of the marks as he had supposed. The significance of this fact was unclear to him.

Dr. Franklin, again noticing James's incomprehension, asked in his politest tones, "Does it not strike you as odd, James, that there should be four parallel bruises on Mrs. Coons's throat, one above the other? The hands, after all, have but two digits powerful enough to choke off a person's breath. The thumbs. The eight other digits merely anchor the thumbs so their force can be applied to close the windpipe. Perhaps," he added, in a bantering tone, "we should be looking for a man with four thumbs. Otherwise, how are we to account for four parallel bruises?"

When James did not respond, Franklin continued, "Was she strangled from behind with the thumbs at the back of her neck and the fingers across her windpipe? Or, was she throttled *twice*? The first of these suppositions fails to make sense, because eight fingers would overlap and not make four distinct marks. Besides, the fingers are, as I said, incapable of exerting the deep, concentrated pressure needed to close a person's windpipe.

"This afternoon, after receiving your report describing Mrs. Lyons's observations, Mr. Mahoney and I tried the experiment of each putting our fingers across the throat of the other from behind. We agreed that the fingers, anchored by the thumbs from behind, could not strangle a person to death. The pressure of the eight fingers would be too diffuse. The idea that Mrs. Coons was choked twice is a much simpler idea, and in studying the phenomena of nature I have always found that the simpler the explanation the more likely it is."

"But why would anyone strangle a person twice?" James interjected.

Dr. Franklin replied, "Perhaps Mrs. Coons managed to break her assailant's grip the first time he attempted to throttle her. But that theory is not consistent with the absence of scratches, wounds, or abrasions on her corpse. Nor were there any tears in her clothing to indicate a desperate struggle. Had there been such signs, the observant Mrs. Lyons would have noticed them in disrobing and washing the corpse, and told you of them.

"I have thought, however, of three other possible answers to the objection you raise, James. One is that the strangler repeated the strangulation to make certain that death had occurred because some reflex in Mrs. Coons's body after the first strangulation made him wonder whether she might still be alive. Or, the second throttling might have been the behavior of a distraught, confused person who did not act with natural purpose. Or, conceivably, there might have been two different stranglers, acting at different moments. This latter possibility, however, contains, in the nature of things, too much of the bizarre to warrant much consideration, and it would be best to exclude it as a possible explanation for the redundancy of the bruises on Mrs. Coons's throat."

Dr. Franklin paused at this point to take a drink of his French spring water before resuming.

"An irrational redundancy is also evident in the manner in which Mrs. Coons's body was tied up. If the purpose of tying her hands and feet was to make a compact bundle of the corpse for carrying, as I think probable, then there was no need to tie the arms to the sides of her body, as was done. Either binding the wrists behind the body or the arms to the body would have sufficed to achieve the desired compactness. To do both was unnecessary."

Dr. Franklin invited James to stand up and try the experiment of what he had just described, and when James had done so he instantly felt the truth of what Dr. Franklin said. With his hands clasped behind him as if tied together, his arms became pinned to the sides of his body.

When James resumed his seat he remarked, "So you believe Mrs. Coons's assailant did not act with deliberate, rational intent."

"It would appear so. If restraining Mrs. Coons was his purpose, then you could suppose that was the reason for binding her hands behind her back and tying her ankles together. But consider this. She could not have been restrained —especially not the ankles tied together—and have given birth. And why would it be necessary after the baby was born to restrain a woman weakened by the ordeal of giving birth?"

Dr. Franklin then took up the related questions of the missing stockings, the petticoat being on backwards, the shift being over the petticoat, and the shoes being on the wrong feet. He agreed with James's reasoning in his report, that these facts all pointed to the conclusions that Mrs. Coons had been

disrobed the night she disappeared and someone else—
someone not familiar with female undergarments—had re-
clothed her while she was unconscious or already dead. Dr.
Franklin stated again that the bloodstains on the shift and the
petticoat which Mrs. Lyons reported and the absence of any
wound to Mrs. Coons's body from which that blood could have
come, led to the surmise that she had bled from a natural
opening in her body.

"But if she was disrobed," Dr. Franklin pondered out loud,
"why did the person who killed her think it necessary to dress
her again, since the corpse was found wrapped in canvas?
That, too, is an odd redundancy."

Dr. Franklin stopped speaking for a moment, then said, "It
almost seems that on the night she died she was involved with
someone subject to wildly fluctuating moods. The more we
learn in trying to understand the character of her killer and
what happened that night, the more it seems that further
questions arise. We do not know, for instance, why she took
her blue doll with her, or the connection between her giving
birth and her murder."

"I have supposed," James said, "ever since hearing your
argument that Mrs. Coons was with child and gave birth the
night she died, that the man who impregnated her was the
man who strangled her."

"That may well prove to be the case," Dr. Franklin said.
"But we do not know that as a fact. All it is, is a plausible
conjecture. We lack proof as yet that her lover was her killer. It
may have been a jealous rival of the lover who found out she
had betrayed his devotion to her. The only thing we can say
with some certainty at present—or at least with some degree of
plausibility—is that she left the Mauls' house in a pregnant
condition of her own free will and went somewhere to get help,

taking her precious doll with her. And that she was disrobed, including her stockings and shoes, most likely to facilitate childbirth. That she gave birth to her baby. That someone dressed her again and tied her up. And that someone strangled her. Whether the strangulation preceded her being dressed again or the other way around, has not been established."

"What is your opinion, sir, of the theory proposed by the proprietor of the Blue Anchor Tavern that a seaman murdered Mrs. Coons?"

Dr. Franklin smiled broadly in amusement.

"I dare say that if the good Mr. Cratty looked in his own storeroom at the Blue Anchor Tavern, he would find pieces of old sail and a coil or two of the cord called marline, which both seamen and river men use. In a busy seaport like Philadelphia —where a dozen ships come into port or leave every day, and where many ships are built and sea stores abound—sails and marline are commonplace, as are opportunities for obtaining them. It is therefore exceedingly presumptuous to say their presence in this crime indicates the criminal has to be a sailor, though that is one possibility."

Franklin then went over to the cabinet in his study and opened its top drawer and removed from it a worn leather case, which he handed to James.

"Here is a portable escritoire which you will find useful on your travels into New Jersey. In it are pens, paper, and ink with which to write your reports to me during your journey. Now, if you will excuse me, I will get another purse of money for you, James, to pay the expenses of your trip, including the purchase of a saddle horse in Princeton."

The elderly gentleman went into his bedroom with the aid of his cane, and soon returned with a small cloth pouch bulging with hard money, which he handed to his associate.

"This should cover your expenses for coach fare, lodgings, and a horse and its equipage," Dr. Franklin said.

"I will return to you whatever I do not spend," James rejoined.

"We can speak of that later. Now, I want to discuss with you Robert Maul's letter to Mrs. Coons and the answers you have had to our advertisement."

"Yes," James said, "it would please me to know your opinions on these matters, since one of the answers to our ad seems to threaten my life."

"As to that, it obviously comes from someone who hates Quakers. How dangerous the man who wrote it might be is, of course, not predictable. But if I were you and had a pistol that could be carried in my coat without becoming obtrusive, I would go armed during the rest of our investigation. For it is possible this letter writer poses a true threat to you. The letter could even have been written by the man who killed Lizzy Coons, rather than just someone who hates Quakers because they opposed our war for independence.

"The other anonymous letter expressing hostility to our investigation was too mild, I think, to warrant thinking of it as coming from a person who is capable of violence, and Joseph Ayles's note is of no consequence in light of what the worthy Mr. Scull, the dairyman, told you about him. You must expect to receive false leads when money is offered as a reward for information."

"What did you make of the letter from Robert Maul?" James asked. "Should I give it to his brother William as proof that Robert survived the war and is contemplating a return to Philadelphia? I rather think I should."

"I am of two minds as to that, James," Dr. Franklin replied. "On the one hand, William Maul's anxiety is a consideration.

But he has lived with uncertainty concerning his brother for some years now. A few more weeks will hardly matter. On the other hand, Robert Maul's letter manifests an abiding interest in Elizabeth Coons, a passion that makes me wish to find out where he presently resides. He is the only man we know of who had a definite, self-confessed attachment to the murdered woman. We also know through his brother William that Robert was jealous of the attentions the Hessians paid to Elizabeth Coons. If somehow, in the past several weeks, he discovered that she was carrying the child of another man—say, one of the Hessians he disliked—how would he have reacted to such news? Would he have returned to Philadelphia posthaste to confront her? Or would he have maintained his love for her, regardless of her fallen condition? These are speculative questions worth asking. They may help us find the truth. I think we ought to keep his letter awhile without sharing its contents with anyone."

"Robert Maul seems to like living in Virginia," James remarked. "If he is indeed there, as his letter to Mrs. Coons suggests, it will be nigh impossible to find him in such a large state unless we have some inkling of his whereabouts, because Virginia encompasses vast mountains, plains and peninsulas."

The last thing Dr. Franklin did in this interview with James was to return to him the two anonymous communications he had had in answer to the ad, which James had given him to read. "You may," Dr. Franklin said, "want to compare the handwriting in these to any further hostile communications you receive."

The next day, after rising and taking breakfast, James told his grandmother he would be going to Princeton and Hopewell the following day to speak with relatives of the dead woman whose murder he was looking into. She, as was her custom, asked no prying questions, and by not protesting his announcement, consented to it.

Then he rode into town to look for further messages at the City Tavern in response to the ad. Instead, he found that William Maul had left him a note.

> Dear Capt. Jamison,
>
> My wife has told me of the inquiries thee made of her, and of thee wanting to know whether Lizzy was ever absent from Philadelphia after she came to live in my father's house. Lizzy and her child did leave the city once, before Rebecca and I married and she came to live in my father's house. As I recall, it was a week or so after the Hessians were billeted upon us in October 1777. My stepmother told me Lizzy and the child had gone on a visit and would be back within a week. I was not told where she went.
>
> May God prosper thee in thy search for the truth.
>
> William Maul

From the City Tavern James rode to the George Inn on Arch Street and bought his ticket for the following morning's stage to Princeton; then he returned home to speak with his grandmother.

An idea had occurred to him while in town that might hasten his inquires toward their conclusion. He had thought of a way to gather the information Dr. Franklin wanted from the midwives of Southwark regarding whether any of them had attended a woman's lying-in at the time of Mrs. Coons's disappearance. His idea was to have Livy collect this intelligence during the four or five days he would be away from the city. So as soon as he arrived home, he spoke to his grandmother to get her opinion of the idea.

"It seems, Grandmère, from information I have received," James said, "that the dead woman, Mrs. Coons, might have given birth to a child the night she disappeared, and that this birth might have had something to do with her murder. I would like to speak, therefore, with any midwife in Southwark, where Mrs. Coons lived, who attended a lying-in around the time she disappeared. But, as I told you this morning, I must leave Philadelphia tomorrow for New Jersey to talk with relatives of Mrs. Coons. It has occurred to me that Livy might make this inquiry for me in my absence, perhaps to better advantage than I could. What do you think? Could you spare her from her obligations to you to do this for me?"

James's grandmother laid aside her knitting and rose from her chair, saying, "Olivia might be able to do it better than you, James, as you say. On some matters women speak more easily to other women than to men. I can certainly spare her from her usual work to help you. Let us go and talk with Livy to see if she's willing to do this."

Livy and Grandmère had already discussed James's project of aiding the Maul family, and sympathized with it, and when Livy heard from Grandmère James's proposal to enlist her in his effort, she found the offer exciting. It was the first time James had ever asked her to do something of personal importance to him outside her household duties.

"Oh, I would be glad to see if I can get the information you need, James. It will allow me to leave the house and use my wits. When should I begin?"

"Tomorrow would be soon enough to talk to the midwives of Southwark. When you speak with them, make it seem that you are looking for a runaway wife who was with child when she ran away. Ask each midwife you find if she attended a woman's lying-in two weeks ago. Say the husband will be coming to Philadelphia in a few days to look for his wife, and that he will pay anyone who can tell him anything useful in helping him locate his wife and their baby. Say you are a cousin of the husband."

Grandmère added, "Be sure, Olivia, that you find all of them. The last I heard, Southwark had half a dozen midwives."

"Do you have any questions, Livy?" James asked.

"No, I think I understand the information you need, James."

Later that afternoon James returned to the City Tavern and found an order for three hundred blue apothecary bottles and three hundred amber bottles from a Mr. Shallowford in York, Pennsylvania. He took the order to the Jamisons' glass house in the Northern Liberties and discussed it with Lawrence and Mr. Bartlett. He also informed Lawrence that he would be out of town for a few days, but assured him that he had not forgotten his promise to be on hand for Jane's lying-in.

He then returned to the City Tavern and wrote a reply to Mr. Shallowford, promising the delivery on his order by Conestoga wagon in three weeks. He specified the cost and that Mr. Shallowford would have to remit half that amount before the bottles he wanted would be blown and the remainder of the money was to be paid as soon as he received the merchandise in good condition in York.

Chapter 14

The morning of James's departure from the city dawned cold and dismal. A steady light rain was falling, and by the time he arrived at the George Inn, where he was to get the stage for Princeton, his boots were soaked through from walking the puddled, wet streets.

To dry his boots and restore his dampened spirits, he extended his feet toward the blazing oak fire in the inn's cozy taproom and ordered a hot flip.

Because James had purchased his ticket from the stage-line agent the previous day, he felt certain of getting a seat inside the coach. While savoring the spicy taste of his hot flip, he noted that two men who had bought their tickets at the last minute were discomforted by their imprudence because a party of four women came in after them and purchased tickets to Bristol. Therefore the two men had to ride with the driver outside the coach, exposed to wind and rain, for the rules of the stage line required gentlemen to give up their seats to ladies in the order in which they had bought their tickets, so that the fair sex might always be assured of riding snug and dry inside the coach in inclement weather.

The city's streets were beginning to stir with pedestrian activity as the stage pulled away from the front of the George Inn and turned up Second Street to Vine. There the driver headed the horses east toward the Pool Bridge and then rolled through the Northern Liberties. After fording the creek past Kensington, the city's manufactories and houses were soon left behind and replaced by a countryside of farms and woods.

An hour north from Philadelphia, on the hard highroad that no amount of rain ever mired, the stage was stopped at the village of Frankfort to let another passenger get on. No further delay occurred until an hour before midday, when they arrived at Bristol, within sight of the Delaware River. The party of four ladies got down there, as Bristol was their destination. The remaining passengers got a bite of food at the New Bristol Inn while the horses were changed.

The departure of the ladies allowed the men who had been riding outside in the rain to come inside the coach for the next leg of the journey. But three new passengers got on, and two of them had to sit in the outside seats of the coach. Luckily, the rain ceased as the road headed north and inland from Bristol before swinging down the long, winding valley that terminated at the Trenton Ferry.

Crossing the Delaware on the ferry took the better part of two hours, the passengers and horses being taken over first, before the barge brought the coach over. But finally everybody was back on the coach on the east bank of the river.

After negotiating the gentle incline up into the town of Trenton, the stage stopped at the sign of the Fig and Vine, where three more passengers got on and two got off. Then began the trip under sodden skies, through autumnal woodlands and alongside puddled fields across the monotonously rolling plain that made New Jersey a prosperous agricultural province. The rich smell of decaying leaves lay heavy in the air. Every little while the landscape's sameness was varied by a brook or stream, which the coach splashed across without pause if it was shallow or forded slowly and deliberately if it was deeper and there was no stone bridge.

James was seated next to the right rear window, away from the wind, which allowed him to keep the window's heavy leather curtain rolled up and have an unobstructed view of the countryside. The landscape he saw reminded him of the forced march he and the rest of the Continental Army had made to Princeton on the Quaker Bridge Road, parallel to the Post Road, following the Christmas morning victory over the Hessians at Trenton.

George Washington's attack at Princeton, James recalled, had been a complete surprise to the British troops stationed there. Consequently, they, too, had been routed, as the Hessians at Trenton had been, after stiff fighting that cost the life of Brigadier General Hugh Mercer, the brave Scotsman and naturalized Virginian who had been one of the Continental Army's most gifted, most experienced, and best loved general officers.

The sun was halfway down the western sky when the stage descended to the bridge crossing the large brook south of Princeton, and began the long, hard pull up the opposite slope. Five of the passengers, including James, got out and walked to ease the strain on the horses as they got the coach up this steep incline.

The stage halted at the inn called The Sign of the New Jersey College only long enough for the passengers going on to New Brunswick to snatch a quick bite in the inn's taproom while fresh horses were brought up and hitched to the coach. But James was in no hurry. He had arrived at his destination.

After hiring a room at the inn for the night, he decided to stretch his legs before supper, and asked Mr. Beekman, the innkeeper, what was worth seeing in the town.

"Nassau Hall, the seat of the College of New Jersey and the largest stone building in America, is certainly our most interesting sight," replied Mr. Beekman. "You will surely want to see that. It's just over the way, on the other side of Nassau Street. You cannot fail to recognize it, it is so imposing. Then there is Morven, the mansion-house of Richard Stockden. He was one of the signers of the Declaration of Independence. The British general Lord Cornwallis used Morven for his headquarters during his military campaign in New Jersey. As it is a private residence, you will not be able to enter the mansion, but the external view is worthy. There are several other fine homes at the upper end of Nassau Street, Mr. Jamison, and you could, if you wish, walk out to Mercer's Heights to see where Washington whipped the Redcoats. I believe you would have time to get there and back before dark, if you hurried."

"Thank you, Mr. Beekman, but I prefer to see something in the town without visiting the Princeton battlefield." He did not tell the innkeeper he knew that historic site from having participated in the battle.

"I understand," James added, "that a family named Rundell lives in Princeton. The wife's name is Elizabeth, I believe. Do you know where they live?"

"The Rundell House is the yellow clapboard with the white trim at the head of Nassau Street, on the right if you were going out toward the battlefield. Old Amos Rundell's been dead since before the war, but his widow lives in the house. They never had children. I mean no offense, Mr. Jamison, should she be kin to you, but Elizabeth Rundell has a reputation of being miserly."

"I do not know the lady. I only have some business to discuss with her. There is another question, however, I wish to ask you, Mr. Beekman. I need to buy a saddle horse to continue my travels after leaving Princeton. Do you know of a good horse for sale?"

"I do, indeed, sir. Mr. Gooch, a master of Greek and Latin at the College, has had a sorrel mare for sale the past few weeks. I know the animal. She was bred in Virginia, which is where Mr. Gooch is from, and would, I think, suit you. You can find Mr. Gooch at Nassau Hall."

"One last thing," James said. "I understand the College has Mr. Rittenhouse's orrery demonstrating the orbits of the planets around the sun. Can you direct me to it? I have a great desire to see this ingenious machine. I heard Rittenhouse talk on astronomy before the American Philosophical Society in Philadelphia a few months before the start of the war."

"You will find that, too, in Nassau Hall," Mr. Beekman replied, "in the library on the second floor. But I'm afraid, sir, that the orrery was damaged by some of the soldiers billeted in Nassau Hall during the war, and is not now in working order. I saw its movements exhibited once, years ago, and it was, as you have heard, a most marvelous instrument. It was used before it was damaged to teach the young gentlemen of the College their astronomy."

"Still, I would like to see what so renowned an example of American ingenuity looks like, even if it is not in working order."

James found the motions of the famous orrery being described by the College librarian to two gentlemen from Holland who had come to Princeton on their tour of the

United States expressly to see this manifestation of eighteenth-century astronomical knowledge and ingenuity, created through David Rittenhouse's skill in fabricating precision instruments. The instrument's round, steel rim appeared to have a diameter of some four feet and was mounted on a large, vertical square painted dark blue and spangled with pointed white stars. Between the curve of the orrery's calibrated rim and each corner of the panel were painted cumulus clouds. The steel arms representing each planet moved in coordination around the center representing the sun, the librarian explained. They were positioned by a series of intricate, finely machined small gears, which were set in motion by a mechanical crank attached to the rear of the wooden panel.

The machine was designed to represent the relative motions of the planets and of solar and lunar eclipses for a period of 5,000 years either backwards or forwards in time, its custodian explained. But because of the missing gears which American soldiers billeted in Nassau Hall had taken as souvenirs, neither James nor the two Dutchmen were able to see the orrery in motion. James left the library when the librarian was still answering technical questions put to him by the visitors from Holland.

Mr. Gooch was not in his room, and James had to content himself with leaving a note explaining his interest in buying a horse and promising to return the following morning.

On his way to see the architectural beauties and grounds of Morven, the home of Richard Stockton, James passed the Rundell mansion-house, which was only a short walk from his inn.

Returning from his excursion about the town just after sunset, James found no table was free in the crowded dining room of The Sign of the College of New Jersey. As he stood perplexed, a gentleman and a lady who had shared the coach from Philadelphia with him, a Mr. and Mrs. Carver who were on their way to New York but were breaking the trip in Princeton, noticed him surveying the room and waved to him to join them. They were seated with another gentleman, and there was a vacant chair at their table.

When James came to the table, the unknown gentleman was introduced to him as Mrs. Carver's brother, Andrew Parsons. Mr. Carver called over the waiter who had taken their order, and James ordered roast veal for his meal on the recommendation of Mr. Parsons, who said he ate at the Inn often because he was the bursar at the College and a bachelor.

Lydia Carver, a woman in her early thirties, elegantly dressed in a forest green Brunswick traveling gown, asked, "And what do you do in Philadelphia, Mr. Jamison?"

"My family owns a glass house in the Northern Liberties, which I and my brother-in-law manage for my grandmother," James answered.

"I know that house," Thaddeus Carver said. "I run ships to bring timber from Maine and tar from North Carolina to Philadelphia. I'm thinking of starting up a barrel-making operation."

"Is this a good time to start a new business in Philadelphia, Mr. Jamison?" Andrew Parsons asked.

James was just about to give his opinion when Mrs. Carver said, "Oh, please, Andrew! Business is so tiresome a subject."

"What then shall we talk of, Lydia?" her brother asked.

"Oh, anything but business and politics. Having to listen to men speak of those topics is wearisome. What is the latest religious news in New Jersey, dear brother? Is the Second

Coming imminent? Has the Inner Light of the Quakers illumined anyone hereabouts lately?"

"Odd that you should ask, Lydia," Andrew Parsons replied. "There just happens to be some news on that front."

"Tell us the news," Lydia Carver said.

"Well, it seems that from a study of the Scriptures a Presbyterian minister from Elizabeth Town by the name of Stout has come to believe the Lord will return to Jerusalem four years hence, on the third Sabbath of the fourth month of 1789. Stout is preaching his conviction to everyone who will give him heed. And he is not just preaching it, he is doing something about it."

"A sign of true conviction," Thaddeus Carver interjected. "You have to applaud a man for that. What is he doing?"

"Well, with the consent of his wife, who is completely devoted to him and his ideas, he is spending the considerable fortune she brought him in their marriage to prepare for the glorious event. He has purchased a large ship and refitted it to make the voyage to the Holy Land for the Second Coming and has constructed a special wharf for mooring it at New Haven, Connecticut, where a number of his most active supporters live. And he has ordered two large dormitories built, one for women and one for men, next to the wharf to receive the Jews of America—from their various communities in Newport, New York, Philadelphia, and Charleston—whom he is inviting to join him on the voyage to Palestine, to be on hand for the Messiah's return. He has renamed the ship *The Second Coming*, I understand."

The Carvers and James had no immediate comment on this strange story of sincere faith. They did not seem to know whether to be amused or saddened by it. Just then their meals were brought to the table, and further converse on the

Reverend Stout and his conviction was suspended in settling into the substantial fare placed before them.

At last Lydia Carver said, "But how wrong this Presbyterian minister is, no matter how sincere he may be. He would have done well to remember the scriptural passages where the Lord tells his disciples that no man knows the day or the hour of the Final Judgment. We must be always prepared for the Lord's reappearance, like the wise virgins in the parable who had their lamps trimmed and ready for their master's return. For someone to think he can calculate God's appointed times is simply vanity, if not blasphemy."

"You're right, of course, Lydia," her husband said. "Nonetheless, I have a certain admiration for this Reverend Stout and the sincerity of his disregard of worldly interests. He is willing to give all that he and his wife have for the sake of his conviction. Few men today, I think, are willing to sacrifice everything for what they believe to be God's will. But let us speak of other matters. It appears, Mr. Jamison, from the condition of your hand, that perhaps you may have seen service in the late war."

The three men discovered that they were all veterans of the war. But Carver and Parsons had served in their state militias, while James had been in the Continental Army. This led them to speak of war and politics, and the future of the nation.

James was for creating a new national government to replace the Articles of Confederation, a government that would afford more unity and strength, and thus allow the nation to better defend itself against foreign enemies, he said. His two male companions favored continuing under the Articles which made each state virtually an independent government unto itself. Then the three of them began to discuss what sort of new general government would best serve the interests of commerce.

At that point Lydia Carver, who had not participated in these discussions, declared that she wanted to retire for the night, and bid her husband, brother, and James goodnight, saying she would see them all in the morning and admonishing her husband not to stay up too late—advice that he and his companions did not heed, for they had many opinions to thresh out on many important subjects.

When James arose the next morning he discovered the Carvers had already departed for New York and that it was almost time for him to go to see Mr. Gooch about his horse. As soon as he had enjoyed a bowl of tea and some baked eggs, he set out for Nassau Hall.

He found Mr. Gooch in his room, tutoring a student in Greek, and had to wait until he was free to accompany him to the livery stable where he kept the sorrel mare. Once at the stables, Gooch urged James to take the horse, whose name was Jenny, for a good run on the towpath of the canal a mile below the town, to find out whether he liked her gait.

This exercise proved to James that every feature of the mare was more than satisfactory. Finding on returning to the livery that the price was, as Dr. Franklin had predicted, far below what a sound, well-bred horse of good temperament and gait would have cost in Philadelphia, James concluded the bargain and gave partial payment for Jenny and all her equipment, which unexpectedly included—besides saddle and bridle—capacious saddlebags. He arranged with Mr. Gooch to meet at the inn at one o'clock to provide the remainder of the payment for the horse in exchange for a bill of sale and possession of the animal.

Chapter 15

James's experience on his visit to Dame Rundell's mansion, where a wan, nervous maidservant answered his knock, was less satisfactory.

"Good morning. My name is Captain Jamison," James began. "I'm from Philadelphia. I'd like to speak with your mistress if she's at home."

"Just a moment, sir. I'll go see." James waited. Quite a few minutes passed before the maid returned and reported, "She says she's not at home," and started closing the door. James interrupted her action, since it was obvious from the way the maid had phrased her statement that Mrs. Rundell was at home.

"Excuse me, miss! Please be so kind as to explain to Mrs. Rundell that I've come all the way from Philadelphia only to talk with her about her niece, Elizabeth Coons." The maid, seemingly amazed that anyone would challenge her mistress's authority—if she said she wasn't at home, she wasn't at home—stared at him, but went off to deliver his message, leaving the door ajar.

When she returned, she said, "Mrs. Rundell says to tell you, Captain Jamison, she won't give Lizzy Coons and her child a farthing, not even a ha'penny or a mill—not nothing—if you've come to beg money from her for them."

"What is your name, miss?"

"Caroline."

"Well, Caroline, please be so good as to inform Mrs. Rundell that her niece is dead—murdered, in fact—and that I've come all the way here from Philadelphia at considerable expense in travel and lodging just to know what she can tell me of Elizabeth Coons's character and history. Tell her that for me. Please."

Caroline's face looked like she had been made to take a draught of vinegar, but she went. Upon her return, the maid said, "Come this way, sir. The missus says she has plenty to tell you about her niece."

Considering what the innkeeper had said about Dame Rundell's miserliness, James surmised that he had perhaps gained admittance to her presence by telling her maid to say he had expended a considerable sum of money in coming from Philadelphia for a few moments of conversation with her, which established him in the lady's eyes as a man of means rather than a mendicant.

Elizabeth Rundell received him in her morning room, reclining on a chaise longue. She was a rather shriveled woman who, possibly because of poor eyesight, used rouge too freely and in places where it didn't belong. She also wore a pale blue turban, perhaps to hide a deficiency of hair she did not wish the world to notice.

Before even offering James a chair, she started their discourse with the abrupt remark, "Thee says thee is from Philadelphia."

"Yes, Madam."

"And, pray, tell me, does thee know my old friend Mrs. Colonel Andrew Jones?"

"No, Madam. But I have met the lady's husband."

"Well, I am surprised. I thought everyone of quality in Philadelphia knew Mrs. Colonel Jones. What is that thee hides behind thy back?"

The reference was to the habit James had formed of keeping his disfigured hand out of sight.

"It is only something that discomforts some persons of sensitive feelings," James replied, removing from behind his back what remained of his left hand, with its three missing fingers and half the palm, in its specially sewn, black kid glove.

Mistress Rundell's aversion to the sight of the maimed claw instantly registered on her face, but she bravely compressed her lips so no word or exclamation of her repugnance was heard to escape her.

"Caroline!" she cried in commanding tones to her pale maidservant who stood anxiously by the door awaiting orders.

"Yes, mum?"

"Put a chair for this gentleman over yonder, on the other side of the chimney, so he and I can both have the benefit of the fire."

"Yes, mum."

And then to James, in a hardly less commanding tone, she said, "Please have a seat, sir."

Once he was seated at a distance, she remarked, "Thee says my niece is dead?"

"Yes, she died a terrible...."

But Madam Rundell did not let him finish. She was not interested in the circumstances of how or when her niece had died.

"The last time I saw Lizzy was years ago," Mrs. Rundell said. "She was on her way with her brat to Philadelphia from New Ark. Of a sudden they showed up on my doorstep, unannounced, expecting lodging for the night. The rudest thing thee could imagine, not to write to me beforehand to ask if she could stay the night. Her husband had just died, she said. Nor did she have the decency to write to me afterward to thank me for the bed and board I provided her. But then what can be expected from the daughter of the sort of woman my brother Edward married? Our father forbade him to take a wife from the lower orders who was not a Friend. But Edward went ahead anyhow and forfeited his inheritance. It nearly killed Mother. Some people can be so inconsiderate and self-interested!"

As James listened to this speech, he thought to himself, she's finding fault with herself. The vain man faults vanity in others. Liars denounce lying. The miser complains of illiberal treatment. It was evident to him why Elizabeth Coons had sought shelter with her cousin Katherine Merkle who kept a vegetable stand in one of the market houses in Philadelphia rather than with this wealthy, childless aunt for whom she had been named, who was mistress of an opulent, empty house.

There was not much point, James thought, in continuing the conversation with this woman who had not been in touch with Lizzy Coons for eight years. So, as soon as he could, he thanked her for speaking with him and left. He returned to the inn and had his noon meal, and as he was settling the bill for his food and lodging Mr. Gooch showed up with his horse and its equipage and a bill of sale.

James paid him in the hard money Dr. Franklin had provided and took possession of the horse. Then he continued on to the village of Hopewell, riding the sorrel mare.

It was the most soul-refreshing day imaginable for a ride through the New Jersey countryside. One of those perfect days of Indian summer—sunny and mild with a refreshing breeze and a deep-blue, cloudless sky. The woods were splashes of vivid orange, yellow, and red, accented with scattered touches of dark green from the pines which made the gaudy autumn colors even more pronounced.

As James jogged along on his new horse, the splendor of the day, the sight of an abundant harvest in the fields, and his horse's smooth gait made him feel buoyant, and he did not worry about the problem Mr. Beekman had apprised him of when he was paying his bill—the fact that there were no travelers' accommodations in Hopewell. He would be entirely dependent on the generosity of Mrs. Leet and her husband for bed and board. But he had an intuition that Hopewell would live up to its name, perhaps because he could not believe a New Jersey farmer who was also a Christian minister would begrudge a traveler hospitality at harvest time.

Only a couple of hours of daylight remained by the time he got to Hopewell, which was a handful of houses, a store, a blacksmith shop, and two churches. From the first man he asked, James got directions to the home of the Baptist minister named Leet, and after a twenty-minute ride from the village, he came upon the farm where the sister of Lizzy Coons lived. He dismounted to open the gate and walked his horse toward the house. The gate, the lane to the farm, the outbuildings and barn, and the house—all had a well-kept appearance.

Mary Leet, a strong, healthy-looking countrywoman of middle age, came out to see why the dogs were barking. She stood outside her house's backdoor, wiping her hands on her apron and telling the dogs to be quiet.

"Good afternoon, sir. How may I help you?"

"I'm from Philadelphia, Mrs. Leet. My name is James Jamison. I'm an acquaintance of the Maul family—"

As soon as he mentioned the Mauls, she interrupted him.

"Come in, come in. If you've ridden all the way here from Philadelphia, you must be tired."

"I've only ridden over from Princeton. I spent the night there so I could talk with your aunt, Mrs. Rundell."

"Ah, Aunt Elizabeth," she said in a knowing tone. "Come in where we can talk. I'll give you a cup of tea and something to tide you over 'til supper. Any friend of the Mauls is most welcome, most welcome. They took in both my sisters, as you may know."

Mrs. Leet was in the midst of preparing supper for her family with the help of her daughter and told the twelve-year-old girl to set another place for Mr. Jamison. James saw there were already eight plates at the long, well-scrubbed kitchen table.

"My husband," she said, "is still out in the fields shocking the last of the corn with our boys. But they'll be coming in pretty soon because it will soon be too dark to work. You should water your horse and put her up in the barn, Mr. Jamison, while I fix your tea and cake.

"Mary, go with him. Show him which stall to use. Be sure to give the mare a good measure of oats, Mr. Jamison. Come back in after you've taken care of your mount."

Her directions made it clear to James that he and Jenny would be the guests of the Leet family that night, and the delicious odors of her kitchen made the prospect pleasing.

Little Mary Leet took an instant liking to Jenny, petting her neck and muzzle and talking to her while James removed her saddle and bit. He baited the mare with oats as he had been told to do and rubbed down her sweat-darkened withers with handfuls of sweet-smelling clover hay. By the time he was through tending to his horse, the talkative little girl had told him all about her father and mother, the farm, and her five brothers, the oldest of whom was to marry in the spring and would be moving out west to the Ohio territory.

When James returned to the kitchen from the barn, Mrs. Leet had a pot of hot tea, a slice of fresh-baked cinnamon bread, and a slab of country butter for him at the table.

James hardly knew where to begin making the inquiries that had brought him to Mrs. Leet's house. So he simply said, "I suppose you've heard of your sister's death."

"I had word of it from Cousin Katherine," Mrs. Leet said, her voice thickening as she said this. "I agree with Katherine. I do not think Mr. Maul could have been the cause of Lizzy's death. He was very kind to Lizzy and Margaret, and both of them had a high regard for him."

"I am of the same opinion," James said. "I, too, have a high regard for the Mauls. The oldest son of that family saved my life at the battle of Monmouth. For this reason I'm making it my business to see whether I can find out who truly killed your sister Elizabeth, which is why I am here. I want to learn as much as I can about her and her acquaintances."

"Our family history is a bit complicated, Mr. Jamison," Mary Leet replied. "You probably know my maiden name and that of my sisters was Gilbert. Our father was from Princeton, and Lizzy and I were born there. I was the firstborn. Before Lizzy came, Mother had four children who died. Then Margaret came into our family. So I was much older than Lizzy and Margaret. Margaret was just a year older than Lizzy. I was more like a second mother to my sisters when they were little, for I was seventeen when Lizzy was just seven and Margaret eight. We were living in Philadelphia when I married and came here."

"But if your mother had several children who died in infancy between your birth and Lizzy's birth," James asked, "and Margaret came into your family after Lizzy, how could Margaret have been one year older than Lizzy?"

"Well, that's because Margaret was adopted. And the reason for that was that Mother was raised by Margaret's parents when she was orphaned."

"How did your family come to be in Philadelphia?" James asked.

"Father was the son of a wealthy Quaker land jobber in Princeton. My grandfather disinherited him for marrying a non-Quaker from a lower order of society than he was. Because of that we never knew our grandfather and grandmother Gilbert. For a while Father, who wanted to learn a trade, worked as an apprentice to the clockmaker in Princeton. Then he came into an inheritance—a farm near Princeton and some money—from one of his great uncles. But he failed as a farmer. What was left of his inheritance he used to set up as a clockmaker in Philadelphia, where he believed there would be enough custom to support another clockmaker. But though Father had a natural gift as a mechanic, he could not compete with the established master craftsmen of the city and soon had to hire himself out to others. Within two years of arriving in the city, he found it difficult to support his family. Lizzy was sent to live with Mother's sister in New Ark, who had joined the Society of Friends and married a Quaker. Margaret, because of her frail health, was kept at home in Philadelphia, where she grew to womanhood.

"When Lizzy's husband died, I wrote to her to come with her little girl to live with us, that we would make room for them. But she preferred to try life in Philadelphia to being on the farm and went to stay with Cousin Kate, and then with Margaret."

"Your cousin in Philadelphia told me your sister visited you here in Hopewell during the war, while she was living with the Mauls," James said.

"She did. Lizzy brought her little girl here to see if she would stay with us, because the two German soldiers billeted on the Mauls were crowding them so much. Lizzy and I were hoping Sarah would take to my little Mary, since they were the same age. And they did like each other. But Sarah said she didn't like it. So Lizzy took her back to Philadelphia and put her with Kate."

"Tell me something about your sister's character," James said.

Mrs. Leet mistakenly thought he had asked her about both of her siblings.

"They were very different in some ways. Margaret was skinny as a rail, but Lizzy made a good figure. Both of them were good-hearted and apt to pity stray dogs. I wasn't the least surprised when I heard Margaret had taken to nursing the sick of her Weekly Meeting. Mother was that way, too. Lizzy was the smartest of us. She had a good head for managing things. If her husband hadn't died young, they would've succeeded, I think. He must have been a good man from what Lizzy told me about him."

"I understand you may have letters your sister wrote to you when she lived with the Mauls," James said. "Did she say anything in any of them, or when she was visiting you here in Hopewell, about the two Hessians living in the Maul household? Or any other man of her acquaintance?"

"I do have Lizzy's letters. She never spoke of anything like that while she was here, but I think I remember her mentioning the Germans in one or two of her letters. If I recall, she said one of them made a grab for her once when no one else was around."

"Might I see the letters to read them and have the loan of them for a few weeks?" James asked. "Information in them might help me in my search for the man who killed her, when combined with other things I've learned."

Mrs. Leet was perfectly willing to have James see and read the letters. But as to taking them away with him when he left, she was not so sure. They were all she had left of her sister, she said.

Just then the sound of voices and wagons coming into the yard was heard, and Mrs. Leet took James out to introduce him to her husband and her five sons, three of whom were full-grown men. They entered the house after washing their hands and faces in the tin basins by the back door. Their faces glowed from their work in the fields, and they filled the kitchen with the smell of fresh air. The field workers immediately went to the table and stood quietly at their places while their father gave the blessing for the supper which their mother and sister had prepared; then they all sat and noisily began passing the numerous dishes around, talking as they began to eat.

During the course of the meal, James learned that John Leet was more farmer than minister, and that he had been elected at the outset of the war with Britain to lead a company of militia raised in Middlesex County, New Jersey. He had been in nine battles, and before the end of the war had risen to the rank of Colonel in charge of several companies.

His three grown sons, John, James, and Joshua, were, like him, tall, broad-shouldered men. They were full of lively speech among themselves and with their sister and their younger brothers, Jesse and Seth, but quiet and respectful in speaking with their parents. All of them, even Seth, the youngest, who was a chatterbox, fell silent when their father said anything to the whole family. This honest tiller of the soil and preacher of God's Word brought to James's mind one of the sayings from *Poor Richard's Almanac* by Dr. Franklin. "Don't judge a man by what he does on Sunday," though its usual meaning was as an admonition to be wary of hypocrites.

The Reverend John Leet's church, which James learned was at a crossroads three miles from his farm, was open only on Sunday. Tomorrow being the Sabbath, James was invited to worship with the family and he readily accepted Leet's invitation, being curious to know what sort of sermon a man like John Leet would deliver.

The most serious matter discussed at the supper table by Mrs. Leet, her husband, and James was what America had won by the sacrifices of the recent war. They were in agreement that the independence of the States would one day produce a mighty nation on the northern continent of America, and Reverend Leet stated that he thought the United States would become an example of freedom and self-government to the whole world.

"But," Mrs. Leet reminded James and her husband, "we must eliminate slavery or we will never amount to a hill of beans."

"You're right, Mary," her husband agreed. "The Bible tells us, in the book of Jeremiah, which is the text for my sermon tomorrow, that it is not His will that any man should own another man's body, or the bodies of another man's children, in perpetuity. What are your views on slavery, Captain Jamison?"

"I'm hopeful it will be gotten rid of state by state through legislative acts, as is happening in New England. I also find the idea that is being talked of, of excluding slavery from the

Northwest Territory—which will one day furnish new States—would be a hopeful step. Slavery is contrary to our country's principles of liberty and equality. It must be gotten rid of one way or another. It cannot persist in a country like ours founded on God-given, equal birthrights."

"Admirably stated, Captain Jamison," John Leet said. "I think you are going to like my sermon tomorrow. By the way, my son John here has decided to migrate to the Northwest Territory after his marriage next spring. Tell our guest your plans, John."

"Yes, sir," the stalwart young man answered. "Martha and I want to take up some of the rich bottom land out west. I've already gone out to the Ohio with Archie Cox, who lives on the next farm over and is also getting married in April, like me. Archie and I want to go together to the Northwest Territory. He and I saw land along the Muskingum, a tributary of the Ohio just west of Virginia, which we think will make us good farms. My parents and Martha's approve our enterprise, and Archie's father is even talking of moving with us."

After further talk on the future of the country and the opportunities it held for the rising generation, the head of the house said it was time for everyone to be in bed to be fresh and rested for Sunday worship.

James retired for the night to Mary Leet's spacious pantry, which she had set up for him as a place to sleep using the canvas camp bed her husband had used on his military campaigns. She loaned him her sister's letters before he went to this improvised bedroom. He read them by the light of the candles she furnished him.

There were ten letters, the most recent dated March 29, 1783—two and a half years previously. Evidently, Mrs. Coons had been less communicative with her sister in the final years of her life than she had been earlier.

The contents of the letters consisted mostly of domestic events in the Maul household. One letter, however, contained a reference to the possibility of marrying again. There were continual references to the kindness she received from the Mauls. Another letter described the circumstances of her sister Margaret's death and insisted that Jacob Maul could not have been the cause of it.

James took the greatest interest in Mrs. Coons's passing references to the Hessians in three of her epistles. She reported that the two Hessians came from the same village in Hesse and had known each other since boyhood, and that the corporal of the pair had tried to kiss her. Once, she said, she happened to walk in on an angry exchange of words between the two Germans in their native language. From the way they'd reacted to her sudden appearance, she thought the argument they were having might have been over her. It climaxed with the sergeant striking the corporal across the mouth with the back of his hand.

The third and final reference to the Germans was that Sergeant Weber had said she should be his "little housewife" after the war and live with him on his Uncle Polzer's farm near German Town.

Chapter 16

The Leets and James went to church in two farm wagons. John Leet sent his sons John, James, and Joshua ahead in one wagon to unlock the church, open its shutters, build fires in its two Franklin stoves, and put the hymnals on the benches. He and his wife, with their three youngest children and their guest, followed in the other wagon an hour later.

On the way into church, James was introduced to John Leet's deacon, Philip Beale, the family of young John Leet's fiancée, and others of the congregation.

The service began with the invocation and the singing of "O God, Our Help in Ages Past." After these opening exercises led by his deacon, John Leet stepped to the pulpit, and read from Jeremiah, Chapter 34. "Thus saith the Lord, the God of Israel; I made a covenant with your fathers in the day that I brought them forth out of the house of Egypt, out of the house of bondmen, saying, at the end of seven years let ye go every man his brother an Hebrew, which hath been sold unto thee; and when he hath served thee six years, thou shalt let him go free from thee."

The minister closed the Bible and stood silent a moment at the pulpit with downcast eyes, concentrating his mind on the main points of the sermon he had written in the evenings of the previous week, after coming in from laboring in his fields.

Then he looked around the church at the upturned faces and began to preach.

"My dear friends and neighbors, the almighty Creator, whose eternal power has spangled the heavens with stars and governs the motions of the earth, the sun and the moon, has been our help in ages past. But will He be our hope for years to come? That depends on us, dear neighbors and friends.

"In ancient times in the land of Judea, the Jews made sacrifices to God by killing and splitting in two an animal without spot or blemish, and burning its two halves on the altar of sacrifice. They called such sacrifices a 'holocaust.' Sacrificing valuable animals from their flocks and herds was part of their covenant with the Almighty. These sacrifices prefigured the final and ultimate sacrifice that God made of Himself on the Cross. In the first instance, the holocausts the Jews of old performed, mankind made the sacrifice to God. In the second instance, the reverse was true. God sacrificed Himself to make a new covenant by which mankind everywhere, not just the twelve tribes of Israel, might find forgiveness for their sins through believing in what God had done for them in offering himself in atonement for man's sins. We have only to believe in that sacrifice to find redemption and have salvation."

At these words, exclamations rang out in various parts of the congregation. "Amen!" "Praise Jesus!" and "Blessed be His Holy Name!"

"But hearken, dear neighbors and friends!" the Reverend Leet's voice rose above the shouts. "The Jews of old broke their covenant with God, and God punished them! That is why a new covenant was needed. How did they break their covenant? They broke it by not freeing their fellow Hebrews who had labored for them for seven years. They did not show the mercy to their bondsmen that God showed them in bringing them out of bondage in Egypt.

"So God allowed King Nebuchadnezzar of Babylon to overrun the land of Israel and destroy the cities of Judea. Those who survived the slaughter, the prophet Jeremiah tells us, were taken captive and became slaves, and were sent into exile in Babylon.

"The seven years Jeremiah refers to is what you and I call 'indentured servitude.' Some of you who sit here before me in this church this morning crossed the ocean to America, this promised land flowing in milk and honey, as indentured servants, which Israel's covenant with God made lawful. Since you could not afford to pay your way to America, you sold your labor for a fixed number of years in exchange for obtaining passage. How would you have felt if, after fulfilling the years of your indenture, you had been unjustly retained in perpetual bondage? That was the sin the Jews of old committed, the sin that God punished. They kept their servants in bondage beyond the lawful term of their service.

"That a man should own another man's body and keep him in perpetual bondage, and put his children in bondage all their lives, is not God's will, nor God's law. A nation which does that will not escape His wrath. We may be certain of that. The day of reckoning for that nation will come, sooner or later. We have the example of the Babylonian Captivity of the Jews of old in testament to that truth."

On this note of solemn warning, John Leet ended his sermon. Deacon Beale then came to the pulpit and led the congregation in the hymn which begins with the words "Blest be the tie that binds our hearts in Christian love."

John Leet closed the service with a benediction delivered with upraised face, closed eyes, and outspread arms.

"Almighty God, our help in ages past, our hope in years to come, may the living truth that your prophet Jeremiah has made known to us enter our hearts and through your Son, our Lord and Savior, bring us redemption. Amen."

On the way home in the wagons, nothing was said by either the Leets or James. They were all of them pondering the sermon and the biblical lesson it explicated.

After a Sunday dinner of food from the previous evening's supper, James took his leave and started on his return to Philadelphia by way of German Town. As he was saying his goodbyes, Mary Leet put into his hands the letters from her sister Elizabeth he had returned to her that morning before going to church. "Take these, Captain Jamison. Use them to bring the man who killed my sister to justice. John has persuaded me to loan them to you for that purpose. Return them, please, when they have served their purpose."

James's saddlebags, as he set out for Philadelphia, bulged with the provisions Mary Leet insisted he take from her larder to sustain him on his journey.

It was another glorious afternoon, the morning fog having dissipated hours before, leaving a deep blue sky and sunny atmosphere. On some stretches of the woodland track James traveled in following the directions John Leet had given him, he saw large stumps and blackened circles where great piles of tree branches had been burned—evidence that the immense forest the first European settlers had beheld when they came up the valley of the Delaware River had not yet been completely destroyed to clear the land for farms.

He came across no other travelers on the back roads he traversed and around the middle of the afternoon he reached the main traveled road next to the Delaware, and turned south toward Trenton. Not long thereafter the riverbank took on a familiar appearance. He stopped for a closer look and saw the stubs of the brush that had been cut down and set to one side, years before, to make a landing place on the east bank of the Delaware for Washington and his army when they crossed the river for their attack on the Hessian garrison at Trenton. The ruts made by the gun carriages in pulling them up the embankment were still visible.

As he rested in the saddle by the riverbank that bright autumn day, gazing on the scene, what he saw brought back vivid memories of that perilous night. He remembered the foreboding they had all felt during the crossing, for they knew that if they failed to surprise the Hessians and were defeated by them in battle, the war and the cause of American liberty would be lost. But Colonel Glover's boatmen had not been discovered, and the Army made it safely over the river and defeated the Hessians. They had been victorious, thanks to God's blessing and Washington's plan of attack.

James remembered the swirling black waters of the river that winter night, and the banging of the chunks of ice against the boat in which he had crossed. He remembered the biting sting of sleet on his face and manhandling the heavy tubes of the cannons—slick with sleet—out of the boats, to be mounted on the gun carriages and wheeled up the riverbank and down the road to Trenton.

And in the lantern light of his memory, he saw once more himself and three of his artillerymen, trying to lift one of the cannons from a boat and felt it slip from their grasp to crush Nathan Manning's thigh, lying athwart the gunwale of the boat. He heard once more Nathan's scream and saw again his splintered bone in the lantern light, surrounded by bloody fat, tearing his skin and breeches.

The last he saw of Nathan he was being carried off somewhere in the night. The Army could not pause over the fate of one young man. It had to hurry to get to Trenton before the Hessians woke from their drunken celebration of Christmas Eve.

An eagle screamed on the far side of the river, waking James from his reverie, and, looking over, he saw the bird flying north between the woods and the water, and he turned his horse's head and continued southward on the river road.

At Trenton, he stopped at the Buck's Head Inn, where the mail was made up, and wrote his report to Dr. Franklin on what he had learned in Princeton and Hopewell. Bundling the report with the letters he had gotten from Mary Leet, he gave the packet to the postmaster to wrap, address and seal.

When the postmaster learned that the packet was going to Dr. Franklin, he became noticeably cordial, and informed James he had received his appointment as postmaster from Benjamin Franklin when Franklin had been Postmaster General of the United States. The man said he would forward the packet to Philadelphia at his own expense, and wanted to know what friend of Dr. Franklin's he had the honor of addressing. Not wanting even someone living outside the city to know of his connection with Franklin, James gave the first name that came to mind, which was "Seth Leet." And it was as Seth Leet that he had his hand shaken by the grateful postmaster in honor of Benjamin Franklin.

James crossed back into Pennsylvania on the same barge that had ferried him over to Trenton on his way to Princeton three days earlier before he had bought Jenny. Once safely on the Pennsylvania side of the river, he set off for Bristol and reached there without mishap in time to obtain a clean, warm bed for the night at a tavern called the Black Bear.

Chapter 17

James resumed his journey Monday morning, the weather holding clear but turning cold. On the way to German Town, he stopped once by the road to make a blazing fire of tumbled-down, old fence rails to warm himself and eat the last of Mary Leet's cloth-wrapped morsels of veal, crusty bread, and homemade cheese. After leaving Bristol he encountered nothing but the most wretched public houses along the road and was exceedingly glad to have these tokens of her good housekeeping in his saddlebags.

In Frankfort he halted long enough to have a hot drink and get directions to German Town. An hour after that halt, he dismounted in front of the Union Inn which his informants in Frankfort had mentioned. He intended to ask the keeper of this tavern, which was two miles short of German Town, where the roads to Philadelphia and Bristol intersected, and if he knew the location of a farm owned by a German named Polzer.

When James entered the Union Inn and its lovely aroma of beer, four men were having an animated conversation in German at a table. The foursome ceased speaking the moment James came through the door. No one else was in the taproom. One of the men, who had an almost childlike stature, slenderness, and look of innocence, got up from the table and went behind the bar to wait on James.

Wishing the traveler good day in English spoken in a deep voice that had no trace of a Teutonic accent, he immediately asked, "Are you from the country or the city?"

The question struck James as impertinent, coming as it did from a person who was keeping a public house, who ought to have at least asked how he could be of service before inquiring about his place of origin. But, not wanting to give offense himself, James replied that he lived in Philadelphia but was just now coming from Bristol on his way to German Town.

"If you're from Philadelphia," the slender proprietor said, "then you know all about the Quaker Murders, unless you've been away from the city for a considerable time."

This comment surprised James even more than the question about where he was from. A reference to the Quaker Murders was the last thing he had expected to hear when he'd entered this taproom. But he again answered in a civil manner, "I've heard a Quaker was arrested in the city on suspicion of strangling a woman."

"And what's your judgment in the matter? Was the man guilty? These men and I have been disputing the case. Three of us are of the opinion the man was guilty of murder. The other one says he was innocent. What do you think?"

It took James a moment to decide how to reply to this interrogation. He did not want to refuse to answer. But neither did he want to give his actual opinion, which might involve him in the dispute the men were having and a discussion of his reasons for his judgment. So he decided that his best course would be evasion.

"I think," James said, "a man is innocent until he has been proven guilty on evidence in a court of law. On the other hand, the authorities would probably not have made an arrest unless they had some reason for it."

These truisms seemed to James to be perfectly neutral. But his words caused a stir among the trio at the table, who had been listening attentively to the conversation between him and the innkeeper. On hearing what James said, one of the rustics at the table gave the man sitting next to him a whack on the shoulder and said something in German, as if James's platitudes were the pronouncement of a sentence by a judge because he came from the city of Philadelphia.

The proprietor of the inn likewise made a remark in German to his companions, which caused two of the men at the table to laugh heartily and take a swig of beer from their steins. But the other man—the one whose shoulder had been whacked—neither laughed nor drank, but only looked sour.

Then the proprietor turned to James and said in English, "The man arrested for the crime will never be tried for his crime."

He left his place behind the bar and went over to the table, where he retrieved a newspaper that had been lying there, and brought it to James, saying, "He's escaped the hangman."

Thus James learned that there had been a riot at the Walnut Street Jail in which Jacob Maul and his protector Robert Cash had both been killed, along with other persons. It was this news that the men had been discussing. One of them had just returned from the city with the paper containing the news.

According to the account in the newspaper which James read, the riot had occurred the day he'd left Philadelphia for Princeton. Pennsylvania militiamen had been sent in to quell the riot and restore order. Three rioters had been shot and killed and five wounded. Because of the confusion in the prison during the uprising, the persons who bludgeoned Maul and Cash to death, the paper said, would probably never be identified and brought to justice.

Reading this news brought to James's mind the impression he had had of the prison, and his memory of the distraught Quaker stonecutter and his Negro protector. These recollections were followed by his remembrance of William Maul and his gentle wife. William must have already interred his father's body in the burial ground of the Free Quakers. He and Rebecca now had a further occasion for grief. James wondered if Cash's body had been given Christian burial.

With his father dead, William and his younger brother Robert were all that remained of their family.

James also wondered what Dr. Franklin's reaction would be to the news of Jacob Maul's passing. Would he want to give up further inquiry into the murder of Elizabeth Coons? Now that Maul was dead, was there any reason to search out the farm belonging to the German named Polzer? What use would there be to get information on Polzer's nephew, the former sergeant August Weber, who had expressed an interest in Lizzy Coons? Was there any point in continuing an investigation to obtain justice for a dead man?

James did not know what to do. But he knew he didn't want to converse any further with anyone at the Union Inn and laid the newspaper on the bar and left the tavern. Mounting his horse, he continued to think about what he should do, and for no particular reason turned the horse's head in the direction of German Town, letting the horse walk along at whatever pace she pleased, while he thought.

Perhaps it would be best to return at once to Philadelphia to seek instructions from Dr. Franklin. Or perhaps he should go ahead and complete the plan they had made the last time they'd spoken. In mulling over these questions, he reviewed

Dr. Franklin's reasons for investigating the murder of Mrs. Coons, which included his disgust over the expulsion of William and Rebecca Maul from their Quaker church because William's father had been arrested on suspicion of murder. That reason was still valid. Whether Jacob Maul was dead or alive, his reputation remained a concern for his son. If Maul was proven innocent, it would show that the Quaker Elders had been wrong in their prejudice against the Maul family.

Then, too, there was the question of justice for the murdered woman. If Maul was not her killer—as James now believed he was not—then Lizzy Coons's killer was still free, and justice would not be done until he was found and punished. Now that Maul was dead the Commonwealth of Pennsylvania would take no further interest in looking for another suspect in the death of Mrs. Elizabeth Coons. It bothered James to think of her killer going undetected and unpunished. This thought more than anything decided him to continue his inquiries for Dr. Franklin.

It also occurred to him that to be dissuaded from continuing by a mere speculation that Dr. Franklin might have lost interest in the investigation would make him look foolish. The decision to desist or proceed was Dr. Franklin's, not his. Having reached this conclusion, he gathered up the loose reins and put Jenny into a canter.

The decision to continue his inquiries cleared his mind, and he remembered that at the Battle of German Town in '77 there had been a German miller from the place who had guided the army's advance through the foggy maze of ravines north of the town. It occurred to him that this miller would surely know the German farmers in the area and would therefore be able to tell him the location of the Polzer farm.

James arrived in German Town a little before noon, and the first three men he asked for help in finding the miller he sought spoke no English. It then occurred to him to find a grocer, someone who bought flour from local millers and would be acquainted with the farmers who brought grist to their mills. Such a person would almost certainly speak English, as well as German, since some of his customers at least would use English.

This strategy worked. The first grocer he found could converse in English. But he laughed when James told him he was looking for a German miller.

"Which one? There are three of them," the grocer said. "Which one is your business with?"

The question posed a problem for James. He could hardly claim acquaintance with someone whose name he did not know. So he told the grocer that he was looking for the miller who had served as Washington's scout before the Battle of German Town, and said that he had an interest in "the payment of commutation." The two statements separately were true enough. He was looking for the man who had guided Washington so he could ask him where the Polzer farm was, and he did have an interest in the payment of the bonuses in land being distributed to veterans of the war—his own bonus. But the implication he created in making the statements at the same time was that he was an agent of Congress looking for the miller to compensate him for his services to General Washington during the war.

The deception had the intended effect.

"Yah. The one ye're wanting is Otto Blymueller. His mill is on Gunner's Creek. Just follow the road north beside that creek, the one over there beyond the street," and he pointed out his window. "Ye're sure to come upon it."

James thanked the grocer and went in search of Otto Blymueller's mill, which he soon found.

When James identified himself as someone who had been with the Army and knew of the miller's special service to General Washington, Blymueller turned the milling job he was doing over to his apprentice to finish and invited his visitor to have a drink from his jug. He said he was about to sit down to dinner with his family and his mill hands, and insisted that James join them.

The miller's English was broken and heavily accented, but no one else at the table spoke any English at all or, if they did, they were not interested in conversing in it. That made it easy for James to speak exclusively with Herr Blymueller without seeming to be impolite. He was pleasant with the others at the table by means of friendly smiles and nods. The good Frau Blymueller, who sat by his side, likewise bestowed on James an abundance of nods and smiles while carefully pronouncing the German names of each dish she handed him as if concerned to teach him her language as well as feed him.

James and the miller spoke of what had happened at the battle of German Town, but at last James obtained the information he desired.

Blymueller, it turned out, ground the grist for Sergeant Weber's uncle, Anton Polzer. And when asked by James if he knew Polzer's nephew, August Weber, he said he did, and also Weber's friend Diedreich Schmidt. Both of them had been taken prisoner during the war, James learned from the miller, and both had been paroled by signing a pledge to work for Weber's uncle for the remainder of the war and not return to British military service, such paroles being a common practice as a way to avoid having to guard and feed captured enemy soldiers.

"August Veber he ish not longer vit his oncle on der farm," Herr Blymueller said.

"No longer on the farm? Where is he?" James asked.

"He ish gone ter der city."

"How long has he been there?"

"Oh, I suppose id mus' be mos' uf vun yahr now dat he lef Anton to go into der city. De uder vun, Diedreich, he ish still at der farm. He ish marriet now vid de *tochter* uf olt Anton."

Blymueller had no information to give James as to where Weber lived in Philadelphia or what he did there, but he thought he might have gotten a job in a rope walk.

This report, that Weber might be working in a manufactory for making cord and rope, interested James more than Otto Blymueller could possibly appreciate, given that Lizzy Coons's corpse had been found trussed up with marline twine.

After dinner, the miller went back to work, and James went to find the former corporal, Diedreich Schmidt, highly grateful for Frau Blymueller's hearty food and her husband's information.

Chapter 18

As he rode off into the countryside, following the directions he had been given to the farm of Anton Polzer, James felt he might be going to make a prodigious discovery.

The Polzer farm lay northwest of the town, miles from a traveled road. The narrow wagon track to it from the main road was entirely shut in by forest trees. James saw no other habitation or even any fields as he jogged down the miles-long lane through woods that he had been told led to the farm.

A forlorn silence invested the Polzer homestead as he rode into the barnyard. The unpainted house looked dingy and in poor repair; the barn was in even worse condition and showed large cracks between its weathered vertical boards. A rooster and four hens were stepping in jerky unison along the grassy margin of the barnyard, scratching and pecking for seeds and insects. No other animated being was in sight. A smell of hay and manure permeated the air in the vicinity of the barnyard. The light wind rustled the gorgeously arrayed maple trees surrounding the house and sent a few bright leaves twirling down.

Without dismounting, James repeatedly hallooed the house and the barn, but got no response.

His expectations had been too thoroughly aroused, however, and he had ridden too far, to be easily discouraged.

Sooner or later, he knew, Polzer's cows would have to be brought in to be milked from whatever pasture they were on. But that might not happen until dusk, which would leave too little time for a talk with Anton Polzer and a return to German Town before nightfall; and the general aspect of Polzer's house and barn made it clear to James that he was unlikely to receive an invitation to spend the night here. Nor from the look of the place would he be inclined to accept such an invitation.

James therefore rode around behind the barn, looking for the way to the fields belonging to the farm, and found a track that went off into the woods. From the deposits of fresh horse dung on it and the deeply crushed weeds along its edges, the track appeared to have been recently traversed by a heavily laden wagon drawn by horses.

After several twists and turns to avoid boggy ground, for the terrain was flat and poorly drained, this woodland track led James onto a sloping, stubbled field of some thirty acres, enclosed on all sides by trees. A second, larger field was visible on the other side of a thin line of trees dividing the fields. At the far edge of the field he had just ridden into, he saw two men standing by a wagon driven by what looked like a boy. The men were spreading something from the wagon onto the field with pitchforks.

The man facing James became aware of his presence as soon as he emerged from the woods and both men stopped what they were doing to stare at him. The driver of the wagon likewise turned around on the seat to look, and he saw that the driver was not a boy, as he had thought, but a young female dressed in male clothing. She was as ill-kempt as the men and nearly as stained as they were by the manure being spread onto the field.

James felt certain the two men were the farm's owner, Anton Polzer, with his new son-in-law whom Herr Blymueller had mentioned, Diedreich Schmidt. The young woman, who had eyes the color of a robin's egg he saw as he drew close, had to be Polzer's daughter, Schmidt's recently wed bride. Coming to a halt beside the threesome, James said pleasantly, "Good day."

The older of the two men, a tall, raw-boned man in his fifties, nodded his head in reply without speaking, all the while gazing at James, as did the much younger man on the other side of the wagon and the plain-featured female rustic on the wagon's seat.

"Fine field, you have here," James continued. "I see you had it planted in wheat last year, from the look of the stubble."

"Rye," Anton Polzer said matter-of-factly. "Ve had it in rye, *zwei* yahren past, nut last yahr."

Deeply suspicious, Polzer waited for this strange American gentleman on horseback to make known the reason for his sudden, unexpected appearance in this remote spot.

"I'm Captain Jamison. I'm from Philadelphia. Can you tell me where I can find August Weber, Herr Polzer? I'd like to talk with your nephew. No one was at the house, so I came looking for you."

This speech caused an immediate reaction on the part of the young woman, who began speaking forcefully to her father and husband in German, in what sounded to James like an alarmed tone.

While she was speaking, Diedreich Schmidt, a well-set, blond-haired man in his early thirties, stuck his fork in the load of manure on the wagon and came around to stand next to his father-in-law.

The discussion among the three in their native tongue continued for several minutes; and as they spoke back and forth, though they sometimes glanced at each other, they mostly kept their eyes fixed on James. What they were saying to each other he had no way of knowing, but it was evident they were discussing the question he had asked.

Finally the young woman, who seemed to have been chosen to speak for them all, said to James, "What you want with August?"

While they'd been talking amongst themselves James had thought of a half-truth to tell these country people, which he believed would be acceptable to them. "The family of a widow in Philadelphia who is missing has asked me to find her, and since Herr Weber once expressed an interest in marrying her when he was with the British army in Philadelphia, I want to speak with him." In saying this, he assumed that because they lived an isolated life remote from Philadelphia, they would have no knowledge of Elizabeth Coons's murder.

Upon this statement from James, the young woman and her male companions had another, lengthier discussion, after which their speaker asked, "What is the woman's name?"

"Mrs. Coons. I believe your husband knew her, too," James said, looking at Diedreich Schmidt. "You and August Weber lived with the woman's family during the war. Isn't that true, Herr Schmidt?"

Schmidt did not answer James, but instead launched into a long discourse directed at his young wife, in a tone that sounded to James to be nervously explanatory. James heard the name "Charlotte" used several times, which was evidently the name of the young woman on the wagon, who interrupted Schmidt's speech several times with questions.

At last, Schmidt ceased speaking, and Charlotte Schmidt summarized the result of the colloquy by turning toward James and saying, "We don't know a Frau Coons."

"Her first name was Elizabeth," James said. "Elizabeth Coons."

But without discussing this further information with either her husband or her father, the young woman seated on the wagon simply repeated her previous categorical denial, "We don't know any Mrs. Coons," which certainly could not have been true of her husband, however true it was for her and her father.

"You do know August Weber, don't you," James stated rather than asked.

After a moment of hesitation, she replied, "Yah, we know him."

"Then please tell me where I can find him in Philadelphia."

More discussion among them followed this politely worded request.

Finally, Anton Polzer spoke. And as he did so, James thought that he might at last be getting at something that might further Dr. Franklin's investigation.

"August, he left a long time back. He haf de parole, same as Diedreich, unt stay here 'til de war end; den vun day he say he vant ter go tu de city unt lif. He don't like, he say, de farm. It don't suit him, he say. I try keep him here tu vurk. I say it goot tu own land, an' some day de farm be his maybe. But he get mad unt say tu me dat de farm unt me can go tu hell. He say he got petter t'ings tu do; he don't vant tu be farmer. He start tu leaf unt I grab him tu talk sense tu him, unt he push me down, unt go avay. I don't know vhere he is.

"Diedreich, he different"—and with this Polzer put his arm around his son-in-law's shoulders—"he like de farm. He marry mine Charlotte. He goot vurker. He vurk hard. Some day de farm be his."

So James learned that Sergeant August Weber seemed to be an ambitious man who preferred life in the city, and discovered for the second time that Weber could be violent in arguing with someone close to him. For Lizzy Coons had said in one of her letters that she had seen him strike his boyhood friend, with whom he had grown up in the same village in Germany, the man Diedreich Schmidt now standing before James. And now James had learned that Weber had once in anger laid hands on his uncle. He wondered if a man with a temperament such as this, if opposed by a woman in something of serious import to him, might be capable of greater violence than slapping or pushing.

The long speech in English that Anton Polzer had made on his nephew's behavior seemed to have exhausted his patience with this American stranger, and he told James dismissively, "Ve got vurk tu do."

Then he said something in German to his daughter that caused her to put the horses in motion, while he, with his arm still across his son-in-law's shoulders and his pitchfork in his other hand followed alongside the wagon, talking to Schmidt. By thus ignoring James, the Germans ended the interview.

James turned Jenny around and rode back the way he had come. The gloom of the coming night was already evident in the woods as he left the field, and he put his heels to the mare to quicken her pace.

Retracing the lane back to the Polzer farmyard, he returned to the high road where in the gathering twilight he urged his horse on at a swifter gait. He wanted to get to German Town before complete darkness set in, to obtain a bed for the night, which he managed to do.

After having supper, he wrote a detailed report of his eventful day in German Town to leave for Dr. Franklin as soon as he got back to Philadelphia the next morning. He went straight to bed after writing his report.

In his account of his interview with the Germans, James allowed himself the deduction that, having observed Diedreich Schmidt's relations with his wife, he could no longer consider him a suspect in the murder of Mrs. Coons. Being the husband of Polzer's only child, he in effect was a partner in the operation of the farm, and from what James had seen in the woodland field Schmidt's life on the farm afforded him little opportunity for carrying on amours in Philadelphia. Heavy continual work seemed to be his entire life. And from the impression the forceful, apparently jealous and suspicious young woman driving the wagon had made on James, he did not think she would permit her husband out of her sight long enough for him to dally with another woman.

At first light the next morning, without waiting to take breakfast in German Town, James was in the saddle on his way back to Philadelphia. He took the direct road into the city rather than the roundabout, picturesque route alongside the Schuylkill River.

As he got to the center of the city on his way to take breakfast at the City Tavern, he spotted Dr. Franklin coming toward him in the sedan chair he had brought back with him from France. His bearers were four debtors from the Walnut Street Jail he had recruited to carry the chair, to give them a chance to earn money to pay their debts and get out of prison. This lucky turn of events, James thought, would allow him to indicate to Dr. Franklin his return to the city and show him the horse he had bought with Dr. Franklin's money. So he dismounted to lead Jenny as close as possible to the sedan chair coming toward him, to make certain the man inside it saw him and the horse. But though Dr. Franklin was plainly visible through the sedan chair's windows and glanced in his direction, he showed no sign of recognizing James as he passed within a few feet of him in the street. He seemed to be completely absorbed in his own thoughts.

James remounted and continued on to the City Tavern, where he inquired whether there were any communications for him. The Tavern's day manager, Mr. Proctor, said that just before he'd relieved Mr. Morley, the night manager, a man had asked for Captain Jamison, but had not left anything for him. When James requested a description of the man, Mr. Proctor had no information because Mr. Morley had not mentioned the man's appearance.

After taking breakfast, James wrote across the top of the first page of his report: "Tues. Am back in town. Saw you on the street. Will come tomorrow at the usual hour to find out how I'm to proceed now that J. M. is dead." He then delivered the report to the post by the boundary wall of Franklin Court.

Having discharged this duty, he went home and was welcomed by Grandmère with happy affection on his safe return from his journey. When he took Grandmère and Livy out to the stable to see Jenny, they had nothing but praise and admiration for the sorrel mare.

Back in the house, James asked Livy what she had learned from her search among the midwives of Southwark while he'd been gone. Had any of them attended a woman's lying-in the night of September seventh?

"One of them did," said the fair-skinned, brown-haired maid, beaming with pleasure at being able to report her success to James. "It took me most of a day to get the names of the midwives and where to find them. Then I went around and talked with each of them. The first one I went to find, her family told me she was at Chester on a visit, and they didn't know when she would return. The next three didn't know of any birth that occurred at the time you are interested in.

"The last one on my list said she had attended a birth above a tavern the night of September seventh. But she said the woman wasn't from the country because she had seen her before, walking on the streets of Southwark.

"I didn't care about that, since I knew you were interested in a woman who lived in Southwark. So I told the midwife, just as you told me I should, that I would get word to the husband —meaning you—and you would come by to see her in a few days. So you must talk to her as soon as you can, James. Her name is Martha Shields. She lives off Pine Street in Anthill Alley, the first house to the right, second floor on the right."

"Livy did very well, James," Grandmère said proudly, "don't you think?"

"Oh, very well indeed. Thanks to what you've accomplished, Livy, I may get the information I need on the last hours of Lizzy Coons's life."

"I also have news," James's grandmother said, handing him a letter. "This came for you just a little while ago."

The letter was really a short note in a neat, clerkly hand. "Capt. Jamison, a boy in a white hat will attend you tonight at ten by the Watch where you usually eat in town & will bring you to me. I have information." The note was not signed.

When James asked his grandmother to tell him how she had come by this note, she said it had been brought by a street boy who asked for money for bringing it, which she gave him. The ungrateful urchin had complained that what she had given him was not enough, but she refused to give him more, as he demanded.

"Was there anything about this boy that was different from other street boys?"

"His hat," Grandmère said. "He had a white chapeau with a wide brim and round crown. The hat was less grimy than his face."

"Grandmère, thank you for taking the letter. It may lead to something. I think I'll go upstairs a moment before I go out again."

"But, *mon cher*, you just arrived home! These comings and goings will ruin your health. You are not eating proper meals, James. Tell him what you told me the other day, Olivia. Tell him."

But before Livy could make any reply, James said, "Whatever the two of you think of my habits we can talk over later. Right now, I must go see this Mrs. Shields, and before I do that, I have to go upstairs for a moment."

When James got to his bedchamber, he unlocked his writing desk and took from it the two hostile replies he had received in response to Dr. Franklin's newspaper ad, and compared their handwriting to the note he had just received. Neither one matched the handwriting on the note.

Several things bothered James about this note delivered by the boy wearing a white hat, who was to guide him to a rendezvous with a man who would not sign his name. Whoever had employed the boy to deliver his note knew where James lived and where he habitually ate his meals when he did not take them at home. Given these facts, it seemed likely that his movements were being watched, for the note had been brought to his house soon after his return to Philadelphia from an absence of several days but while he was not yet at home, and therefore unable to question the messenger when he delivered the note. Its peremptory tenor and ungracious command to be in front of the City Tavern at a late hour when few people would be abroad was unworthy of a gentleman, James felt.

Chapter 19

Following Livy's description of where Mrs. Shields lived, James had no difficulty finding the midwife's residence in Anthill Alley.

She received him with the deference and expressions of sympathy proper for the alleged husband of a wife who had run away from home while pregnant. She asked to please be excused for a moment while she spoke to her neighbors. James could hear her knocking next door and saying, "He's here," and a woman's voice answering, "I'll be right over," and he heard her going down the stairs and knocking at doors there. While Mrs. Shields was below, a woman came and stood in the open doorway, smiling sadly at James, who acknowledged her presence with a nod of his head.

Mrs. Shields came back upstairs with two other women, who joined the woman in the doorway. One of them curtsied to James.

"Well, sir," Mrs. Shields said after she had settled herself again in a chair in front of James, "what can I tell you?"

James glanced at the three women looking in at him from the doorway like three wide-eyed, solemn owls blinking on the limb of a tree.

"Oh, don't pay them any mind, sir. Them's neighbors. They know all about your visit. I told them of it after I spoke to that pretty cousin of yours—I believe she said she was—who told me you'd be by to see me someday soon."

Regardless of the audience, there was nothing for James to do but go ahead with the pretense he had adopted to get information from this woman without revealing that the object of his inquiry was the murdered woman whose identity had become known to everyone in Philadelphia.

"I understand," James said, "that you attended a lying-in on the night of September the seventh, and I'd like to make sure that woman was my wife. Please describe her for me."

Mrs. Shields's description of the woman whose childbirth she attended that night could have fit Elizabeth Coons, or any number of other women her age. But when she added to the description, in her eagerness to be helpful, the information that she had seen the woman a few days before in the Southwark Market with her newborn infant in her arms, and that both of them seemed to be "in fine condition," James knew he was barking up the wrong tree and that this midwife could not give him information pertaining to Elizabeth Coons. He quickly improvised a question to put a stop to any further conversation.

"What color of hair did you say the woman had, Mrs. Shields?"

"Why, it were light brown, sir, a lovely light brown."

"Then I'm afraid that could not have been my wife, Mrs. Shields. Her hair is bright red." James added as he rose to leave, "But I do thank you for your willingness to help."

James was even more disappointed by the outcome of this interview than Mrs. Shields and her cronies were. He felt he had been deprived of information that would have been of considerable value had it pertained to Elizabeth Coons, while they had only been deprived of their anticipated entertainment on hearing a husband narrate the circumstances of his wife's running away from home. His expectations had been much more aroused and more consequential than theirs had been.

Upon James's arrival home, Livy and his grandmother saw at once from the expression on his face that he had met with disappointment, and asked to have the details of his visit with Mrs. Shields, which he quickly provided.

"You've had another letter," Grandmère said. "It came while you were out. Perhaps it has something that will raise your spirits. The man who brought this one would not take the coin I offered him for his trouble. He said he had been well paid to bring it and had been told not to take anything more for delivering it."

The letter was addressed in Dr. Franklin's handwriting, which James had come to recognize. But it contained no comforting news.

> My dear James,
> Your report on the German boors is most interesting, but I must decline keeping the appointment you propose. My old enemy the Gout, assisted by his ally the Stone, has me under siege, & I have not left my bed for three days past until this morning, when I had to go out to attend to some business that absolutely could not be put off. That effort has prostrated me to a greater degree than before my sally.
> Be assured, my interest in our investigation has not flagged. It is as keen now as before the sad death of Jacob Maul. We will continue to push ahead to find out the truth concerning the death of Mrs. Coons, if for no other reasons than to restore the Quaker stonecutter's

once impeccable reputation for his son's sake, & to do justice to Mrs. C.

We have much to discuss, & I regret it may be days yet before I am sufficiently recovered to see you. I have had these attacks of gout & stone before and know their probable duration. I assure you we shall converse as soon as possible, for your efforts on my behalf have been heroic and have given me a considerable feeling of obligation toward you. In the meantime, please accept a word of advice. Refrain from any effort to find the Hessian here in Philadelphia. Let us consult before you look for this man of unpredictable temper & violence. Direct your efforts toward locating the midwife who attended Mrs. Coons the night of her disappearance.

You understand, I trust, why I did not give any sign of recognition when we passed each other this morning in the street. You made a good bargain on the mare from the passing glimpse I had of her.

B.F.

Dr. Franklin's indisposition could not have come at a worse time for James. He felt an urgent need to consult his director because, unbeknownst to Dr. Franklin, he had already, through his surrogate Livy, drawn a blank in his attempt to locate a midwife who had attended Elizabeth Coons. Other than the appointment with the writer of the anonymous note summoning him to a meeting that night, he had no prospects for further information. Except for that summons, he seemed to have reached a dead end.

He wondered whether he should ask his brother-in-law Lawrence to accompany him to meet this man who appeared to have been spying on him, but decided he could not involve

Lawrence in possible danger when he was about to become a
father again. Nor could he risk the possibility that the
interview with his summoner might reveal to Lawrence his
connection to Dr. Franklin. It occurred to him that Mr.
Mahoney, who already knew of that connection, would be a
dependable, sturdy companion for the interview that night.
But there was no certainty of getting a message to him and
receiving an answer in time. Besides, Dr. Franklin in his
present condition needed his manservant more than James
did. He would have to keep this assignation alone.

That night, on his way to meet the boy who would guide
him to his appointment with the man who claimed to have
information, James saw that the tin disk with the Roman
numeral IX painted on it was still displayed atop the watch box
at Fourth and Chestnut streets. He recognized the watchman
who stood inside the box, with his rattle, club and lantern
hanging from his belted coat, as someone he had spoken with
in passing by this watch box on former occasions. However
this time he did not tarry to exchange pleasantries with the
watchman, but simply waved to him in greeting, from the
other side of the street and kept going. He wanted to station
himself at the front window of the City Tavern to observe
whoever might pass by before his meeting with the boy in the
white hat.

But except for a limping, horribly emaciated dog, he saw
nothing out of the ordinary in the street before noticing the
watchman at Walnut and Second change the Roman IX on top
of his box to an X. At nearly the same moment, he saw a boy—
who must have been eyeing the box from around the corner—
come from the direction of Front Street toward the City
Tavern. The first lamp he walked beneath showed the color of

his hat, and James knew from its whiteness that this was the usher he was awaiting.

He went out on the street in front of the Tavern to meet the boy and find out who had sent him on his errand and where he was going to take him. But the boy, as soon as he saw James coming toward him, halted too far away for James even to have a clear view of his face, let alone speak with him. Then he turned around, motioning with a swing of his arm and slight motion of his head that James was to follow him, and went back in the direction from which he had come.

James started after him, walking rapidly, intending to diminish the distance between himself and the boy and get a better view of his diminutive conductor. But the boy, perceiving this intention, broke into a trot to prevent any narrowing of the interval between them and increased the distance to more than it had been at the outset. James therefore contented himself with staying at the distance the youngster wished to keep between them.

When they reached Front Street, the boy turned south past the watch box there, which was empty, the change of the hour being the time the watchmen walked their rounds to make sure everything was safe and secure in the part of the city that each was responsible for.

James's guide continued down Front past the boat basin of dressed stone by the Blue Anchor and for three more city squares beyond that, where he left Front and went toward the river on the little street named for William Penn that was barely the width of an alley.

The great city squares of Philadelphia were now behind James and his guide, and with them the illumination of the whale oil lamps that lighted the center of the city on nights when there was no luminous moon. The two of them proceeded by the feeble illumination of a small moon to the bottom of Penn Street, where the boy turned abruptly onto a path that punched through the dense screen of brush along the river. The damp smell of the river's muddy verge was strong.

James hesitated to follow the boy into the brush but had no way of reaching him short of shouting into the darkness, something he was loath to do. Even had he called out, he was sure the boy would have ignored his call. So James turned onto the path.

He discovered it to be worn smooth by the passage of many feet, which reassured him because it suggested that the path led somewhere frequented by men. The thick undergrowth on both sides continually brushed against his coat. Then, abruptly, the brush fell away, and James found himself in a stand of giant willow trees free of undergrowth. The boy was nowhere to be seen.

The faint moonlight filtering down through the trees allowed James a dim view of the nearby river, which appeared to be in the grip of a full tide. Upswelling whorls of water roiled the river's surface, as its powerful stream encountered the irresistible incoming flow from the ocean's rising tide. A chill wind was coming off the river.

He took a few steps into the stand of trees and saw the figure of a tall man at the edge of the river, standing next to a boat drawn up beside other boats that were fastened by ropes to the boles of the willow trees along the riverbank. The man had his boat's painter in his hand and was looking at James.

The sight of this solitary figure waiting motionless against the backdrop of the river arrested James's steps. For a moment he and the man regarded each other in silence; then the man said "Come" and turned slightly toward the boat whose painter he held, as if ready to launch it out onto the river.

James was not so far from this dusky figure as not to be able to see the clothes he was wearing, which appeared to be the same as respectable men wore every day on the streets of Philadelphia.

"Who are you?" James asked across the space that separated them.

The man replied, gesturing toward his boat, "Come, Captain Jamison. Please."

James knew to a certainty that this man who was telling him to join him in his boat to go out on the river was the employer of the boy in the white hat and author of the summons that had brought him to this lonely spot. Why he did not refuse this second, more polite entreaty from this dimly lit figure, James would not have been able to say. But he found himself walking toward the boat and climbing onto the seat in its stern, keeping a watchful eye all the time on his summoner.

In passing close to the man to sit in the boat, he saw that he was in the prime of life, strongly built, and had thick blond mustaches.

As soon as James was seated, the man tossed the end of the painter into the bow of the boat and with a strong push shoved it into the river. With one smooth motion, he swung himself lithely in without getting his feet wet and took the boat's middle seat. Fitting the oars into their thule pins, he gave one of them a powerful pull and the other a push to turn the boat around, and using both oars to pull in the same direction propelled the boat bow-first into the river. He paid no heed to James as he rowed, nor did he speak. All of his attention was concentrated on his rowing, as he looked first over one shoulder and then the other to see where he was going.

They went a good ways out onto the river in this fashion, angling slowly upstream with the tide, leaving the

Pennsylvania side of the river and passing Windmill Island. The boat drew opposite the dark mass of the city's buildings and its lighted streets and the quiet wharves densely packed with ships. The man seemed to have a particular place in mind as he rowed, but where that might be puzzled James. For clearly he was not seeking some landing on the Pennsylvania side of the Delaware; nor did he seem intent on crossing to the Jersey side of the river.

Suddenly, without any sign that he was about to do it, the silent oarsman gave a mighty pull on one oar and an equally vigorous push on the other, the same maneuver he had used before, which swung the boat across the current and arrested its motion through the water. At the same instant, and equally to James's surprise, he shipped his oars, pivoted in his seat, and heaved the boat's anchor—a large stone in a rope web—into the river with a resounding, thumping splash. This stoppage of the boat in midstream and the sudden tossing out of the crude anchor were startling, not only for their unexpectedness but because it did not seem that such an anchor, with perhaps only two fathoms of rope attached to it, could find a purchase in the middle of the Delaware River.

But from the rapidity with which the heavy stone anchor did take hold and did make the boat fast to the river bottom, it was clear that the oarsman had stopped them over shoal water.

Then James recalled the bluff sandbar that lay at about this point in the river opposite the city, just beneath the surface, which more than one ship captain foolish enough to come up the Delaware without hiring a pilot had discovered to his regret by running aground on it.

James's nameless boatman appeared to have put his boat over the sandbar's downstream point. He had positioned the stern of the boat, where James sat, so that it swung slowly back and forth like a pendulum over the deep water against the anchor, while the bow of the boat, where he sat facing James, held steady over shoal water.

Having anchored precisely, the man looked at James for the first time since launching the boat with them in it. James could dimly make out the man's rugged features by the faint light from the moon and the city's lamplight gleaming across the water.

The man said, with a slight foreign accent, "My friends tell me you were looking for me in German Town, Captain Jamison. I saw your posters on the walls in Philadelphia."

Under the circumstances—alone at night in a boat anchored in the middle of a broad river without access to anyone's aid—this pronouncement made James instinctively grip the pistol he was carrying in the pocket of his officer's greatcoat. He doubted, however, that at such close quarters he would be able to withdraw the weapon and cock it with sufficient alacrity to do him any good if this strong, active man wished to assail him, should that be his purpose in bringing him out on the river.

So James withdrew the pistol from his coat and cocked it, to have it ready for use in case of need.

For it was clear to James that the man sitting opposite him in the boat was Sergeant August Weber.

Chapter 20

August Weber saw James draw his pistol and cock it with the heel of his left hand, but the gesture did not seem to alarm him in the least. The situation of two men alone in a boat anchored in the middle of a big river in the dead of night seemed to have its own protocols, which included one of the men holding a loaded pistol leveled at the other and ready to use.

"I know you saw Diedreich," Weber said. "He told me your questions about the Quaker's wife."

James now understood how wrong he had been in his perception of Anton Polzer and his connection to his nephew. Polzer had lied. He had said he didn't know where August Weber lived in Philadelphia. But the truth was that for Weber to have written the note summoning James to this meeting on the river, the residents of the Polzer farm had to have immediately informed Weber of James's visit. This meant that Diedreich Schmidt had probably ridden posthaste into the city from the farm and had spoken to Weber while James was still in German Town having supper, writing up his report to Dr. Franklin, and sleeping soundly. And James remembered that in leaving the field he had seen Polzer and Schmidt walking beside the manure wagon, the older man's arm around his son-in-law's shoulders as he spoke to him.

It was also evident to James, from Weber's reference to "the Quaker's wife," that the three people James had spoken with on the Polzer farmer had mistaken his interest in Lizzy Coons for an interest in her sister Margaret Maul, who had died while Weber and Schmidt lived with the Mauls. So, besides deceiving James, they either had misunderstood him or had decided to believe his real interest was in Margaret Maul's death, not the death of Mrs. Coons, as he had said.

Whatever Weber's former comrade in arms and his uncle had thought of James's questions, however, the man sitting with him in the boat knew about the murder of Lizzy Coons because everyone in Philadelphia was talking about it; and Weber had said he had seen James's handbills placed around town soliciting information on the murdered woman.

"Diedreich and me had no part in killing the Quaker's wife. It is wrong for you to say we did and hound me for it."

So far, the German had been doing all the talking, and James wanted to keep him talking. The woman Weber kept referring to as "the Quaker's wife," Margaret Maul, was not Dr. Franklin's primary object of investigation. But James hoped that by running on about Margaret Maul's death, Weber would say something of consequence regarding his connection to Elizabeth Coons. Weber had control of the boat, but James had the weapon, and as long as he had it he felt he had the upper hand, though he hoped the German would make no threatening move that would require shooting him at such close quarters.

"Our officer ordered us not to harm the American *haus frauen*, and I was a sergeant who always obeyed my officer. I was Diedreich's officer, but he did not always obey me. He had the eye for the sister of the Quaker's wife. When the Quaker killed this woman, it shows he also killed the wife. It is the same thing everywhere. A man who is not punished for a crime will do it again. They ought to have hanged the Quaker the first time. Then he would not kill again."

Weber paused as if expecting a response, but James remained silent. He could not tell whether the former sergeant was being honest. Maybe Weber was saying this to deceive him. Maybe the purpose of the arrangements he had made was to put James in a situation where he would have to listen to what the German had to say without interruptions. The arrangements for this conversation at night out on the river showed he had a talent for stagecraft. Weber continued, like an orator who has rehearsed a speech.

"Only the American judge would say God strangles the woman. Only the crazy man stays in the room where he did a killing with the door bolted. But the judge was more crazy. He let the Quaker go. In Hesse, our Prince would never allow a judge like that authority."

Weber paused again before saying in an indignant tone, "Now the Americans send a captain from their army to hunt me, and accuse me, because I am an *auslander* who fought them in the war. But I obeyed my parole. I am the man of honor. I am the obedient soldier, now an honored clerk."

James decided Weber was at least being sincere in regarding him as a government agent. He appeared to think no private person would ever take an active interest in a matter that was the responsibility of state authorities. Therefore in Weber's eyes James had to be an agent of the state.

But James felt no obligation to explain himself to this equivocal man. He did, however, feel an obligation to Dr. Franklin to find out as much as he could from Weber regarding the Hessian's connection with Elizabeth Coons.

"Did you," James asked, "propose marriage to Elizabeth Coons?"

With the quickness of a rattlesnake striking a stick presented to it, Weber struck with the flat of his hand the thwart of the boat on which he sat. The unexpectedness of the blow made James recoil. It was only by the grace of God that Weber's sudden, violent movement did not cause him to squeeze the trigger of the pistol he had leveled at the Hessian.

Weber let go a volley of oaths in German; then, in a controlled but vehement voice, he said, "*Mein Gott* in heaven, that's a lie! I never look at the woman! Elizabeth played the strumpet with Diedreich and me, always talking to us and asking us questions it was not correct to ask. She gave us no peace. She even made a fight between us who had been friends since we was boys."

"When did you come to Philadelphia to live?" James asked.

"One year before this June."

"Where do you live in the city?"

"Pewter Platter Alley."

"Were you on good terms with your uncle when you left his farm?"

"No, I want something better than to be a farmer. He want me to stay and work for him for nothing. He say I owe it to him because he give Diedreich and me the place to stay on parole."

"That was all? You never had a fight? You never pushed him?"

"Yah. I push him. Once when he grabs me by the arm."

"What work did you do when you came to the city?" James asked. "Did you stay with someone?"

"I was cleaning church. I am the Catholic and priest give me job. I stay with priest at the church of Saint Joseph. Then I take job with Mr. Schomacher at his rope walk. Now I am clerk in a counting house because mine German is good and my English pretty good, and I write a good hand and know to keep accounts. Becker and Fleiss have much trade with Hamburg and the Baltic ports."

"After you came to live in the city, when did you see Elizabeth Coons?" James asked.

August Weber took a deep breath and let it out, saying calmly, "I never see her, not once since Diedreich and me live in the Quaker's house. She is not good woman. I got me good job now."

Then he fell silent, and James let him have time to think and to say whatever he pleased. After awhile, he went on.

"It was bad for us when they put us to live in that family. Never I spoke to Elizabeth. She spoke to me. Always asking me and Diedreich where we live in the old country, what we do there, how was our families, do we like America. *Mein Gott*, we was soldiers sent here by our Prince under orders! There is others could tell you what kind of woman she is. She plays the strumpet with Diedreich and me."

All of this, of course, contradicted the uniform testimony of neighbors, friends, and family—what William Maul had told James, Kate Merkle's report that Elizabeth Coons had said one of the Hessians was "mooning" over her, and Elizabeth's letters saying that one of them had tried to grab her and kiss her when she was alone. But James had to admit that Dr. Franklin's conclusion that Mrs. Coons had been pregnant out of wedlock and had borne a child the night she was murdered supported Weber's contention she might dally with a man.

"Why do you say she was a strumpet?" James asked Weber.

"I know more than some who think they know everything. But I keep my mouth shut. I do not say what hurts another. You must stop hounding me. I have good job now. I am guilty of nothing. Herr Becker would send me away if he knew you were after me."

"To whom are you referring when say you know more than others who think they know everything?"

"I do not say what hurts another," Weber repeated.

James didn't understand what this meant, but didn't comment further on it.

"Have you been spying on me?"

"*Nein.*"

"How could you know where I eat in town," James asked, "and where I live, if you haven't been spying on me?"

"The poster say where to bring information to you. I go to City Tavern and ask for you. The man say to me you take meals at that place, and he saw you eat there this morning. The new City Directory has your house."

For a few minutes neither man spoke. James kept his eyes on Weber, and Weber, with his eyes downcast, leaned forward with his elbows on his knees. Then the German looked up. "Can I have permission, Captain Jamison, to leave the river?"

James consented, but added, "Be careful what you do with those oars, Weber. Don't make a sudden move. This pistol might go off."

Weber merely grunted in reply, and, turning around in his seat, began pulling up the anchor. Once the anchor was in the boat, he fitted each oar slowly and carefully between its thule pins and began rowing back to the Pennsylvania side of the river.

"Put me in at the boat basin next to the Blue Anchor Tavern," James said, "above where you picked me up."

Weber grunted his assent again and headed the boat in the direction of the Blue Anchor Tavern, which stayed open through the night for whatever custom offered off the river.

The tavern's lamps, visible in the distance, were the only lights showing below the center of the city. The German rowed toward them.

As the boat glided into the still waters of the boat basin next to the tavern, Weber grabbed an iron ring set in the stones and held the boat to the side of the basin. James stepped out onto its pavement without speaking again to Weber. The Hessian rowed out onto the river without looking back and was soon lost in the darkness. The American uncocked his pistol.

Out on the river in the boat Captain James Jamison had been so focused on Weber that he had not noticed the river's chill dampness. Now he felt cold to the bone, and his teeth began to chatter. Time and again, during his winter campaigns with the army, he had noticed that despite his susceptibility to cold it did not affect him until after a battle was over. He had concluded from these experiences that the mind dominates the body's ordinary susceptibilities.

James entered the Blue Anchor's taproom and found only a barman, drowsing in a chair next to the fireplace.

James ordered a hot rum and while the drink was being made he stood in front of the fire, as close as he could get without singeing his clothes.

When these remedies for his profound chill had had their effect, he asked the barman to bring him paper, pen, ink, and another drink, and drew up a table and chair near the fire to write his report for Dr. Franklin concerning his encounter with Weber. He wanted to do this while the expressions the former sergeant had used were still fresh in his mind, and to put the report in the secret mail drop at Franklin Court on his way home, so Dr. Franklin would get it as soon as possible. He hoped the good doctor would be able to receive him soon, without much further delay, to discuss where they were in their investigation, because having spoken with Weber and having failed to find the midwife who had attended Mrs. Coons in her birthing, James felt he was at an impasse and did not know what he should do next. He seemed no closer now to knowing by whose hand Mrs. Coons had met her death than he had been at the outset of his inquiries, ten days before.

In going from the Blue Anchor to Franklin Court with his report, he decided to stop at the City Tavern on the way, to speak with the night manager, Mr. Morley, who had not been on duty earlier that night. He wanted to get Mr. Morley's recollection of the man who had asked for him without leaving any written message.

The description of the man, it turned out, fit August Weber —tall, muscular, thick blond mustaches, respectably dressed.

The next day brought no word from Dr. Franklin.

James decided to send Livy back to Southwark to look for a wet nurse who might have taken to breast the baby born to Mrs. Coons on the night of September seventh, on the theory that her killer could have put the baby with a wet nurse. But Livy's efforts in this regard proved as unsuccessful as her previous efforts to find the midwife who had attended the dead woman's childbirth. Livy's further attempts to talk with the midwife who had gone to Chester were also unavailing. The woman had not yet returned to Philadelphia.

The day after Livy canvassed Southwark a second time for James, word came of a disaster at the Jamisons' glasshouse in the Northern Liberties. The furnace had cracked. This made the manufacture of glass impossible. Mr. Bartlett and Lawrence were examining the crack, thinking how to repair it. They wanted James to come up and see it, and give his advice.

Later that afternoon, while James was still at the glasshouse, Stephen Lunt rode Jenny into the yard of the Jamison house in the western suburbs.

James had sent him to tell Grandmère that Jane was in labor.

Grandmère ordered Stephen to go to Mr. Morton's livery near the Schuylkill Ferry to tell him to send a chaise to drive her and Livy to the Northern Liberties. Stephen was to return to Lawrence's house with all haste to tell everyone that she and Livy would be there as soon as they could.

Grandmère and her maid hurriedly packed a small trunk with things they would need while they stayed in the Northern Liberties to be with Jane during her lying-in. They locked the house and were waiting out front with the trunk when the chaise arrived.

Chapter 21

The rest of that day was an extraordinary one for the Jamisons. Jane and her baby were their first concern, but the threat posed by the shutdown of the glasshouse, the foundation of the family's livelihood, could not be ignored.

When Grandmère arrived at her former home, where Jane and Lawrence now lived, her old friend Eleanor Stone, Jane's midwife, assured her the baby's arrival was not imminent and possibly would not happen until the following day. Mrs. Stone went home, having instructed Grandmère to send Livy to get her when Jane's pains became more frequent and regular. Nonetheless, there was much coming and going in preparation for the birth on the part of Jane's special friends Lucy Alison and Catherine Tollman, who had pledged to stay with her until her baby came, and on the part of the recent arrivals on the scene.

As was customary, James and Lawrence and other men were barred from seeing Jane and could not enter her room. They were, in fact, prohibited from seeing Jane for an entire week after her baby's birth.

Grandmère went out to her damaged furnace to discuss the problem of repairing it with her grandson and Lawrence. After also soliciting the opinions of Mr. Bartlett and the other veteran glassblower of the house, Mr. Tipton, she decided that it would be better for the future of their enterprise to build a new and bigger furnace rather than to attempt to repair the crack in the old one.

"With the war finished, the number of people living in Philadelphia will increase and the need for glass will grow," she predicted in justifying her decision. When she was informed of the probable cost of constructing a new furnace, Grandmère surprised them by declaring her capital a good deal more than sufficient to cover such an expenditure.

James and Lawrence began calculating how long it would take to dismantle the old furnace and construct a new one, and discussed how to procure the necessary materials to build it, and which bricklayers should be recruited.

Mr. Bartlett, the Tiptons, Mr. Tift and the juvenile workers of the glasshouse began at once tearing out the old furnace, salvaging as many of its firebricks as they could.

There was little sleep in the house that night. Jane's baby arrived at four o'clock in the morning. Livy brought him out from the room where he had been born for his father and uncle to see and admire, her face filled with love, despite her fatigue, as she looked on the tiny, red-faced person with closed, puffy eyes and clenched fists before handing Lawrence his new son to hold. She gazed fondly on the two men, but especially on James, as they took turns holding in their arms the little lump of humanity that was to be given the name Franklin Sheraton, asleep in his little white wool cap and jacket and wrapped in the wool blanket his great-grandmother had knitted for him.

The next morning James rode Jenny home to give Cheval his feed and water, going by way of Market Street to see if the carriage gate peephole was open in signal that a message from Dr. Franklin had been left for him at their secret mail drop.

But the peephole was closed. These obligations fulfilled, he returned to the Northern Liberties to help in the removal of the old furnace his grandfather had built. He spent the whole day at the glasshouse engaged in this hard physical labor, returning home again that evening because Grandmère did not feel she should leave her house untenanted a second night. Once again he passed by Franklin Court and looked for a signal from Dr. Franklin without seeing one.

James spent the next day, Saturday, in the same fashion, only Livy, on instructions from her mistress, was sent home with him that evening, riding tandem behind him on Jenny, her arms clasped around his waist. Grandmère was concerned, she said, that James was not getting a proper breakfast when he had to prepare it himself, and Olivia's presence would remedy that. As Livy had gotten up on Jenny from the mounting block, aided by the pull of James's right arm, Grandmère had also instructed her maid to be sure to prepare James's usual Saturday night bath, which she said he would probably forego if he had to heat the water himself.

On the way to the house in the western suburbs, Livy complimented the sorrel mare's movements and how easy they made it for her to ride tandem. She asked James to tell her how he had acquired Jenny, and he narrated the particulars of his journey to Princeton and Hopewell and everything he had seen, done, and learned in those places, including a full account of John Leet's sermon. He said nothing to her, however, of who had given him the money for the horse and its saddle, nor did he mention his trip to German Town and the encounter he had had there with the family of Anton Polzer.

James had never ridden tandem with a female before; nor had Livy ever been on a horse with a man. And though her father had many times let her ride his workhorses in from the field bareback when she was a girl, she had never been on a well-bred, lively saddle horse. By the time they arrived home, James and Livy were on more personal terms than they had ever been before, and she wondered during the ride how she would feel sitting in the parlor by herself, without Grandmère, knowing James was just a few feet away in the kitchen, naked, taking his bath.

In addition to preparing James's bath every Saturday, Livy always heated the water for her bath on Mondays, the day she did the household washing and ironing, and for her mistress's bath on Wednesdays. The water for the baths was prepared in the kitchen, where the house's biggest fireplace was. The big tin tub for bathing, with the flaring high sides, was kept in the washhouse where the clothes washing was done, just outside the kitchen door. But she had never been alone in the house with James on his bath day. As soon as they got to the house, James offered to draw the water for his bath from the well in the back yard, and did so as soon as he had taken care of the horses. It seemed to Livy that he, too, was a bit embarrassed by their situation.

The next day being the Sabbath, no work would of course be done on the new furnace, but James and Livy rode back to the Northern Liberties after breakfast so they could go to church with Lawrence and Grandmère while Jane's maid Abigail stayed with her, the twins, and the new baby. As always, Livy and Grandmère cooked the family's Sunday supper. But that night Livy and James returned to Grandmère's house in the western suburbs.

Since Monday was washday, Livy stayed at Grandmère's house to tend to that major chore and did not go with James to the Northern Liberties. James, on his way to and from the

Northern Liberties to help with the furnace, found no message from Dr. Franklin.

When he got back home Monday evening, he heard women's voices coming from the parlor and found Livy taking tea with an unknown woman of middle age. In introducing Mrs. Opdahl, Livy told James, "She is from Southwark and wishes to speak with you."

The woman herself added to this introduction, "I did not know of the Quaker Murders until this afternoon, Captain Jamison. I've been out of town for some weeks, visiting relatives. In giving me the news, my family showed me your notice in the papers asking for information on Lizzy Coons, and I looked you up in the Directory."

Whatever information Mrs. Opdahl had on Elizabeth Coons, she had withheld it from Livy and was keeping it for James. She clearly enjoyed having the attention of an officer and gentleman who was becoming well known in Philadelphia.

"I knew Eliza Coons," she said, "only from seeing her go about her errands in Southwark. We were not friends. I knew her by sight, and I dare say she knew me in the same way. She seemed respectable enough, though I never understood why she held Maul blameless in the death of that sister of hers, the nurse. That did strike me as queer. I always suspected the man was worse than he seemed. Eliza's murder shows how right I was."

Mrs. Opdahl accepted Livy's offer to fill her cup of tea, then continued.

"I am not a person who mixes truth with fancy, Captain Jamison," she declared, with becoming self-importance, "and I can say in all truthfulness that the day before I left on my trip, when I passed Eliza Coons on the street, she had the look about her. My family said you might not be interested in this information anymore, now that Maul is dead. But I said you were keeping your ad in the newspapers and that meant you were still interested. So I have come to you, and here I am."

What did Mrs. Opdahl mean in saying Elizabeth Coons had "the look"? James did not understand at all and wondered whether this woman was simply a busybody. But his first impression of her had been that she was a woman of sense; so he asked her to explain what she meant by "the look."

"Why, my lands, ain't that like a man," Mrs. Opdahl said, addressing Livy. "Like I said, I passed Eliza Coons in the street just days before she was killed, and she had the look of a woman in the state or I wasn't baptized Katrina Opdahl. I can tell by just looking at them, the ones that's with child. It's stronger in some than others, but even the ugly ones get the glow. It's like a flower coming into full bloom. You can tell they're in the state just by looking at them if you know what you're looking for, even when they may show no outward sign of the embarrassment."

In agreeing with these assertions about the aura pregnant women often have, Livy said she had first noticed the phenomenon when an aunt of hers was "in the state."

James thanked Mrs. Opdahl for this information regarding her impression that Mrs. Coons had been pregnant at the time of her death—information that confirmed the impression Philomen Lyons had already conveyed to him and Dr. Franklin —and told her it might lead him to further discoveries in his attempt to find out how Mrs. Coons had met her death.

Livy sat with downcast eyes taking little sips of tea. But as soon as James finished thanking Mrs. Opdahl, she spoke up and said—even though Mrs. Opdahl had not informed them of where she had been on her visit out of town—"I believe you said you have been visiting relatives in Chester, Mrs. Opdahl?"

"Yes, that's true. I have been to Chester. My niece lives there, and she had a difficult lying-in. I went down to help, and stayed on to lend a hand in nursing her back to health."

"So you are a midwife?" Livy asked. "Have you, since your return from Chester heard that a countryman whose wife ran away while near to her lying-in has been asking around among the midwives of Southwark to learn whether she had the baby?"

"Yes, I am a midwife, and my familiars did inform me of those inquiries."

James, in listening to this exchange, suddenly realized that Livy was telling him that this woman was the midwife she had failed to interview because the woman had gone down to Chester.

"I believe," Livy said, "the man from the country was interested in any births that might have occurred the first week in September."

"So I heard," Mrs. Opdahl replied. "It's a pity I wasn't in town when the poor man was making his inquires. I might have directed him to a former midwife, a woman named Hannah Farthing, who is rumored to have attended a woman giving birth about that time."

"Could this Hannah Farthing have known Eliza Coons, do you think, Mrs. Opdahl?" Livy asked.

"Why, I suppose she might. For her brother worked for the Mauls once, the people Eliza lived with. He was their hostler, if I am not mistaken."

Livy, having elicited this momentous information, said, "I see," and took a long sip of her tea while looking at James with merry brown eyes over the rim of her teacup.

James stared back at her. Then as he realized the import of what she had just uncovered for his benefit, he broke into a broad smile of appreciation. And Livy slowly nodded twice in silent acknowledgment of his realization. That Hannah Farthing was a former midwife, rumored to have helped a woman in labor around the time Elizabeth Coons disappeared, and was a sister of the Mauls' former hostler. This might well be the information James had been looking for that would unlock the mystery of Elizabeth Coons's final hours.

"Why doesn't this Hannah Farthing practice midwifery any longer?" James asked.

Mrs. Opdahl replied, "She didn't have the skill, Captain Jamison. She lacked ability. She's a wool spinner now. None of the midwives the young woman made inquiries of mentioned Hannah because none of us thinks of her as a midwife anymore. Besides, it's only a rumor she attended a woman's lying-in earlier this month. No one *knows* that she did. What is certain, though, is that no woman has asked Hannah to be at her baby's birthing these five years past. What woman, I ask you, would go to a wool spinner when there are more than enough good midwives in Southwark to choose from?"

Before James could ask how he could find this former midwife, Livy again went to the heart of the matter by saying, "Perhaps it might be worth Captain Jamison's time to meet Mrs. Farthing, since she could have known Eliza Coons through her brother, the hostler. Unless he is of the opinion that nothing would be gained by doing that."

"Yes, I would like to speak with this woman," James quickly interjected. "Where might I find her, Mrs. Opdahl?"

His affirmation seemed to flatter the midwife's sense of importance, and she replied, "I would be glad to make the connection for you, Captain Jamison. The location of Hannah Farthing's apartment is too complicated to explain. But I could take you there. I'd be most happy to."

This was not at all what James wanted, but there was nothing he could say to prevent Mrs. Opdahl from taking him to Hannah Farthing's apartment if she wouldn't tell him how to find it.

Accordingly, an appointment was made for eight thirty the next morning, for Mrs. Opdahl to go with James to meet the sister of Jacob Maul's former hostler.

As soon as the midwife departed, James exclaimed, "Livy, you're a wonder! I feel like hugging you," and he looked at her longingly, but made no move to hug her; nor did she make any move to encourage the idea. Then he went up to his room, wrote the report to Dr. Franklin on this tremendous discovery, and took it immediately to Franklin Court to leave in Dr. Franklin's post.

Mrs. Opdahl accompanied James on foot the next morning to the apartment of the former midwife Hannah Farthing, which was at the end of a warren of passageways having many turns. But there was no response to Mrs. Opdahl's knock. However, she was not to be put off in a matter that involved her appearance of importance. She simply opened the door of the apartment, which had no lock, and went in, declaring that they would wait for Hannah Farthing's return, claiming in justification of this extraordinary conduct her long acquaintance with the woman.

James protested that he could return later, on his own, now that he knew the way. But Mrs. Opdahl would have none of that and declared anew her intention that they both should wait for the wool spinner's return. James resigned himself to the wait but silently hoped Hannah Farthing would not return while he was in her room with Mrs. Opdahl.

The meanly furnished apartment of Mrs. Farthing was at the back of the building, which was off a small, nameless alley by the river near South Water Street. Besides the plain wooden chair Mrs. Opdahl occupied, there was no other accommodation for sitting except the woman's bed, which James was averse to sitting on, so he stood the whole time he was in the room.

The rest of the apartment's meager furnishings appeared to consist of the belongings of a person with few material resources. There was a spinning wheel that had seen hard usage and a scarred table having on it a tin bowl and plate and a guttered candle in a tin holder. There was also a water pail and dipper, a bent poker, a three-legged cast-iron frying pan of the kind called a spider, a Dutch Oven, a pile of miserable kindling, a short broom worn down to a nub, a food box with a lid, a spoon, a knife, a fork, a cup, scissors and a wool comb, a crude, doorless clothes press, and the jorden. The bedclothes were patched but clean; the floor, swept.

The only light coming into the room was through a shoulder-high, dusty window in the wall farthest from the entrance. In idly walking over to the window to see what sort of view it offered, a bit of color on the shelf inside the doorless clothes press caught James's eye. It was the blue dress of a doll with a porcelain face.

Only iron control kept James from stepping over to the clothes press to inspect the doll, but his awareness that Mrs. Opdahl was watching his movements got him past the open clothes press to the window. He stood at the window, pretending to look out its dusty panes at the view of the river they offered, while the portentous fact of the presence in this apartment of a doll matching the description of the one missing from Elizabeth Coons's bedchamber animated his mind.

The silence in the room grew oppressive since neither James nor Mrs. Opdahl had anything to say to each other or any interest in making an effort to cultivate a friendship. Only the circumstance of his wanting to talk with the woman who lived in this dingy room and Mrs. Opdahl's tenacious curiosity to hear what he might say to the woman, and what she might say to him, had brought them together.

Finally, James turned from the window and told his companion he would wait no longer. He did not think Mrs. Farthing would be returning any time soon, and he had other things to do. Mrs. Opdahl reluctantly agreed with his evident resolve to leave.

In saying goodbye to her out on the street, James thanked Mrs. Opdahl for taking an interest in his affairs and promised to return on another occasion to talk with Mrs. Farthing, now that he knew the way. Mrs. Opdahl said it had been her pleasure to be of service to him and expressed a hope that he would inform her of the result of any conversation he had with the former midwife. He said he would, and they parted on amicable terms.

James walked as quickly as he could to the City Tavern, asked if he had any messages, which he did not, and requested the use of a private room and writing materials. He wrote to Dr. Franklin saying he had seen a doll in a blue dress where Hannah Farthing lived and describing her apartment's poverty and giving its location. He also said in the report that he would return to the woman's home to have a word with her as soon as he could.

In leaving his message for Dr. Franklin, James found that his report of the previous evening, saying he was going to see

Mrs. Farthing in company with Mrs. Opdahl, had been removed. In its place was a slip of paper dated that morning saying, "Come tonight at eleven if you receive this in time—if not, tomorrow at that hour."

Chapter 22

Dr. Franklin's message appointing a time to confer produced great elation in James. It would allow him the benefit of his director's advice on how to deal with Hannah Farthing before calling on the woman.

James walked to the Northern Liberties and spent the rest of the day working there on the new furnace. He went home to eat the supper Livy had prepared for him and rest. On going to Franklin Court that evening, he took with him the portable escritoire Dr. Franklin had lent to him for his trip to New Jersey.

At the appointed hour, he rapped rhythmically at the back door of Dr. Franklin's mansion-house and was instantly admitted by Mr. Mahoney, who escorted him up to his master's study on the second floor. The bespectacled Dr. Franklin was taking a bath in a bulky copper tub shaped like a shoe. The furniture in the room had been moved back against the walls to clear a space for this curious tub, which had been set on a large sheet of oiled paper in the middle of the room.

Only Dr. Franklin's white shoulders and arms were visible above the tub's leather-padded rim. He was wearing a fur hat and reading some papers fastened by cloth tapes to a sloping shelf across the tub's opening.

"Greetings, James!" Dr. Franklin said in a hearty voice. "It is good to see you. Please take the chair I had Mr. Mahoney put by my tub so we may converse easily."

James did as directed, and said, "It is a pleasure to see you looking so well, Dr. Franklin. I compliment you on the return of your health."

"Yes, it is a blessing," Dr. Franklin replied. "I don't believe I have ever felt better in my whole life than during the day just ending, and this refreshing bath is making me feel even better. You, too, look well. Your journey to New Jersey on my behalf has not disagreed with you. Has your sister's baby been born?"

"Yes, sir. It was a boy. A fine big boy. They named him Franklin."

"Did they now. That was nice of your brother-in-law and sister. The world needs more Franklins. You know, I suppose, that the word means a property owner or freeholder."

Mr. Mahoney, unlike his behavior on James's previous visits, did not withdraw but rather sat on a low stool on the other side of the tub so he could respond to any need of his master, who, being in the tub, could not reach the cord against the wall to summon his servant.

"I have been reading your reports," Dr. Franklin said. "Your description of Hannah Farthing's apartment and Mrs. Coons's blue doll."

James then noticed that the papers on the sloping shelf of Dr. Franklin's ingenious, cozy bathtub were his.

"We now know where Mrs. Coons's blue doll ended up that night," Franklin said.

"Then you think, as I do, that the blue doll I saw belonged to Mrs. Coons?" James asked.

"It would be strange indeed if there were a pair of blue dolls in this case, one belonging to Mrs. Coons and another to the former midwife Mrs. Farthing. We can safely assume, I think, that there is only the one, the one Mrs. Coons took with her the night she left Jacob Maul's house."

"But why would she take it to Hannah Farthing?" James asked.

"Why, indeed? You ask the question that is of most importance, I think," Dr. Franklin rejoined. "And in this connection, let us consider these related questions: Did Mrs. Coons take the doll with her that night because it was an irreplaceable memento and she did not expect to ever return to the Mauls'? Or, did she take the costly French doll because it was the only thing of value in her possession that she could lay her hands on, and took it to barter for Mrs. Farthing's services as a midwife?

"The fact that she did not take any clothes with her suggests the latter conclusion. All the information you have gathered, James, points to the probability that she gave birth the night she was murdered. Your most recent information— the impression of Mrs. Opdahl, an experienced midwife, that Elizabeth Coons was pregnant at the time of her death—jibes with the 'notion' of Mrs. Lyons. The doll being in Mrs. Farthing's possession plus the rumor that she attended a lying-in in early September give further credence to that hypothesis.

"The poverty in Mrs. Farthing's apartment that you observed and described for me, James, leads me to suspect Mrs. Coons believed Mrs. Farthing would have to be given something to perform the services of a midwife. That the brother of Mrs. Farthing was the Mauls' hostler and part of the same household as Mrs. Coons for a number of years indicates she could have learned from him that his sister had been a midwife and lived in poverty. He may also have told her where his sister lived. She could have remembered these things as she felt the onset of her labor. Everything fits a pattern, James. A pattern consistent with the rumor Mrs. Opdahl reported of Hannah Farthing's attendance at a woman's lying-in around the seventh of September."

James asked, "But if the doll is evidence that Mrs. Coons was in the former midwife's apartment the night she died, how can we get Mrs. Farthing to tell us what happened?"

"Since a farthing is less than a penny," Dr. Franklin said, smiling, "perhaps we might offer the woman a penny for her thoughts. Let us suppose poverty has hardened Mrs. Farthing's heart, and made her unwilling to help others merely from a sense of charity. An offer of money so munificent she could not refuse the bribe would loosen her tongue."

As usual, James found Dr. Franklin's advice clear and reasonable. But he thought he also perceived a serious flaw in it.

"But if the extreme poverty in which she lives has made her grasping, why didn't she answer our notice, which promised a reward for information on Lizzy Coons?"

"Ah, my dear James, you have again formulated the question most worth considering. That Mrs. Farthing did not answer our ad suggests that some other factor, a factor more powerful than poverty, weighs on her mind. Fear."

"But why should she fear me?" James asked.

"No, not you, James. She fears the person who strangled Mrs. Coons, or the law, or both of them at once, if she tells anyone what she knows."

At this point, Dr. Franklin informed Mr. Mahoney he needed more hot water in his bath.

As soon as Mr. Mahoney was gone, Dr. Franklin said, "We must offer Mrs. Farthing something besides money to overcome her fear. We must also offer her protection. You must convince her that no harm will come to her from the authorities or from anyone else if she confides in us—provided she has done no one any harm."

Dr. Franklin asked James to go into his bedroom and told him how to release the catch on a secret panel in the wainscoting behind the little tapestry of St. George slaying the dragon, where he would find a green silk bag with coins in it, which he was to bring.

When James came back with the bag, Dr. Franklin took from it three newly minted coins of fine gold, each crisply stamped with the profile of the French king, Louis XVI; then he told James to return the bag to the secret recess and secure it again.

Each one of these gleaming, handsome coins, James thought, when he returned from putting the bag of gold pieces back in its hiding place, had to be worth many months' wages for an ordinary workman. In his absence, Dr. Franklin had placed the three shining coins in a row on the lip of the sloping reading shelf of his tub and was admiring them.

"You are to take these three Louis to Mrs. Farthing tomorrow morning, James," Dr. Franklin said, "and offer them to her in exchange for telling us everything she knows of Mrs. Coons's last hours. I am sure you will find her at home this time. The worthy Mrs. Opdahl was remiss in forgetting that Tuesday is the weekly market for wool in Philadelphia. Mrs. Farthing was not in her apartment when you went there with Mrs. Opdahl probably because she was off buying wool to spin. You will, I think, find her busy at her spinning wheel tomorrow morning, for poverty is a taskmaster of the most severe kind.

"After you have persuaded Hannah Farthing to tell her story, it must be reduced to writing and signed by her. To carry out this part of the plan, use the portable escritoire you have brought this evening to return to me. Give the woman no money unless she signs her confession. Please be very particular about that."

Dr. Franklin handed the gold coins to James who put them in the deepest pocket of his coat, where he felt the pleasant heaviness of their combined weight.

"After she has signed her confession, bring it to me directly, James. I think the time has come for us to move swiftly."

The hard and fast rule Dr. Franklin had laid down—that James's visits to Franklin Court were to be made only under cover of darkness at an appointed time—did not square with this order to bring Mrs. Farthing's confession to Franklin Court as soon as he had obtained it. James therefore asked him if he had understood his host correctly.

"Yes, come straight here tomorrow as soon as you have Mrs. Farthing's signed testimony. Mr. Mahoney and I will be alone for the next several days. My daughter and her children are leaving at dawn tomorrow for a stay of a week at the farm in West Jersey that my grandson Temple is in charge of. My son-in-law, Mr. Bache, is away on business at Wilmington for several days more, and has taken his slave, Rob, along with him. I have given the other servants leave with pay for the next few days, telling them that in the family's absence I can get along with just Mr. Mahoney to serve me, and that they will be paid their wages all the same. Until the eleventh of October, I have Franklin Court entirely to myself to finish this business of ours."

In concluding his conversation with James, Dr. Franklin advised him to encourage Hannah Farthing to experience the smoothness and weight of the three gold coins herself. He was to promise her two of the coins after she signed her testimony and the third coin on condition that she not communicate with her brother or allow him to speak to her during the next two days. James was to emphasize in his conversation with Mrs. Farthing that no harm would come to her provided she herself had done no harm to anyone.

"I will send Mr. Mahoney to stand watch at the door to the building where Mrs. Farthing lives to prevent her running away if she takes alarm and tries to flee. He tells me he knows the building you described in your report and says that it has but one entrance. If you succeed in your endeavor with the woman, pause at the door as you leave and remove your hat. That will signal to Mr. Mahoney that he can leave his post."

Mr. Mahoney reentered the room at this moment, carrying a basin and a large kettle of steaming water. He placed the basin under the spigot in the "toe" of the shoe-like bathtub and drew off some of the tepid water. He then poured the hot water from the kettle slowly into the tub through a small lid in the tongue of the "shoe." As he lifted the lid, James saw what made the shoe so bulky. The copper tub was lined with cedar wood.

When he arrived home, James found Livy asleep on the parlor sofa, just inside the front door. The nub of her candle had almost guttered out. On hearing his footsteps coming into the parlor she woke and stretched her arms.

"James, I'm glad you're home. I was worried, and decided to wait up for you but fell asleep. What time is it?"

"It must be close to three, I think. The watchmen were calling two when I left the city."

"Let me help you off with your coat," Livy said. "Come out to the kitchen, and I'll serve you some of the oyster soup I made, to warm you up after your walk in the cold."

In the kitchen Livy served him a bowl of steaming hot oyster soup and put a spoonful of butter in it. As James sat down to this welcome food, Livy got out the bread she had baked that afternoon and began to cut slices of it for him. While she was telling him of the book of manners she had begun reading that evening to pass the time until his return, she all of a sudden let out a little yelp and threw down the bread knife, exclaiming, "Oh, mercy!" James sprang to his feet and went to her.

Blood was running from a cut to the ring finger of her left hand.

James pulled out the clean handkerchief Livy had given him that morning and wrapped it around her finger and told her to clamp down on the handkerchief. With his left arm around her waist, he moved her to the bench by the kitchen table. "Sit here, Livy. Squeeze the handkerchief. I'll be right back!"

Then James ran into the back yard, pulled up a bucket of fresh, cold water from the well and carried it back into the house, setting it on the kitchen table.

He took the bloody handkerchief from her finger and said, "Put your hand in the water, Livy. It'll clean your wound. I have some bandages upstairs. I'll be right down. Just wait here."

"It's nothing, James!" she called after him as he ran upstairs. "Only a little cut! Your soup is getting cold."

When James returned with the roll of bandages, he straddled the bench where Livy sat and, taking her hand out of the bucket of water, dabbed it dry with some of the bandages. He had trouble getting Livy's injured finger tightly bandaged because besides his good right hand he had only the claw of his left hand to use. She had to help him with the bandaging. Together, they got the bandage on her finger tied, and when they were finished, he raised her injured hand to his lips with his good hand and kissed the bandage.

"It would be awful," he said, "if anything serious was to happen to you."

She leaned forward on the bench and, putting her arm around his neck, gave him a gentle, quick hug, hiding from his sight the tears welling up in her eyes.

Wednesday morning, as Dr. Franklin had predicted, Hannah Farthing—a woman around fifty years of age with a care-worn, small, round face, grizzled hair, and a single continuous eyebrow—answered James's knock at her door. She was highly suspicious of his purpose in visiting her, and he had trouble getting her to let him into her room until he showed her one of the gold coins and told her he might give it to her, along with two others like it, if she answered some questions on midwifery for him that only she could answer.

Once seated inside the apartment—he on the room's only chair and she on the bed—James drew the chair close to the bed and took the other two *louis d'or* from his coat pocket and placed the three gold coins on the patched, clean bedcover. While he told Hannah Farthing he was a private citizen interested in a matter that only she could help him understand, he arranged the gleaming gold pieces into different patterns: a triangle pointed toward her, a triangle pointed away from her, and variously oriented straight lines. She never took her eyes from the fascinating, gleaming discs as he moved them around on her bedcover.

Then James invited her to pick up the coins. At first she touched them tentatively with the tips of her fingers, as if these foreign objects were exotic animals that, despite their beauty and seeming inertia, could be dangerous. She had obviously never seen this sort of money. Then, one by one, she took the three gold coins into her hands. She rubbed each of them between her thumb and forefinger, and discovered the luxurious, sensuous lubricity peculiar to refined gold.

As she did this, James informed her in the plainest possible terms that whatever she might say to him in answer to his questions would never be made known to anyone who would cause her harm. She heard what he said, but only dreamily. The reality she was giving her fullest attention to lay in her hands. Only when he saw she was thoroughly enamored of the trio of regal coins did he mention the name Elizabeth Coons. "I understand that Elizabeth Coons came to visit you the night she gave birth."

This remark made an instant, radical change in Hannah Farthing's behavior. She stopped fondling the coins and put them down on the bed.

"I never had any truck with that woman!" she declared. "Whoever told you I did is lying!"

Without thought or premeditation, and impelled by an overwhelming desire to scotch her denial, because he was tired of not getting at the truth, James strode over to the doorless clothes press and snatched up the porcelain-faced doll in the blue dress he knew was there. Bringing it back to Hannah Farthing, he thrust it before her face, saying angrily, "What's this? Do you have the audacity to say Elizabeth Coons did not give you this?"

At first she made no reply, but simply sat there on the bed looking at the doll as though it were something never before seen and of no concern to her. After putting on this act a moment or two, she began to look around rather aimlessly, as if nerving herself to dash from the room. James hoped Mr. Mahoney was on duty in case she did bolt.

But she remained seated on the bed, and James sat down again in the chair, pocketing the doll as he did so and gathering up the coins.

"What is it you want to know?" Mrs. Farthing murmured.

"I want to know everything concerning the night Mrs. Coons came here and had her baby. Remember, no harm will come to you for telling me everything you know. If you tell only the truth, the gold I have shown you will be yours. But you must promise not to tell your brother Solomon we have spoken. You must not speak to him or let him speak with you for the next two days. Will you promise me that, Mrs. Farthing?"

"You know Solomon?"

"I've met him, and I don't want you to speak with him or allow him to speak with you for the next two days."

"If Solomon knew I spoke to you of that night, he'd tear me limb from limb! He would! He made me swear the most horrible oath you can imagine that I would never tell anyone what happened here that night. He would be the death of me if he knew I'd spoken with you!"

These passionate words loosened a torrent of pent up confession from the former midwife that she was evidently glad to release.

James listened attentively to the story Hannah Farthing told him of that night and the history of her relationship with Lizzy Coons, someone she'd known of but had never met before Lizzy had come to her with the doll, asking for help.

When she finished, James said, "Now I will write down everything you have said, just as you told it to me, and you will sign the paper."

"But I only told you," Mrs. Farthing protested, "because you already knew Lizzy Coons came to me. I swear I have done no wrong! I only tried to help the woman! Why must I sign a paper? I won't do it!"

"If you've done no wrong," James replied, "and, having heard your story, I believe you haven't, then you have nothing to fear. Unless you sign what I will write, I can't give you the gold. If you sign the paper I will write, you will have the three coins I have shown you right now, and please believe me, Mrs. Farthing, they are worth more than you could earn in a year of spinning wool day and night."

Having seen and heard how fearful she was of her brother, James knew he did not have to withhold one of the gold coins to keep her from speaking with him.

After some further resistance, Hannah Farthing finally agreed to sign, and did sign, a written summary of her testimony.

James left the wool spinner a richer woman than she had ever been in her life or had ever hoped to be.

In leaving the building where Hannah Farthing lived, he doffed his hat to signal to Francis Mahoney—whom he did not see—that he could leave his post.

Chapter 23

James took Hannah Farthing's confession to Dr. Franklin as he had been directed to do, entering Franklin Court by way of the locked door in the west boundary wall. But though he had gone straight to Dr. Franklin's from Hannah Farthing's apartment, Mr. Mahoney was nonetheless there ahead of him to let him in by the mansion-house's back door.

On James's previous visits, Franklin had always received him in his study. This time Mr. Mahoney conducted him to Dr. Franklin's bedroom, which was next to his study, and after opening that door for him, left. James found the master of Franklin Court in bed in his nightshirt and cap, propped up by pillows. He had a document in his hands and around him on the bed were scattered other papers.

"I trust, James," Dr. Franklin said, "that you do not mind conversing with someone in a state of undress. I'm lying low to keep the Gout and the Stone from finding me. Mr. Mahoney told me of your triumph. Please be so kind as to let me see the wool spinner's statement."

James put down on the room's little side table the portable escritoire he carried under his arm, removed from it the written, signed transcript of Hannah Farthing's confession, and handed it to Benjamin Franklin.

"Please have a seat, James, while I read this."

The Confession of Hannah Farthing

I first became aware of Elizabeth Coons, though I didn't know her name, when my brother, Solomon Lort, came to me one day some years ago and offered me money if I would exchange my apartment for his lodgings for a night. This was, I believe, not long after he left the stoneyard of the Quaker who was arrested for strangling a woman. These exchanges continued from then on every so often each month for some years, until about half a year ago or so, when they ceased. My brother never gave me much for doing this, but I was glad to have the little he paid me for sleeping in another bed for one night, except that he often came to me with his request at a very late hour, which disturbed my rest.

I never saw Mrs. Coons until the night she came to my door with her doll, which she kept saying was a very valuable article, and offered to give it to me in exchange for my assistance and for a place to stay until her woman's troubles were over. She said she was a friend of Solomon's. I knew she had to be the woman he spent the nights with in my apartment. How else could someone I had never met know my name and where I lived, and that I knew midwifery, and why else would she expect that by mentioning Solomon's name I would help her?

It was while she was begging me to help her and offering me her doll that her water broke; and so I pitied her and took her in. I suspected, later on, she might be the murdered woman written about in the papers since Solomon called her "Lizzy" that night. But

I was not sure she was the woman who was strangled until you came to ask me about her just now. You made me afraid you were going to arrest me, though I did no wrong, as you will see.

None of those midwives in Southwark, so fond of criticizing me, who drove me out of the profession, could have done better than I did that night. I had the woman take off her clothes and shoes so they wouldn't get blood on them, and had her put on the modesty gown that I had kept from my days as a midwife. I propped her up in the middle of the bed with my pillow and another I made by stuffing a pillowcase full of some of the wool that I had for spinning. I put her cloak folded several times under her head. To take the blood, I used a wool fleece that hadn't been combed yet and put it at the foot of the bed covered by my flannel bedspread folded twice. I told her to brace her feet on the rail at the foot of the bed.

It was a breach birth, and there was nothing anyone could have done about that. The baby came out after a great hard labor that took a long time. I kept the woman's cries down by getting her to bite on a roll of cloth. Solomon was there for the worst of it because when I said I needed someone else to help me, the woman made me go get him. He didn't want to come, but I told him either he went back with me to the apartment where his paramour was lying or I would put the woman out in the street, no matter what her condition was. Then he came. The baby was dead. It was a well-formed boy but small.

Solomon left to get something to bury the baby in, and I delivered the placenta while he was gone and put it in the jorden with the bloody flannel and fleece. I had warm water in the Dutch oven and cleaned the woman up as well as I could with that, using the wash basin I keep under my bed and an unsoiled corner of the flannel bedspread that I cut off. The woman was very weak and only half-conscious. I made her as comfortable as I could because I was sorry for her. It was a hard birth, I tell you. I moved her up to the top of the bed so she could use the whole bed to rest on, and spread the wool I had stuffed in the pillowcase under her thighs to take any blood that came after the delivery of the placenta. I laid the pillowcase over the wool so she wouldn't feel it scratching against her skin, and covered her up with my quilt to keep her warm.

When Solomon returned, he ordered me to go to his lodgings, which I was happy to do because I was tired. It was getting on toward daybreak when I left. The woman was weak, but I swear she was alive. May Satan take my soul if I am not telling you the whole truth and only the truth, so help me God.

I have not seen my brother since that night, and I don't want to see him. He made me swear an oath before I left him that I would never speak to anyone of what happened that night. He said he would know if I told and would come after me, and make me pay.

I slept at Solomon's until the middle of the day; then I went back to my lodgings and found things pretty much as I had left them except my best chair was broken beyond repair, and my bowls, pitcher, and teapot had all been smashed against the chimney. The woman, her dead child, and the placenta were gone, but her stockings and cloak were on the table and her doll was in the clothes press where I had put it. My quilt and the modesty gown were flung into the same corner of the room by the foot of the bed.

I swept up the broken crockery and put the pieces with the bloody fleece and the flannel and dumped everything in the necessary at the back of the yard, along with the bloody water in the wash basin. The broken chair was fit for nothing but kindling, which made me sad every time I burned a piece of it in the fireplace. It was a good chair.

And that is all I know of Elizabeth Coons.

Dr. Franklin, after reading this document, laid it aside and said nothing for a moment. When he spoke, it was to tell James, "You have done well. There is much for us to think about in this confession. You heard her tell her story. Do you believe she was telling the whole truth? People often say that they are, when they aren't."

"I do," James answered. "She seemed sincere and appeared relieved to be confessing."

"Confession of wrongdoing," Dr. Franklin with his bemused chuckle, "seems to do good for the soul. I am reminded of a woman I once knew in my youth, when I worked in London. An old maiden lady, an invalid, who lived a most retired life in the garret of the building where I lived, up two pairs of stairs at the back of an Italian warehouse by the docks. She was a Roman Catholic, and although she had about as much occasion to sin as a cloistered nun, a priest nonetheless came every few days to confess her so she could receive absolution for her sins, and have communion. When I asked her why she needed so much confession since she lived such a retired life, she told me it was impossible to avoid vain thoughts."

"What do you propose to do now, Dr. Franklin?" James asked. "Shall I inform the Sheriff that Solomon Lort was the last person to see Elizabeth Coons alive?"

"By no means should we proceed that way, James. We must first consider Hannah Farthing's confession. There are clear signs of pity and charity scattered throughout it. It is no trifling matter that such an impoverished woman should sacrifice both sets of her bedclothes, of which she could not have had more than two. That was remarkable charity on her part. Note, too, that she does not complain anywhere in her confession of the wool, which she spins for her livelihood, that she lost because of tending to the needs of Mrs. Coons.

"Do we want to expose such a woman to the rigors of the law? We have promised her that no harm will come to her if she herself did no wrong. That is how we got her to confess, through that promise. And if we go to the law, both Mrs. Farthing, as a witness, and her brother, as a suspect in a murder case, will be arrested and put in the Walnut Street Jail. He would, once they were both in prison, have access to her every day and be able to wreak whatever vengeance he wanted to take on her for betraying him. No, James, we must devise a way of proceeding other than going to the Sheriff."

Again, James asked what he proposed to do.

"We must get Lort's confession. Then we shall know what to do."

"You intend to question Lort?" James asked. "I can hardly believe that, Dr. Franklin."

"We have to question him, James. He was the last person to see Mrs. Coons alive. How else can we know what happened after Hannah Farthing left her apartment? According to her confession, the last time she saw the two of them they were alone together, and Mrs. Coons was weak but alive."

"You believe, then, that Lort strangled Elizabeth Coons?" James asked. "I certainly do."

Dr. Franklin replied matter-of-factly, "We must learn what happened after Mrs. Farthing left them. The sooner we do that, the better. Therefore, I propose to have Solomon Lort here at Franklin Court tonight."

James earnestly protested this course of action, saying it was highly imprudent. It would be better to inform the Sheriff of what they had discovered about Lort, James said, and have the Sheriff take Lort into custody and question him.

Franklin reminded James again that to go to the Sheriff would result in both Lort and his sister being put together in the Walnut Street Jail, where no inmate was safe from assault by another. He reminded James that Lort had sworn to take vengeance on his sister if she told anyone of what happened in her apartment the night Elizabeth Coons sought her aid.

"I have been thinking of a way to bring Lort peaceably to Franklin Court," Dr. Franklin said. "I will send Mr. Mahoney to find the man at his place of work to tell him, confidentially, that I am thinking of hiring him as my hostler at Franklin Court for a high wage. I will instruct Francis to say the job would also include, besides wages, the use of the attic above my stable and a supply of winter firewood. Mr. Mahoney will tell the man I am thinking of making this generous offer because he has been highly recommended on account of his skill in handling horses, and his discretion. That will appeal to the man's vanity. Mr. Mahoney will emphasize that no one else is being considered for the job until I have first spoken with him to see if we can come to terms. And that as a condition for being considered for the job, he must not speak to anyone of the interview he is to have with me, so that in case we cannot come to terms and someone else has to be hired, no one will know of my generous offer to him. To guard against someone seeing the man enter my grounds, I will have him come here the same way and at the same hour you first came, James."

"But," James protested again, "if he is Lizzy Coons's murderer and comes to Franklin Court, your part in bringing him to justice will become known eventually, which you do not want to happen. He will, in the end, have to be arrested and tried in court, and if you have him at Franklin Court your part in bringing him to justice will be known."

Dr. Franklin replied, "That may not necessarily happen, James. There may be another way of seeing justice done. And remember, it has yet to be determined definitively that Lort is Mrs. Coons's killer. That is why we must obtain his confession."

James, though still not convinced of the plan's prudence, saw that Dr. Franklin was determined to arraign Solomon Lort at Franklin Court. So he resigned himself to being an accomplice to a rash enterprise.

Dr. Franklin, with his usual acumen, perceived that he had failed to persuade James of the need to bring Lort to Franklin Court. He therefore informed his younger confederate that he would have two of his chair bearers, Albanius Parker and Richard Somers—who were trustworthy, strong men—within easy call, in case Lort became unruly. Mr. Mahoney would also be on hand.

"Besides, James, I will have you, a veteran of many battlefields, by my side when I speak with this man, should he become obstreperous. And though I lack the strength I had in my youth—when I thought nothing of carrying large forms of lead type, one in each hand, up two flights of stairs, and considered it mere sport to swim the Thames from Chelsea to Blackfriars—still, I might not be entirely useless in a fracas. Surely, you would agree that five men, albeit one of them old, are more than a match for one man. I will receive Lort here in my bedchamber, as you see me now, to put him at ease and make him more amenable to speaking with me. Who would suspect an old man in his nightshirt, sitting up in his bed, as having the power to do him harm?"

James, by way of reply, merely smiled. Dr. Franklin had made his strategy seem so reasonable it was impossible to dispute him. James felt he had to humor him with as good a grace as he could summon and protect him from harm as best he could.

James was to return to Franklin Court at half-past nine o'clock that evening to be in readiness for Lort's appearance at eleven. In the meantime, Dr. Franklin advised him to get some rest and inform his family that he might be gone most of the night.

When James departed Franklin Court it was nearly noon, and he went to the City Tavern to have some dinner.

James had not intended to ask whether he had any messages. But Mr. Proctor, the daytime manager of the Tavern, stopped him as he was going into the taproom to say he had a letter for James, which the manager retrieved from his desk and gave to him.

James glanced at it without opening it and stuck it in his coat. No response he might have now from the advertisement in the papers was going to affect his promise to Dr. Franklin to be at Franklin Court at half past nine.

In the taproom he found Robert Evans and Hugh Middleton, two men he had served with in the Continental Army, who were already far enough advanced in their drinking to be telling hilarious tales to a circle of men at the bar. As soon as they saw James, they insisted on his joining them, and introduced him to their acquaintances. In consequence of this chance encounter, James had a diverting dinner standing at the bar eating the free lunches that the amused barkeep kept putting on the counter for the voracious gentlemen who kept calling for more bowls of sangaree. James, mindful that he had to be at Franklin Court in nine hours and might be up most of the night, limited himself to three drinks.

He decided not to go to the Northern Liberties from the City Tavern. Lawrence and Mr. Bartlett would have to get along without him for a day. He wanted to spend some time with Livy before he had to return to Franklin Court.

When James arrived home, Livy, despite the awkwardness of her bandaged finger, was on her hands and knees in the parlor scrubbing the floor. The bandage had already gotten wet, and James made her give him her pail of dirty water to empty around the rose bush in front of the house.

"Let's put a clean bandage on that hurt finger, Livy, and go for a ride up the Schuylkill," he told her. "I feel like going for a ride, and I'd like you to come with me, if you will. We can look at the mansion-houses that have been built up that way. We may not have many of these fine days left before the cold weather sets in."

Livy gladly agreed to go with him—it was his first proposal to her to do something together merely for their own pleasure —and she said she would change out of her working garb and dress in something more becoming for a ride in the country.

"First," James said, "let's change that bandage."

The ride up the valley of the Schuylkill was memorable. The limpid waters of the small river, enameled by rafts of many-colored autumn leaves floating on its placid surface; the stately houses and handsome lawns of the homes wealthy Philadelphians had built along the wooded banks of the river; the sunny, dry day; the pleasant gait of the well-paced horse they rode; being warmly together on Jenny. Everything they saw and felt on their ride along the Schuylkill made Livy and James feel the pure pleasure of being alive.

James told her as much as he knew about the men who had built the big houses they saw, a few of whom he had had business dealings with or served under during the war. He told her about his beloved grandfather, and of his boyhood. She told him of growing up on her father's farm west of Philadelphia, and why she'd decided to come to find work in the city and how fond of Grandmère she was.

They went far up the lovely river valley before turning back, and it was dark by the time they arrived at the house, much refreshed and invigorated.

Livy had made a venison stew that morning, which James insisted that they eat by firelight in the dining room.

They talked of many things during their intimate supper, but not the thing that was most on their minds and in their feelings, which was their relations with each other.

When he left the house to walk to Franklin Court, he told Livy not to wait up for him because he would likely be gone all night. He assured her this would probably be the last time he would have to be out so late, since he felt his investigation into the Quaker Murders was coming to an end. She was apprehensive for his safety as they parted, but did not put her foreboding into words lest it bring bad luck to James.

Chapter 24

When James was again ushered into Dr. Franklin's small bedroom, the papers that had been spread around on the bed were no longer in sight. He now was reading Montesquieu's *Persian Letters*. The portable escritoire James had left on the room's side table under the tapestry of St. George was also gone. In its place was Hannah Farthing's signed confession and a lighted candelabrum. The candles in the sconces on both sides of Dr. Franklin's bed had also been lighted and a large tapestry hung over the door into his study, entirely concealing it.

Before dismissing Mr. Mahoney, Dr. Franklin explained to him and to James what he expected of each of them during Solomon Lort's visit.

"I would like you, James, to station yourself inside there," Franklin said, indicating the closet door next to the head of his bed. "You will be able to hear everything that occurs between Lort and me, but he will not know of your presence. You are my first line of defense, should the man become unruly. But I want you to stay out of sight unless you hear him assault me. No matter how alarming Lort's words may sound, you are not to come out unless he physically attacks me, and I think there's little chance of that.

"Mr. Mahoney, you are to wait with Richard Somers and Albanius Parker in the kitchen after you bring Lort up. Should I need your assistance, I will call you, and the three of you are to come with all speed." As he said this, Dr. Franklin nodded toward a pair of braided cords hanging side by side on the wall within reach of the right side of his bed. "Remember, if I call you, it means I need your help as quickly as possible." The taciturn, burly servant nodded in agreement and went away to carry out his important commission to invite Lort to Franklin Court.

James sat in the small bedroom's only chair to await the arrival of the Mauls' former hostler with Dr. Franklin, who was in a talkative mood.

He told James the story of his chair bearers, Parker and Somers. They were, he said, honest but improvident men who had been imprisoned for debt until their debts were paid. But how could they pay them from prison, Dr. Franklin asked, if they had no family or friends with means to meet their obligations for them? Therefore he had hired them, he said, along with two other debtors in similar circumstances, to carry his sedan chair so they might earn some money to discharge their debts and obtain their release from prison.

He also spoke of how he had founded a society to improve Pennsylvania's system of imprisonment to reform criminals and make them into citizens who would one day be of benefit to the Commonwealth.

He had heard, he said, that his sedan chair—the first ever seen in Pennsylvania—was causing talk in the town that he was putting on European airs. But the truth was that it had been a gift from a French nobleman who knew how painful the jolting of carriages over uneven pavements was to a man who suffered from kidney stones, and he had brought it back with him to

Philadelphia from France because he had found from experience that nothing was less jarring than a sedan chair carried by four men striding in unison. That was the only reason he had brought the sedan chair back to Philadelphia with him.

Dr. Franklin also told James several amusing stories of his youth. One of them was a crime against property which had occurred when he and several companions were trying to get back to the ship that was bringing them home to America from England. They had gone ashore with the captain's permission to see something of the English countryside and had strayed rather far when they heard the unexpected booming of the ship's recall gun and saw its recall flag in the distance, signaling that it was about to weigh anchor and set sail. In hurrying along the shore to get back to the ship before it left without them, they discovered that the tide had filled a wide inlet since they had passed that way. Franklin proposed they steal a boat to get over the water or they would never reach their ship on time, and waded out into the inlet, pried loose the staple of the mooring stake for one of the boats in the inlet, and towed it back to his companions, by which they crossed the water and got back to their ship before it sailed. They left the boat on the far side for the owner to retrieve. This was but one of the several "errata" he had been guilty of in his youth, he said.

It was on that voyage across the Atlantic when he was twenty years old, he told James, that he had learned one of the most important lessons of his life, the necessity of having the good opinion of others. One of the passengers on the ship, he said, was causing continual discord by his uncivil behavior, though he committed no offense that would have justified the captain putting him in irons and locking him up for the duration of the voyage. Such constant irritation in the narrow confines of a ship facing an ocean passage of a month's duration was intolerable. Finally one of the Quakers on board proposed that the misbehaving passenger be shunned.

A week of having his fellow passengers refuse to speak to him, eat with him, or be in his company cured the man of his disruptive conduct, Dr. Franklin said.

At this juncture, footsteps were heard in the hall. Dr. Franklin asked James to hand him Hannah Farthing's confession which he put next to him on his bed face down. He then told his confederate to take up his post in the closet and keep his ear close to the door.

From the closet, James heard Mr. Mahoney's voice announcing the arrival of Solomon Lort and leaving, and Dr. Franklin's voice thanking the man for coming at so late an hour and inviting him to have a seat. Lort said he hoped he would be given the job of hostler.

Dr. Franklin then asked the man whether he had spoken to anyone of coming to Franklin Court, and James heard Lort say he hadn't, adding, "Your man was very plain about my not telling anyone and said I was not even to let anybody see me knock at your gate. I can't see the need for such fiddle-faddle in coming to see a man about a job."

The freeness of this speech suggested to James that Lort was not awed by being in the presence of the great Benjamin Franklin, who had tamed the lightning from heaven and humbled King George the Third.

Dr. Franklin responded by saying, "There is much to consider in hiring a man who will be living on your property. And since I am offering high wages, I intend to be highly particular about the man I hire. Mr. Mahoney told you of the room above the stables and the supply of winter fuel you would have as my hostler."

James heard no reply from Lort to this comment and imagined him nodding assent.

"Tell me, Mr. Lort," Dr. Franklin said, "will your present employer provide you a good character?"

"I suppose I can get one."

"And who is your employer?"

"The shambles where your man, the stocky little Irishman, found me. I thought you knew that," Lort said, rather argumentatively.

"But who is the proprietor of the shambles? I do not know that."

"Mr. Ross."

"And before Mr. Ross? Who was your employer?"

"Mr. Brown what owns the quarry out on the Lancaster Pike."

Then Dr. Franklin said, "I understand you once worked for the Quaker stonecutter Jacob Maul. Is that right?"

Even through the door, James could sense Lort's wariness at the mention of this former employer, and he heard a rustling of bedclothes as Dr. Franklin apparently shifted himself higher against his pillows. A moment of silence ensued before Lort said, "That's right."

Prior to this, except for scoffing at being forbidden to tell anyone of coming to Franklin Court, Lort had maintained a reasonably respectful tone of address in speaking with Franklin, as befitted a man of lesser quality. Dr. Franklin's next question changed everything.

"And if I am not mistaken—please correct me if I am wrong —you also knew Jacob Maul's housekeeper, Elizabeth Coons?"

Through the door James heard the sound of a thud as Lort evidently got up quickly from his chair, overturning it. The sound almost brought James from his hiding place, but he recalled Dr. Franklin's admonition that he was to remain concealed in the closet unless Lort actually assaulted him, and the sound of the chair falling over seemed to be more of a sign of distress on Lort's part than Dr. Franklin's.

Franklin manifested a remarkably amiable tone in what he said next.

"You might have saved me the trouble, Mr. Lort, of asking you here for a talk if you will not conduct yourself in a proper way and provide civil answers to my civil questions. Please set the chair back on its legs and sit down. I have something of utmost consequence to discuss with you after you have read this paper. You may believe me when I say it is in your interest that you do read it. I suppose you can read."

At last James understood why Dr. Franklin had wanted to get a written, signed statement from Hannah Farthing.

No sound but that of Lort setting the chair back was heard, followed by a profound stillness, as Lort evidently began reading his sister's confession which Franklin had handed to him. Then James heard a furious outburst.

"Damn your eyes, you old makebait! You can't make me stay here! You jockeyed me with your piss ant story of a job! I'm leaving!"

Then there was the sound of a violent rattling of the latch on the door to the hall as Lort tried to leave but evidently couldn't get the door open. This puzzled James because he had seen no lock or bolt on the door into the hall.

He wondered whether Mr. Mahoney was on the other side holding the door shut in a contest of strength with Solomon Lort. But that wasn't at all likely.

The rattling of the latch grew louder and more violent as Lort's frustration over being kept in the room against his will mounted.

"Let me out, you leather-headed old bastard!" he shouted with vehemence. No sooner was this expletive uttered than James heard him shout, "I'll fix you!" and the sound of the rattling of the latch abruptly ceased and was replaced by a sound that could have been that of someone jumping on the bed, and Dr. Franklin exclaimed something he didn't quite finish which sounded like it could have been a stifled cry for help.

With that, James rushed into the bedroom and saw Lort straddling the body of Dr. Franklin with a knee at each side of his chest, pressing a pillow against his face. Franklin's legs, kicking against the tucked-in bedclothes, were restrained by them, and his arms were flailing about trying to throw his powerful assailant off his chest, without effect.

James dashed to the fireplace, grabbed the poker, and laid it across Lort's back with all the might of his good right arm. This heavy blow had the desired effect of getting Lort to desist from his attack on Dr. Franklin. He jumped off the bed and hurled himself at James—who was in the act of raising the poker for a second strike—bowling James over and knocking him to the floor. Instantly Lort was on top of his now prone attacker, straddling him, and keeping him down with the weight of his body, as he pummeled his face with blow after blow of his fists. James dropped the poker, which he could not wield, and tried to shield himself with his arms from these heavy blows. Then Lort seized James by the throat with both hands and began choking him.

As James started to feel himself losing consciousness, the pressure on his throat ceased entirely and the weight of Lort's body rolled off him, revealing Franklin red-faced, in his nightshirt, and breathing heavily, minus his bifocals and nightcap, gripping the poker with which he had just rendered Lort senseless.

As James raised himself on one elbow, gasping for breath, the door to the bedchamber opened and Mr. Mahoney and the two chair bearers burst into the room. It was the first time James had ever seen Mr. Mahoney's countenance display anything other than imperturbable calm, as he saw two men on the floor and his disheveled elderly master standing over them with a poker in his hand.

Dr. Franklin, indicating Lort with the tip of his poker, ordered Mr. Mahoney, "Get him out of here! Tie his hands behind him and put him in the icehouse! When you've done that, report to me. I'll be in the study."

Mr. Mahoney responded to these stern orders with an uncharacteristic verbal acknowledgment, a humble, "Yes, master."

As the unconscious Lort was being carried away by the three brawny servants, Dr. Franklin helped James to his feet, saying, "Oh, my, dear James, I hope you're not badly hurt. It's all my fault. Perhaps we should call a physician?"

"I'm all right," James said, opening and closing his jaw to see if he could. "No bones seem to have been broken. Except maybe my nose," he added, touching it and wincing.

"You were right," Dr. Franklin said. "I should never have tried to reason with that lout. It's not the first time I've relied too much on my power of persuasion and have met with failure. But who would have thought he'd attempt to suffocate me in my own bedroom!"

"Nor would I have suspected you, Dr. Franklin," James remarked mildly, "of being capable of the violence you have displayed."

That remark caused Dr. Franklin to murmur, as if pleased with himself, "Even God's meekest creatures may react in defense of themselves when cornered."

As Dr. Franklin, without the aid of his cane, gently walked James into his study and eased him into a chair, the younger man asked, "Why couldn't Lort open the door? Apparently you called Mr. Mahoney only after he left off attacking you and turned on me."

Dr. Franklin chuckled and said, "I've had a carpenter install a hidden bolt that slides into the top of that door, so that when I hear my grandchildren trooping down the hall to see me and I am not in a mood to receive their playful overtures, I can pull one of the cords by my bedside and slide the bolt into the top of the door, locking it. I used the bolt to keep Lort in, with almost catastrophic results, it appears, had you not rescued me."

"You returned the favor, Dr. Franklin," James replied, "by rescuing me."

"Then we are true allies. For that is what allies do, aid each other in times of distress and danger."

Dr. Franklin opened the front of the cabinet in his study, revealing a mixing bowl of cut green glass with a gold rim, two matching green glass tumblers, a bottle of rum, another of brandy, and a small pitcher of water, and proceeded to prepare with these ingredients what he called "Artillery Punch."

Mr. Mahoney came in while Dr. Franklin and James were settling their nerves with this potent mix of rum, water, and brandy. The servant had slippers and a robe for his barefoot master, and reported that Lort was safely jailed in the icehouse, with the two chair bearers standing guard outside the door.

"Is Lort conscious yet?" Dr. Franklin asked.

"More so than not. But he's still groggy."

Dr. Franklin looked at his pendulum clock and told Mr. Mahoney, "When you hear the Watch call midnight bring the man here."

After Mr. Mahoney's departure, James proposed turning the hostler over to the Sheriff, giving as his reason that he could not be kept in the icehouse forever.

"But we have not yet established," Dr. Franklin replied, "that Lort killed Mrs. Coons; nor, if he did, what degree of guilt he may bear in her death. I seldom desist, James, once I am on the track of something. If blocked in one approach, I try another."

James did not argue with his director on this matter, and they spoke instead of their recent experience and Lort's character.

When Mr. Mahoney came back with the hostler grasped firmly by the arm, shortly after midnight, Lort was gagged as well as bound behind by the wrists, and walking unsteadily. He looked completely spent. His head hung on his chest, and he raised it only when he heard Dr. Franklin speaking to Mr. Mahoney, then let it fall again. There was a visible lump on the crown of the hostler's head.

Dr. Franklin resumed his interrogation of Lort by saying, "I am willing to conceive, sir, that you might not have killed Mrs. Coons. I am also willing to admit the possibility that you might have killed her under mitigating circumstances. But I must have the truth."

Lort looked up and peered at Dr. Franklin with bleary eyes.

"Unless you stop your defiance and tell us everything, we will hand you over to the Sheriff, and he will put you in the Walnut Street Jail. The death of Jacob Maul should inform you of what can happen to men in that jail when its inmates suspect a fellow inmate of having killed a woman. They do not weigh fine points of evidence and motive. They execute justice summarily. So let us have no more of your nonsense, sir. Take the gag from his mouth, Francis."

Lort coughed several times after the gag was removed. And it was evident Dr. Franklin's harsh speech had had an effect.

Dr. Franklin repeated in somewhat different terms that Lort could either make a full confession to him, with the possibility of receiving "some consideration" or he could stand trial, if he survived his incarceration in the Jail long enough to be brought into court, and be found guilty of first-degree murder under the laws of the Commonwealth of Pennsylvania and sentenced to hang.

"It is in your interest, sir, to tell us the truth," Dr. Franklin admonished Lort. "I have, as you know, your sister's signed confession, and if you convince us that what you have to say concerning Mrs. Coons's death is the whole truth and nothing but the truth, it could possibly save you from the hangman. But if you lie, or contradict something we know to be true, or withhold information we already have, or give us any reason whatever to suspect you of not telling the truth, the whole truth, and nothing but the truth, you will find yourself inside the Walnut Street Jail within the hour, I assure you."

After hearing the conclusion of this admonition, Lort began his confession. Dr. Franklin directed James to take notes on what Lort said, and told Mr. Mahoney to stay in the room in case the hostler needed to be restrained.

Chapter 25

Solomon Lort's Confession

"I first met Lizzy Coons when she came to live with the Mauls during the war. She was a good woman who always gave me a kind word when I came in from the stable for meals. Lizzy and I got along from the beginning, and she was a likely looking woman besides. Until the night she died we never quarreled but over one thing, and that was whether the Quaker killed her sister.

"She wanted everyone to believe he was lily-white innocent, but I couldn't believe that. How would he be innocent, I asked her, when he was with a dead woman in a room bolted from the inside? I heard Maul draw the bolt. The German sergeant and I both did. We heard it while the sergeant was pounding on the door. I was standing right by the door. Maul had been sleeping with a dead woman inside a locked room! I told the Coroner this, but Lizzy's testimony as the dead woman's sister outweighed mine. And Susan Love wouldn't say at the inquest that she heard the bolt being drawn. The sergeant and I heard it, but he wasn't called to testify. He knew what I said was true. We talked about it more than once. He might have been a German, but he wasn't dumb.

"When we argued over the Quaker, Lizzy could never answer my question: if Maul didn't strangle your sister, how did she die? She always got around it by telling me he was too kind to kill anyone, which was no answer at all.

"The damned war and Maul's religion caused me to lose my job at the stoneyard, which kept me from courting Lizzy in the regular way. We kept on seeing each other, though, after the Quaker discharged me. I told her I was thinking of marrying her after the war, and we began meeting off and on at night in the stable's lean-to where I lived when I worked for the Quaker, as we used to; but Lizzy didn't like that arrangement. She said she was afraid one of the Mauls would see us. So I asked my sister to use her apartment, which was in a big building where hardly anyone else lived. The night Lizzy died there, she and I had not been seeing each other for months."

(Dr. Franklin interrupted at this point to ask what caused them to cease their liaison, and Lort said, "It was Lizzy's doing. I wanted to keep on, but she didn't." Dr. Franklin also wanted to know if he had ever asked Mrs. Coons to be his wife, and he said, "I told her I was thinking of marrying her.")

"After her baby died, I went out to get something to bury it in, and when I got back to the apartment I told Hannah to go to my lodgings. After she left, I was getting ready to wrap the baby in a piece of canvas I had cut from the roll I had brought, when I heard Lizzy making a sort of gurgling noise from the bed and was afraid she might be dying. I got up from what I was doing and went over to the bed and took her by the shoulders and called out her name and gave her a good shaking to bring her out of her faint. That brought her around, and she opened her eyes and looked at me, and I got her a dipper of water from the pail, which made her feel better.

"She asked me where the baby was, and I said it was dead and held it up for her to see. That put her in another swoon, and I shook her by the shoulders again.

"This time, as soon as she came to, she started crying and blaming me for the baby's death and accusing me of getting her in the state and not marrying her. That made me mad, and I told her to be quiet or I'd crop her light. I told her I had come to her when she sent Hannah for me and would stick by her, but she had to stop calling me names and show some gratitude.

"But she kept on, and her voice got loud. That brought the old man who lived down the passage, and he banged on the door and shouted that if we didn't keep quiet he was going to call the Watch. I was afraid if he did that, and the Watch came, they would see the dead baby and get the wrong idea. But Lizzy just kept on screeching. So to shut her up and make her quiet, I took her by the throat and squeezed off her air, and that stopped her from saying anything, and the old man went away.

"But when I released her throat, I saw I had squeezed too hard because Lizzy's eyes were poppy. When she got her breath back, she began crying and giving me more hard words and said I had tried to kill her, and got what you might call the hysterics. She said I was no good and deserved to live in horse muck, and other such things that were hard to listen to; and I told her to shut her mouth. Then she said she was going home to Rebecca Maul, and I laughed at that, which made her mad, and she started ranting in a loud voice. So I grabbed her by the throat again and choked her until she shut her yawp."

(Lort stopped talking here. He seemed to be reliving that moment because his eyes got a sort of faraway look. To prompt him to resume his narrative, Dr. Franklin asked what happened to the baby, but Lort did not seem to hear the question and said, "I didn't mean to crop Lizzy's light. I only wanted her to stop tormenting me." As he said this, he seemed near to tears. Dr. Franklin let the moment pass and asked Lort where he had gotten the canvas and marline that he had used to wrap the baby with. Lort answered that he got it from the shambles where he worked, that they used marline and pieces of old sail to wrap up the carcasses of the beeves to keep the flies and dirt off them. Then Dr. Franklin asked why he had brought back so much canvas and twine, enough for a woman's body as well as a tiny infant. Lort replied that he had grabbed the first roll of canvas and the first loop of marline that had come to hand because he was in a hurry to get back to his sister's. He said he had thought of bringing a shovel from the shambles as well as the canvas and twine but decided not to because he remembered a place where he could put the baby without using a shovel, a place where the ground was always wet and soft. When Dr. Franklin asked him what happened after he choked Mrs. Coons the second time, he went back to telling his story.)

"I didn't believe Lizzy was dead and tried to revive her by shaking her shoulders again, but she was past my help.

"This made me crack-brained, and I started cursing and throwing things around and smashing them. Then I thought I'd better stop making noise or the old man would bring the Watch, and I'd be in trouble. I needed to bury Lizzy before sunup.

"So I dressed her as fast as I could and tied her up and put her shoes back on and tied her ankles together, and fastened her arms against her body and rolled her in a piece of the canvas and tied up the bundle at the top and bottom and around the middle. That was when I remembered I had no shovel, and I couldn't get one before daylight came. I didn't know what to do. I thought of getting some stones and putting them inside the bundle and carrying it to the river to sink it. But I didn't think I had time for that, either. Then it came to me that I could put Lizzy in the old necessary at Maul's place, and it would seem like the Quaker had strangled another woman, and he would get what he ought to have had when he murdered Lizzy's sister. So that's what I did.

"I listened at the door to make sure the old man—who is Hannah's only near neighbor in the building where she lives— wasn't moving around; then I carried Lizzy to the Quaker's stoneyard and put her in the necessary. Then I went back to Hannah's apartment and wrapped the baby and took it to a wharf I know of that has a heavy, flat stone under it, which I heaved aside, and scooped a hole in the wet ground with my hands. First light was just beginning to come into the sky when I heaved the stone back the way it had been."

Lort stopped talking then, and Dr. Franklin asked him which wharf that had been; and he said it was Budd's Wharf near Whalebone Alley. Dr. Franklin bade him continue his narrative, but he added only that after burying the child he had gone back to his sister's apartment and got what was left of the canvas and the marline. Then he went to a taphouse whose proprietor would open for him at any hour of the day or night to serve him drink. When Dr. Franklin saw that Lort had finished his tale, he told Mr. Mahoney to put the hostler back in the icehouse.

At the outset of Dr. Franklin's investigation into the Quaker Murders, James remembered, he had said the tracks of the two sisters' deaths might cross, and they had. Solomon Lort's conviction that Maul had killed Lizzy Coons's sister but had escaped his rightful punishment for the crime had caused him to cast suspicion on Maul for the death of Lizzy Coons, a death he himself had been responsible for. He had thus become guilty, Dr. Franklin said, not only of Lizzy Coons's death but of being an accomplice in the deaths of Maul and his protector, Robert Cash, in the prison riot, though he had not committed those killings with his own hands.

"Lort's confession is an illustration of a principle of human nature I first observed in my youth, James. Our tendency to attribute our misdeeds to the influence of others or to circumstances over which we have no control. In this man's case, he claims that Jacob discharged him when he lost custom during the war because of his religious convictions, thus rendering Lort unable to court Mrs. Coons in 'the regular way.' It is unclear what the man means by 'the regular way.'

"Almost never have I observed a man attribute his virtuous acts to circumstances beyond his control. We tend to take full credit to ourselves for our praiseworthy acts."

Dr. Franklin paused, as if reflecting on what he and James had just heard from Lort.

"What did you think of the man's confession, James?" Dr. Franklin asked. "Do you think it is credible?"

"In the parts of it that overlap his sister's confession," James replied, "I saw nothing of much importance that differed from hers. He omitted that he at first refused to go to Mrs. Coons when she sent Hannah Farthing to bring him. And he failed to mention his threats against his sister if she revealed to anyone that Mrs. Coons had given birth to a child of his.

"With regard to your theory of human nature, Dr. Franklin, that we tend to take credit for our good actions but want to avoid responsibility for our bad behavior, I noticed that Lort seemed to blame Mrs. Coons for provoking him into assaulting her. He also cited the old man's complaints as a reason for choking her to keep her quiet. But what particularly struck me was what he said of his feelings after he killed Mrs. Coons."

Here James consulted the notes he had taken on Lort's confession. "He said she was 'past my help,' as if throttling her twice had in some way been a help to her. It is just as you say, Dr. Franklin, he was avoiding responsibility for a wrong he had committed.

"I also noticed," James continued, "that Lort condemned Maul for murdering a woman, presumably by choking her, while finding excuses for his commission of that very crime. And because of his strong sense of self-righteousness in regard to Maul, when he saw an opportunity to throw suspicion on his former employer for strangling Mrs. Coons, he felt no remorse at all about dumping her corpse in the old necessary on Maul's property. In fact, in that part of his narrative, he seemed to think that this solution to his problem of getting rid of the corpse was an act of delayed justice."

"Yes," Dr. Franklin said, "and when it came to his murderous rage against Mrs. Coons for speaking hard words against him, when he felt he had done her no wrong, the man seems to have persuaded himself that rather than wanting to kill her, he had only wanted to stop her unjustified criticism of him. What seems to have set off his rage was the thought that Mrs. Coons would repeat her accusations against him to the Mauls. His self-esteem, it seems, was what concerned him when he throttled her the second and final time."

The master of Franklin Court then launched into a dissertation on good and evil, and how they applied in this case. He might have been addressing a jury, though his only audience was James.

"Wrongdoing, James," Dr. Franklin began, "consists in harming others and ourselves. Goodness consists of conduct in which we respect ourselves and others as God's creations. Thus the Bible commands us to do what is right and to avoid wrong for our own sake as well as for the sake of others.

"I agree with the doctrine that teaches us that as surely as there are laws governing the Earth's passage around the sun, there are moral laws which when they are violated result in disharmony and calamity, but when respected and obeyed lead to our happiness and the happiness of others. The acts which the Ten Commandments enjoin us to perform or to avoid are not right and wrong because they are commanded or forbidden. They are right and wrong in the nature of things. We ought to honor our parents not because one of the Ten Commandments tells us to, but because in the nature of things, as God has created us and the world, it is right for us to honor our parents. The same is true for each of the Commandments. The God of Nature, in endowing mankind with life and liberty, created the moral laws that govern how we should use our lives and our liberty in the pursuit of the happiness that God wants us to have.

"The misdeeds of the false witness, the thief, the murderer, the blasphemer, were deemed misdeeds before God created the world and endowed us with free will. We may be certain that wrongdoing will be punished either here or hereafter according to the laws of the God of nature, even when they go undetected and unpunished by men. Without doubt, the chance events which happen in nature can harm innocent persons, but accidents appear to be necessary to the goodness and preservation of God's creation. The law of gravity, for instance, cannot be suspended to assist a man who has slipped from a steeple and is falling to his death.

"The willful evil that men do in misusing their freedom is not God's will. Rather, it is the will of those who abuse the liberty God has deemed necessary to our human nature and wellbeing. It is liberty that makes human goodness possible. For without free will, we would be merely automatons, and there would be neither disgrace nor merit in anything we do. Moral judgments in that case simply would not apply to our lives. We would not be accountable for our lives any more than the beast of the field is.

"As for the unintended evils that arise from our actions because we cannot always foresee the results of what we freely do, we must not pass judgment on them. God has reserved judgment on those actions to Himself, for only God is able to know and take into account everything a person knows and intends when he decides to act in a certain way. Hence the biblical injunction 'Judge not, lest ye be judged' pertains only to judgments that God alone is capable of making.

"Solomon Lort's willful conduct, James, both directly and indirectly has caused much harm. First in the death of Mrs. Coons, but also in the deaths of the innocent Jacob Maul and Robert Cash, not to mention the injury done to the happiness of Mrs. Coons's innocent daughter, Jacob's innocent son and daughter-in-law, and the sister and cousin of Lizzy Coons, Mrs. Leet and Mistress Merkle. In throwing Mrs. Coons's corpse into the old boghouse and treating the body of his own dead son as if he were some dead animal, Solomon Lort has also been guilty of violating another natural law, respect for the dead, which is part of respect for human life, in that human beings have been made, as the Bible tells us, in the image of God."

"I would not dispute your philosophy, Dr. Franklin," James said. "But what, exactly, do you intend to do with the man you're holding in your icehouse?"

"How are we to judge Lort?" Dr. Franklin asked. "That is the question. And in considering it, we must also consider this. What we do with him will affect his sister, Hannah Farthing, whose trust in our promise to protect her has been instrumental in bringing Lort's crimes against God and man to light. Should she be turned over to the authorities for punishment because she did not come forward of her own volition to tell what she knew?"

Dr. Franklin was of the opinion that he and James were the best persons to determine Lort's punishment because they alone knew, as no one else ever would, how Hannah Farthing and her brother had spoken during their confessions. That initial spontaneity, he said, could never be repeated before a jury.

"Lawyers know," Dr. Franklin remarked, "how to twist the truth to make it seem something else. Sophisticated reasoners intent on perverting the truth can make even facts appear otherwise than they are. Divorced from the good will of men who love the truth, reason can serve bad ends."

Dr. Franklin gave it as his opinion that, as far as he could see, Hannah Farthing had intended no wrong and had done none. James agreed with that judgment.

They were also in agreement that, apart from knowing her brother had gotten Lizzy Coons with child and not married her, she had no certain knowledge of his other misdeeds.

Indeed, James and Franklin agreed that she had treated Elizabeth Coons with consideration and kindness and had done all she or anyone else could have done to ease her suffering the night of her lying-in.

On the other hand, Dr. Franklin pointed out, it was also true that Hannah Farthing had failed in her duty when Mrs. Coons's corpse was discovered and Jacob Maul was arrested on suspicion of murdering her. She should have come forward then to testify to what she knew, and by so doing eliminate the suspicion against Maul. But, Dr. Franklin also mused, her silence had been coerced by her brother's threats. Therefore, he, concluded, because her silence had been coerced, it would be acting in good conscience and justly to make no report to the magistrates of her part in this business. Besides, there would be dire consequences for her if she and her brother were incarcerated together in the Walnut Street Jail.

James concurred.

"Matters are quite different in the case of her brother," Dr. Franklin said. "That Lort is guilty of having been criminally sinful, there can be no doubt. But what sort of wrongdoing is he guilty of? It weighs in his favor, and perhaps clears him of the charge of premeditated murder, that he has confessed to throttling Mrs. Coons twice, because had he planned her death there would have been no reason to choke her more than once. It is probable, therefore, that he is telling the truth in describing his murderous anger at hearing her 'ranting,' as he called her reproaches. That he did not premeditate her murder is confirmed by his not having a shovel to bury her corpse. Also, if the murder had been premeditated, he would have killed her as soon as he dismissed his sister from the apartment. There is also the matter of his smashing furniture in his sister's apartment after he killed Mrs. Coons, which reflects a distraught rather than a premeditating mind and was not conducive to concealing a premeditated deed. The fact that he did create such noise is confirmed by his sister finding her crockery and best chair smashed beyond repair and good only for firewood when she returned to her apartment.

"But," Dr. Franklin added, "if we were to turn Lort over to the authorities the chances are very great, I think, James, that he would be convicted of murder in the first degree, which would not be a just verdict. Moreover, as I have said, putting Lort in prison would subject him to the risk of being killed by the most vicious inmates of the Walnut Street Jail, who would think they were acting righteously in killing him. And his arrest would inevitably result in the arrest of his sister, with the consequences for her that we have discussed. And that, too, would be unjust.

"As I told you, the conditions that allow the inmates of the Walnut Street Jail to die of hunger and illness and do violence against each other have led me to organize, since my return from France, a society to look into reforming the prison system of our state. At present the Walnut Street Jail is little more than a school for vice in which killers, counterfeiters, arsonists, and thieves are cheek by jowl with mere debtors, disorderly persons, runaway apprentices, vagabonds, and witnesses being held to give testimony in trials."

Having disburdened himself of this discourse on the nature of good and evil and the particulars of Solomon Lort's case and that of his sister, Dr. Franklin declared to James that he was in favor of their deciding the proper punishment for Lort's crimes, instead of turning the man over to the Sheriff and the courts for imprisonment, trial, and punishment.

Chapter 26

James was extremely curious to know how Dr. Franklin proposed to punish Solomon Lort without involving the Sheriff of Philadelphia and the courts of the Commonwealth.

"Dr. Franklin," he said, "you have made, I think, a convincing argument that it would be wrong to turn Hannah Farthing and Solomon Lort over to the authorities. But you can't keep him confined in your icehouse forever, that's certain. What do you propose?"

"There's a Nantucket whaling ship," Benjamin Franklin replied, "that stopped here some days ago to take on sea stores that are unavailable on Nantucket. When it leaves Philadelphia, at first light this morning, this whaler will sail down the length of the Atlantic, round Cape Horn, and make a four-year cruise on the whaling grounds of the Pacific Ocean. My cousin Jabez Folger is captain of this ship, for on my mother's side I descend from that famous family of Nantucket whalers, the Folgers. Jabez called here at Franklin Court his first day in port to say hello, and mentioned that he was shorthanded for his voyage. That has given me an idea. What I propose to do, James, is to put Lort on this whaler."

"But how," James rejoined, "would that be a punishment?"

"Why do you suppose," Dr. Franklin said, "that whalers often leave American shores shorthanded and have to fill out their crews in the heathen isles of the South Sea? The reason is the hard labor and dangers of whaling. To consign Lort to a lifetime aboard whaling ships would be to condemn him to a lifetime at hard labor. It would be to introduce him to the terrors of the deep and the most awesome creature in God's creation, a monster that will put a wholesome fear of the living God in Lort, something he is lacking at present."

"But you said your cousin's ship is making a four-year cruise for whales," James protested. "That is not a lifetime of hard labor. And what is to prevent Lort from finding a chance to jump ship in the tropics which, I have heard, sailors sometimes do, and then live a long life of pleasure on one of those island paradises?"

"Yes, those are excellent points. I invited my cousin to Franklin Court this afternoon, James, to discuss those very questions with him. Jabez told me the ships of the American whaling fleet in the Pacific are always in need of men because of the fatalities that are frequent in the industry. He said it would be easy for him, before returning to the United States, to transfer this man onto another American whaler just arriving on the Pacific whaling grounds, with the understanding that that captain on his return home would transfer Lort into yet another American whaler newly arrived on the Pacific whaling grounds. Through a series of such transfers he would be kept in the American whaling fleet in the Pacific Ocean until he died. And as to jumping ship, Jabez saw no reason why Lort might not be put in irons and locked up whenever the ship he was on happened to be in the vicinity of land, which, my cousin said, would be seldom, since whales are not much known for frequenting land.

"I observed to Jabez, in anticipation of what we have found out tonight, that Lort might be a murderer. That did not seem to bother him in the slightest. He said he was used to dealing with such men. And if Lort became violent or tried to incite others to mutiny, he knew what he had to do. So, also, did his fellow captains in the whale fishery, he said. The perils and mishaps of their business have taught the captains of American whalers how to deal with 'hard cases.' A captain's word is law aboard his ship, Jabez told me.

"Being a frugal man, he was all the more amenable to my proposal when he thought he would not have to pay a man like Solomon Lort more than a three-thousandth lay of the estimated profits of his voyage. And that amount would fall short of what Lort would owe him for his food and clothing during a four-year voyage. When I suggested that Lort sign the ship's papers under a name that would keep him aware of his crime, the name Solomon Coons, Jabez said he didn't care if the man shipped under the name Beelzebub.

"From this day forward, James, Solomon Lort so long as he lives will never set foot on land again and will without cease perform the dangerous and backbreaking but useful work of hunting and killing whales and reducing their blubber to oil to light the lamps of the world."

James agreed with Dr. Franklin's reasoning that Lort had taken the life of Lizzy Coons in a fit of anger, without premeditation, and the more he considered the good doctor's proposed punishment for such a crime, the more he agreed with the sentence to a lifetime of hard, dangerous labor. To expose Lort to the rigors of life in the whaling fishery for the rest of his life, ship after ship, until he died either of natural causes or in one of the mishaps so common to the pursuit of whales, was a punishment suited to his crime. It would also serve, as Dr. Franklin said, a useful purpose and perhaps give the condemned man time to repent of what he had done to deserve such punishment.

Nonetheless, James had an important question to raise before he consented to the proposed sentence.

"How," he asked Dr. Franklin, "will sending Lort to a lifetime of hard labor in the whale fishery cleanse the stain from Jacob Maul's good name and restore to his faithful son William the family's lost respectability?"

"To accomplish that end, James," Dr. Franklin replied, "you have only to present the authorities with Lort's confession —something we will prepare for him to sign as a condition for not turning him over to the Sheriff. His confession will confirm everything you tell the Sheriff about his guilt. And you can say that Lort escaped from your custody after you obtained his confession, which, as soon as cousin Jabez sails, will be nothing but the literal truth. The marks Lort put on your face will support your statement to the Sheriff. The corpse of Lizzy Coons's stillborn child, when you exhume it for proper burial, will fully corroborate the tale. You might even tell the Sheriff that Lort escaped while he was showing you the location of the infant's grave."

Benjamin Franklin then set James to the task of writing up Lort's confession for his signature, while he had the hostler brought from the icehouse and explained to him the choice he now faced. Either accept perpetual bondage in the whaling fleet or face the gallows for the crime he had committed. Lort agreed to leave Philadelphia aboard Jabez Folger's whaler bound for the Pacific Ocean.

After signing his confession, the hostler was taken to his lodgings by Mr. Mahoney and the two stalwart chair bearers to collect his belongings. From there they delivered him to the ship, an hour before its sailing, where he was turned over to the authority of Captain Folger, signed the ship's articles as Solomon Coons, and was put in irons until the ship reached the open ocean.

After Lort left Franklin Court in the custody of Mr. Mahoney, Albanius Parker, and Richard Somers, Dr. Franklin composed a brief notice for James to put in the papers, as though coming from him. It explained to the people of Philadelphia in a masterfully succinct fashion the circumstances of Mrs. Coons's death and Jacob Maul's innocence, leaving out of the account all mention of Franklin and Hannah Farthing.

Following this, James and Dr. Franklin consumed the remainder of the rum-and-brandy Artillery Punch as their reward for solving the mystery of the Quaker Murders. It would, Dr. Franklin said, be a shame—indeed, a rather unpardonable sin—to throw away such an admirable beverage.

They drank toast after toast. First, to "Truth and Justice" and then "The Power of the Press." After these highly satisfying toasts, Dr. Franklin made the observation that his ancient enemy the Gout would doubtless track him down by following the potent fragrance of this pleasant punch. But, he said, when his nemesis showed up, he would persuade the Gout by the aid of reason not to interfere with one of the few remaining pleasures of an old man's life. James therefore proposed that they drink to "The Power of Reason," which was followed by Dr. Franklin proposing they drink to "The Power of Gold and Pokers." The final portions of the Artillery Punch were consumed in toasting "The American Whale Fishery" and "The Midwives of Southwark."

While this merriment was in progress, Dr. Franklin instructed James to give Mrs. Opdahl ten Spanish dollars out of the money he had left from the sums he had received, and to tell her that Hannah Farthing had contributed no intelligence to the investigation into the Quaker Murders—that, indeed, she did not know Elizabeth Coons—whereas Mrs. Opdahl's report of Mrs. Coons's pregnant condition had been of great value in advancing the investigation of the Quaker Murders and bringing it to a successful conclusion. He was also to buy a yellow silk turban for Mrs. Lyons in one of the city's establishments for women's apparel, as an expression of thanks for her aid. The remainder of the money was to be given to Mistress Merkle to put her young ward, Sarah Coons, in a school where she might learn how to keep accounts. Dr. Franklin told James that the ability to read and write and keep accounts were skills a woman should have in case she ever needed to make her own way in the world or to assist a husband in the family business. He also took Mrs. Coons's letters from his cabinet and gave them to James to send back to her sister in Hopewell, New Jersey.

When James brought up the business of selling the horse he had purchased in Princeton, Dr. Franklin told him to keep it as a token of appreciation for assisting him in exonerating his old friend Jacob Maul of wrongdoing. No amount of protest on James's part could alter the firmness of Dr. Franklin's resolve to make him this valuable present.

The conviviality of the conversation over the Artillery Punch emboldened James to ask Dr. Franklin a personal question on a subject that had occurred to him on the occasion of their first meeting at Franklin Court and about which he had been curious ever since. What, James wanted to know, was the secret of Dr. Franklin's cheerfulness? For a general air of contentment seemed to pervade his manner and to be part of his character. Dr. Franklin obliged his confederate with the following anecdote.

The Secret of Benjamin Franklin's Cheerfulness

One summer when I was a boy in my native Boston, a wig maker who had a shop in the next street over from my father's candle shop kept a canary in a cage outside his place of business. The bird was always singing merrily, until one day it stopped singing and assumed a sad appearance and soon afterward fell from its perch, dead. I happened to be standing by the cage looking at the sad canary when it dropped off the perch, and the incident made a permanent impression on me as a boy. From that moment on, I have considered melancholy a state of mind inimical to health and something to be avoided. So instead of croaking as some people do regarding their circumstances in life and what has befallen them, especially when they have some reason to feel sad, which no man can altogether and always avoid, I have made it a rule to count my blessings when I feel a mood of melancholy stealing over me. And this habit has usually served to restore my spirits to their proper tone.

The night was past and the roosters in the vicinity of Franklin Court had all crowed by the time Benjamin Franklin and Captain James Jamison concluded their colloquy in the aftermath of their successful investigation.

Dr. Franklin advised James that it would be best if he rested for a while at Franklin Court before going home, and he had to admit that he was probably in no condition to walk the streets of Philadelphia with proper gentlemanly decorum. So he accepted Dr. Franklin's invitation to repair to his son-in-law and daughter's chamber at the southeast corner of Franklin Court's uppermost floor.

James woke hours later with the sun brightly shining in the room, where he had lain on top of the bed's covers after taking off his coat and shoes. The clock on the fireplace mantle said it was past noon.

James's nose, cheeks, ears, and throat hurt, and when he went to the washstand to splash water on his face, he saw why. His reflection in the washbowl mirror showed two black eyes, bruises to his cheeks and throat, and a cut on his right ear, from the beating and choking Solomon Lort had given him in Dr. Franklin's bedroom the night before.

James threw several handfuls of water on his face and carefully dabbed it dry around his bruises. Then he put on his shoes and coat and went downstairs. The house was completely quiet. There was a note addressed to him in Dr. Franklin's hand stuck in the jamb of the front door. It said he was to keep the key to Franklin Court in case he ever needed to come back.

James let himself out and walked to the door in the west wall of the grounds of Franklin Court—which he opened with his key—and went down the narrow, foul passage on the other side of the door. Hungry and in need of coffee though he was, he went on past the Indian Queen, which was next to where the passage emerged on Fourth Street, and hurried home as fast as he could walk, being worried that his delay in getting back might have been of concern to Livy.

His battered face drew stares and comments as he strode down Fourth Street and turned right on Chestnut.

As soon as he entered his house, he called out Livy's name. But got no reply. The house was empty.

He then went out to the stables behind the house and discovered only Cheval standing in his stall. The sorrel mare was not there.

He was just emerging from the stables when he saw Livy on Jenny coming down the street. He waved to her, and she put her heels to the horse and came on at a fast trot, stopping the mare only as she was almost upon him. She dismounted and flung herself into his arms all in one motion.

"Oh, James, I was so worried! I went up to the Northern Liberties, thinking you might be there."

She pulled her head away from his chest to look him in the face, and, seeing his bruises and the cut on his ear, exclaimed, "You're hurt! What happened? Who did this to you?"

He pulled her back into his embrace and said, burying his face in the fresh, clean smell of her hair. "I'm sorry I worried you, Livy. I hope it won't ever happen again."

"But who hurt you? We've got to go in, James, so I can tend to you."

"Have the horses been fed?"

"Yes, I fed and watered them first thing this morning when you weren't here yet. Let's go in."

"Good. But let's unsaddle Jenny first, and rub her down. It looks like you rode her pretty hard."

"I did," Livy laughed. "She can go fast when you ask her to. People in the streets stared at me, riding like a man. But I didn't care. I was so anxious when you weren't home by the middle of the day."

While they tended to Jenny, he told Livy who had battered his face, but not where or how it had happened. He finished the story in the house while Livy gently bathed his bruises with warm water and soap and then salved them with balm, which she spread with her fingertips. He gave her basically Dr. Franklin's story that was going to appear in the newspapers, which left out all mention of Hannah Farthing, Franklin Court, Benjamin Franklin, and Franklin's three manservants.

He was not sure that what he said was entirely credible. But she seemed satisfied by it. The main thing for her, it seemed, was that he was home and had not suffered serious injury.

Livy told him that she had been careful when she went to the Northern Liberties not to alarm his grandmother. "I tethered Jenny out of sight and walked to the glasshouse. I talked only with Mr. Bartlett, who told me you weren't there. Lawrence was in the house eating dinner, he said. I made him promise not to tell any of them, especially not Grandmère, that I had been there looking for you. He said Grandmère is coming home this afternoon."

After she had salved his bruises, James took Livy into the parlor, where he sat down with her on the sofa. He took Livy's bandaged left hand in his right hand, but she removed it and took off the bandage, and with a warm smile placed her hand back in his. He raised it to his lips, looking affectionately into her now serious eyes. He kept her hand to his lips a long moment before letting their hands rest together between them on the sofa.

Grandmère found them there an hour later, still holding hands. James rose when his grandmother entered the room, but he did not relinquish Livy's hand.

"Grandmère," James said, "Livy and I are going to marry, with your permission."

Grandmère Jamison looked at their clasped hands, the solemn face of her maid, and her grandson's bruised countenance, and said, "Have I ever interfered, Jamie, with your affairs? *Que Dieu bénisse votre marriage.*" Then a warm smile suffused her rosy, unwrinkled visage, and she went to

Livy and kissed her on both cheeks, saying, "It's about time he saw that you love him."

Then she kissed her beloved grandson, saying, "Who did you have to fight to get her, James?"

Chapter 27

The next day, a Sabbath, James went to church with his family, except for Jane. It was a day of rest and thanksgiving for James, spent mostly giving his family accounts of his adventures and the story of his betrothal to Livy. At their family supper, Franklin Sheraton, who was now often awake and had his eyes open a good deal of the time when he was not busy with his main jobs of sleeping and eating, was a bigger center of attention than anyone else, especially for his twin brothers, who thought everything he did was hilarious.

The following day, James dedicated himself to carrying out Dr. Franklin's instructions. Early that morning while the tide was out, he went to Budd's Wharf and made certain Lort had been telling the truth about depositing Lizzy Coons's stillborn infant under the wharf. The flat rock was there and the tiny body was beneath it. He then went to the office of the Sheriff to give him the signed confession of Solomon Lort, and explained without any mention of Benjamin Franklin or Hannah Farthing how he had obtained it. James's character as a gentleman and a Revolutionary War officer who had received the Purple Heart medal in the war gave him a certain credence with the Sheriff who, along with everyone else of quality in Philadelphia, knew of his investigation into the so-called Quaker Murders and his reason for it. But it was his black eyes and the other marks on his face that inclined the Sheriff to believe the story James told of his apprehension of the real murderer of Elizabeth Coons and Lort's alleged escape from his custody.

James then went with the Sheriff and two of his assistants to Budd's Wharf and extracted the remains of Lizzy Coons's baby from beneath the flat rock, which provided, as Dr. Franklin had said it would, full corroboration of the story James told. The Sheriff took custody of the remains to give them proper Christian burial.

Sheriff Tuttleton solemnly congratulated James on solving the mystery of Mrs. Coons's death and proving the innocence of Jacob Maul. He expressed regret that the stonecutter had died in the prison riot and could not resume his former life. The chief law officer of Philadelphia said he would send notices to the newspapers of Pennsylvania, Delaware, and New Jersey and also the largest newspapers in New York, Maryland, and Virginia, advertising that Solomon Lort was wanted for the murder of Mrs. Elizabeth Coons.

"If there were more citizens like yourself in Pennsylvania, Captain Jamison," the Sheriff said, "our Commonwealth would be a better place than it is."

Next, James mailed to Mrs. Leet the letters he had promised to return, enclosing a copy of Dr. Franklin's condensed explanation of who had killed her sister Lizzy. Then he went around to the half-dozen newspapers of the city and left them copies of the explanation to print as news. Mr. Mahoney had made these copies by using the copying machine Benjamin Franklin had invented, whereby tracing a document with a stylus reproduced the words on another sheet of paper by means of a mechanical arm. A messenger had brought the copies to James the evening before.

James dined at the City Tavern and afterwards went to pay a final visit to William Maul and his wife Rebecca to give them the letter from Robert Maul and their copy of Dr. Franklin's account of Lizzy Coons's death. The young Quaker couple was dismayed when they learned from James that Lizzy had been pregnant when she was killed and that the murderer had been the Maul's former hostler, who had been her lover. They were overjoyed, however, to know that Robert Maul had survived the war and was apparently living somewhere in Virginia, the largest state in the Union.

In talking to the Mauls, James learned that they had formed a connection with the Free Quakers and were attending their Weekly Meeting. William and Rebecca Maul appeared much less unhappy than they had been during his last visit with them, and the possibility of Robert Maul perhaps coming back to Philadelphia was a cheering prospect to them.

That evening, James opened the letter he had received at the City Tavern on Wednesday. It proved to be a second threat in the same handwriting as the other letter he had received warning him to desist from his investigation into Mrs. Coons's death.

On Tuesday, James and Livy, riding tandem on Jenny, went to a millinery shop kept by a French woman in Bennett Street, where Livy selected as a gift for Philomen Lyons a very expensive turban of yellow silk. She then accompanied her betrothed to the Negro washerwoman's house to deliver it.

Mrs. Lyons politely turned down the gift when it was first presented to her, as beyond her merits. But after some gentle coaxing from Livy, she finally accepted it with many thanks, though she continued to say it was more than she deserved.

Mrs. Lyons was effusive in her congratulations when Livy announced that she and James were engaged to be married.

Her two little grandsons were fascinated by James's battered face, which Mrs. Lyons was too polite to mention or stare at.

James treated Livy and himself to a dinner of canvasback duck and French wine at the century-old Half Moon Inn on Chestnut Street, across from the front of the State House, where many members of the Pennsylvania Assembly had their noontide meals.

After dinner, he returned Livy to Grandmère and went on carrying out Dr. Franklin's directives. He delivered to Mrs. Opdahl the ten Spanish dollars and, to protect Hannah Farthing from gossiping tongues, Dr. Franklin's message that the former midwife had never known Elizabeth Coons and had provided no information as significant as Mrs. Opdahl's impression that when she died Lizzy Coons had been "in the state."

The final commission James discharged was to give Mistress Merkle the remainder of Dr. Franklin's funds for the education of her ward, Sarah Coons, a sum that exceeded the gifts to Mrs. Lyons and Mrs. Opdahl combined. In making this present, James carried out a mission of his own. He presented the daughter of Elizabeth Coons with the French doll with the porcelain face and blue dress that her mother had cherished and took the little orphan aside. Holding a private colloquy with her, he told her that she should consider it a blessing that she had known one of her parents, a blessing the blue doll would always remind her of. He also told her that should she ever feel angry or sad, she should remember that some little boys and girls have no recollection of either their mother or their father, and she should count her blessings. The little girl hugged the doll to her breast as she listened to this speech, solemnly nodding her head several times. At the end, she thanked James by throwing her arms around his neck and kissing his cheek.

In the days that followed, as the explanation of Mrs. Coons's death appeared in the papers and word spread that the Mauls' former hostler had strangled the Quaker housekeeper, James's fame increased prodigiously, and he began to understand Dr. Franklin's having insisted on remaining the anonymous director of their collaboration.

James did not see Dr. Franklin again until the 29th of October, and then it was as part of the massive public gathering to honor Dr. Franklin's elevation by the Assembly and the Supreme Executive Council to the highest office in the state. His election to the presidency of Pennsylvania at age seventy-nine was unanimous, except for the vote of one member of the Assembly, who abstained, saying no man, not even the great Dr. Benjamin Franklin, deserved absolute approval. The election took place in the same chamber of the State House where, in 1776, Franklin, then seventy years old, had signed the Declaration of Independence.

Following the vote, a grand procession of officials and dignitaries escorted Dr. Franklin to the Court House in Market Street, where the result was to be formally proclaimed. The first contingent in the grand procession consisted of the city's constables, bearing their staves. Next came the Sheriffs with their wands of authority; then Philadelphia's chief notaries and robed judges. The Marshal of the Admiralty, the Warden of the Port, the Collector of Customs, the Naval Officer, the Secretary of the Land Office, the Master of the Rolls, and the Registrar of Wills followed the judges. Then came Dr. Franklin, walking with his gold-headed cane and wearing a splendid gray suit of fine material with cloth buttons, holding onto the arm of Vice

President Biddle. Following these two chief executives came the Sergeant-at-Arms of the Assembly, bearing the heavy mace of his office against his shoulder and leading the Speaker of the Assembly, the Governor of Pennsylvania, and the members of the Supreme Executive Council and the Assembly. These were followed by the Provost and the professors of the University in their academic gowns. Officers of the Pennsylvania militia, including Captain James Jamison, in their full-dress, embroidered military uniforms, with drawn swords perpendicular to their shoulders, brought up the rear of the procession.

As this stately procession went up Fifth Street and turned down Market on its way to the Court House, Dr. Franklin was the center of attention. Crowds even larger than those that had welcomed him home from France thronged the parade route. Men and boys were perched in every tree strong enough to hold their weight. The multitudes crowding the sidewalks and dangling from every window along the way greeted the venerable gentleman with loud huzzahs and sustained applause as he came abreast of them. Several times young women smilingly dashed out from the sidewalk and kissed the smiling Dr. Franklin. These expressions of affection were greeted each time by loud roars of good-hearted approval.

At the Court House, Governor Mifflin, Vice President Biddle, the Clerk of the Assembly Mr. Bryan, the High Sheriff, and other principal dignitaries ascended with Dr. Franklin to the balcony on the building's second floor. There the Sheriff called out repeatedly in his stentorian voice to the multitudes jamming the streets below the balcony, "Silence! Silence under pain of imprisonment!" and gradually a hush spread through the throng.

When all was quiet, the Clerk of the Assembly extended his outstretched hand toward the elderly man standing at the front of the balcony and, looking out at the crowds filling the streets as far as one could see, proclaimed: "His Excellency Benjamin Franklin, Esquire, President of the Supreme Executive Council of the Commonwealth of Pennsylvania, Captain-General and Commander-in-Chief in and over the same!"

Whereupon Dr. Franklin raised his hand in salute to the people, and they in turn shouted their joyful appreciation of Philadelphia's most famous citizen and one of the two most famous citizens of the United States of America.

A small cannon below the balcony was fired to signal to the churches of the city that had bells—Gloria Dei, St. Mary's, Christ Church, and a few lesser places of worship—to peal forth in glad jubilation. And the chorus of bells was joined by the stern, martial reports of the minute guns on the ships anchored in the Delaware and moored to the many wharves of Philadelphia, where every ship of any importance was festooned with flags.

In all that jubilant, numerous throng, only Francis Mahoney and Captain James Jamison knew of the pains and expense this internationally famous scientist, statesman, inventor, and revolutionary leader had taken to see justice done for a humble family of leather-apron Quaker stonecutters.

In the second week of January, 1786, four months after James and Dr. Franklin began investigating the so-called Quaker Murders, James received a letter in a familiar hand containing copies of two letters just received from Europe. These were answers to the inquiries Dr. Franklin had made in

September, asking all of his most eminent medical friends in Europe if they had knowledge of any fatalities from spontaneous rupturing to the blood vessels in the throat and, if so, requesting that they please communicate the details of the cases to him.

One of the letters was from the Dutch physician Jan Ingenousz who reported that he knew of one such death that had produced bruises to the throat. The case was that of a cloistered nun who had died in her sleep at her convent and was found dead in her cell.

The other letter was from the London physician Sir Charles Fauxhall. He had knowledge of two such deaths. A spinster who lived with her married brother and an elderly viscount who died in his sleep next to his wife.

In all three instances, the victims in life had had a pronounced appearance of melancholy and the same elongated limbs, hands, and feet that characterized the physical appearance of Jacob Maul's second wife.

Dr. Franklin suggested that James should make a synopsis of these letters and publish it in the newspapers, with the opinion that they indicated that Margaret Gilbert Maul had died a strange death from natural causes.

The End

Editor's note:

Marfan's Syndrome, a genetic disease affecting connective tissues, skeletal structure, and the cardiovascular system, can cause fatal ruptures to blood vessels. The disease was not clinically recognized until 1896. Abraham Lincoln is believed to have had this malady.

Author's Note

Biographers are committed to representing the reality of history. Writers of historical fictions have the somewhat different goal of creating the illusion of a past experience. Experts on Benjamin Franklin's life will readily spot where I depart from the truth of history. But some things that might strike some readers as made up are actually among the historical facts of the narrative. Franklin Court. The horrors of the Walnut Street Jail. The Glass Harmonica which Franklin helped to perfect and played. Franklin's sedan chair. The thieving British general. Franklin's years as a legislative agent. His role in negotiating the original boundaries of the United States. His creation of a mutual-improvement club known as the Junto, a volunteer fire company, and an association for prison reform. The intention has been throughout to achieve "verisimilitude" in representing Philadelphia in 1785 and, more importantly, Franklin's genius, interests, and convictions. Francis Mahoney, the Maul and Jamison families, the Gilbert family, and Philomen Lyons have all been created as means to display eighteenth-century Philadelphia and Franklin's character.

J.H.M

About The Author

John Harmon McElroy

John Harmon McElroy was born in a small glass-manufacturing town on the banks of the Allegheny River in Pennsylvania, and two of his ancestors fought for American Independence in the Revolutionary War. A graduate of Princeton University, John spent two years as an ensign on a destroyer escort radar picket ship in the mid-Atlantic, keeping watch for Soviet bombers. He is a Professor Emeritus of American Literature at the University of Arizona, was twice appointed a Fulbright Professor of American Studies, and is the author of four books on American cultural history. For over twenty years he taught Benjamin Franklin's *Autobiography* in a course he created called "Literature of the Early Republic."

John and his wife, Onyria Herrera McElroy, PhD, were married in Havana, Cuba in 1957. Their adventures together include spending an afternoon conversing with Ernest

Hemingway at his home La Vigía outside Havana; planting 500 redwoods in Galicia, Spain, to commemorate Columbus's world-changing voyage of discovery; making a 480-mile pilgrimage on the Camino de Santiago and John's fire walking at a festival in Soria, Spain, that has celebrated the summer solstice since time immemorial. They live in Tucson, Arizona, and have four children, eight grandchildren and two great-grandchildren.

If You Enjoyed This Book

Visit

PENMORE PRESS
www.penmorepress.com

All Penmore Press books are available directly through our website, amazon.com, Barnes and Noble and Nook, Sony Reader, Apple iTunes, Kobo books and via leading bookshops across the United States, Canada, the UK, Australia and Europe.

The Chosen Man

by

J. G Harlond

From the bulb of a rare flower bloom ambition and scandal

Rome, 1635: As Flanders braces for another long year of war, a Spanish count presents the Vatican with a means of disrupting the Dutch rebels' booming economy. His plan is brilliant. They just need the right man to implement it.

They choose Ludovico da Portovenere, a charismatic spice and silk merchant. Intrigued by the Vatican's proposal—and hungry for profit—Ludo sets off for Amsterdam to sow greed and venture capitalism for a disastrous harvest, hampered by a timid English priest sent from Rome, accompanied by a quick-witted young admirer he will use as a spy, and bothered by the memory of the beautiful young lady he refused to take with him.

Set in a world of international politics and domestic intrigue, *The Chosen Man* spins an engrossing tale about the Dutch financial scandal known as tulip mania—and how decisions made in high places can have terrible repercussions on innocent lives.

PENMORE PRESS
www.penmorepress.com

KING'S SCARLET

BY

JOHN DANIELSKI

Chivalry comes naturally to Royal Marine captain Thomas Pennywhistle, but in the savage Peninsular War, it's a luxury he can ill afford. Trapped behind enemy lines with vital dispatches for Lord Wellington, Pennywhistle violates orders when he saves a beautiful stranger, setting off a sequence of events that jeopardize his mission. The French launch a massive manhunt to capture him. His Spanish allies prove less than reliable. The woman he rescued has an agenda of her own that might help him along, if it doesn't get them all killed.

A time will come when, outmaneuvered, captured, and stripped of everything, he must stand alone before his enemies. But Pennywhistle is a hard man to kill and too bloody obstinate to concede defeat.

PENMORE PRESS
www.penmorepress.com

Penmore Press

Challenging, Intriguing, Adventurous, Historical and Imaginative

www.penmorepress.com

CPSIA information can be obtained
at www.ICGtesting.com
Printed in the USA
FFOW03n2016231017
41382FF